Plagued

J. L. Sugden

Plagued

Olympia Publishers
London

www.olympiapublishers.com
OLYMPIA PAPERBACK EDITION

A CIP catalogue record for this title is
available from the British Library.

ISBN: 978-1-80074-527-8

This is a work of fiction.
Names, characters, places and incidents originate from the writer's
imagination. Any resemblance to actual persons, living or dead, is
purely coincidental.

First Published in 2023

Olympia Publishers
Tallis House
2 Tallis Street
London
EC4Y 0AB

Printed in Great Britain

Acknowledgements

By far the most problematic part of being a dyslexic author is that, when you don't completely understand the words in the first place, spell check becomes confusing at best, thus, I'd like to acknowledge the proofreading skills of my mother, Jo Sugden, without whom I strongly believe the task of getting thought on page would have been far more difficult and problematic. For their support throughout the process of writing this book, I'd like to thank David Sugden, Terry and Janet Altoft, as well as my friends Matthew Renaud, Weronika Baranowska and Bambi Marhold. For their expert advice, I'd like to also acknowledge Jessica Fear and author Joe Hakim, without whom I'd have had far less ability in creative writing and getting published. Finally, I'd like to make a special thanks to my best friend, Mariamah Davey, who inspired me and set me on my writing career, as well as providing support, motivation and a second pair of eyes on my work and writing.

Back Story

The Draden

The Draden are the race of immortal, youthful beings that govern the happenings of the universe. Their name, in their language, Dradenic, means divine-beings, and that is the best-known word of their language, as they keep it very quiet and only speak it to each other. They prefer to speak 'mortal tongue' when they are in the presence of the mortals, though many tongues and languages across the universe that are spoken claim to be, by them who speak it, based highly on Dradenic, so putting its speakers much closer to their gods. Indeed, the Holy tongue, Taraong, is said to be the closest to it, and this may be true since it is spoken, much the same, across many worlds in the universe to a great degree. Even though this is used very little, and even fewer that hear it understand it, for it is never spoken outside of a temple dedicated to one of the Draden, and most sadly, it has never been heard on Earth.

The Draden themselves are greatly powerful but are also much older and wiser as compared to any mortal, and, though they are much stronger and more divine, (filled with immortal years of learning) they are also very humble. Very rarely will you see a Draden kneel or ask another to kneel, and if a mortal were to kneel to them then they would simply be laughed at. However, this is the case of most Draden, but not all, for some among them are much younger than others, and, as they are omniscient due to millions of earth-years of experience. The younger among them are often less wise, make more mistakes, and are more egotistical than their seniors. Even if many don't look it, there are often many years of separation between them, with the oldest and first of their race being over four millennium (cosmic years) older than the rest.

As a result, the Draden, particularly the more youthful of them, are far closer to humans than one may think. They are rash and hot-headed. They are vain and sinful, however, most quickly lose these, becoming more cunning, witty and benevolent in their rule. For it is, after all, the original Draden, the one known in the English tongue as Life, that created all life in the cosmos.

The Draden themselves have roles and responsibilities, often assigned to them at birth by Faith after consulting All One. A Draden's name often corresponds to the thing that it is in charge of, for example Health is in charge of healing all illnesses, however, her true name, which would be the translation of Health into Dradenic, is unknown to nearly all mortals, as are that of most Draden. As a result, a Draden may become known by more than one name, depending on where a mortal comes from, or whether or not there are multiple words for the task that Draden is responsible for. Equally, not all Dradens have their own tasks. Many Dradens, such as Health, has helpers, servants and monks working under them, and so these Dradens are not called for a specific task they are required to watch over, but are given names much like mortals by their creators. Such as the monks of Helothom, who serve Health in helping to bring healing to mortals. (This system of servants and helpers is part of the Titan system, which will be described later.)

Equally, among the much older Draden, (in particular the Octull,) they share the same name as the thing they're responsible for, such as the Draden Life, however, it is the thing that takes its name from them, not them from the thing, for it is them who created it, such as Society, Life, War, Death and Hope.

About the All One

The Draden themselves are not entirely atheist. The religion of the Draden worship is a single being they call Trihonus (it is known as Alhonus in Taraong, though they say it's blasphemy to pray directly to Alhonus). The beings most simple name is the All One. The All One, is said to be the personification of the whole cosmic tree and everything in it, including the Draden themselves. They say it is from this that Life was first created, (and the other Octull) as well as the rest of the cosmos and the different realms of existence.

There is not much known about the All One, and very few stories ever passed onto mortals or involving mortals. What is known is that few among the Dradens have actually seen it, or rather, its personified form, limited to Life, Faith (whom is the chief communicator with All One) and one or two others who claim to have seen it. They are very rarely taken seriously by the other Dradens, and never has it been said to have been seen by any mortal, though some claim to have seen it, and others have been near a Draden when it has appeared.

However, there are many Dradens, and indeed one or two very important mortals, that tend to end up living with the Draden after their death, that have heard the All One talking to them. It has come as a gentle yet powerful voice in a dream after a heart full of long prayer, and, for the most part, these claims are believed, for Draden who have seen the All One (personified) and heard it speak can safely confirm that the voice described matches the one they had heard themselves. For it is very particular, unforgettable and unmistakable. The only problem with the All One is that, like many oracles and extremely wise people, it only ever talks in riddles, which is easy for the wise to understand (most of the time) but not for the younger and less experienced Draden who can easily mistake its meaning. It is even harder for a mortal to understand, which is why the All One very rarely talks to them, and why priests of Taraong say that one should not pray directly to Alhonus.

As for what is described about the All One, it is much the same as what is described about most modern Earth religions, saying that as the All One is everything in the cosmos, then it is omniscient as it knows itself entirely, it is omnipresent as everything, including you and me, are part of it and make it up, thus it is everywhere all at the same time. It is omnipotent, as it has full control over itself and so has power to do anything it likes, putting it above all other things.

Politics of the Draden

The Draden political system is simple in the fact that there are four lead Dradens, called the Quadrel, who discuss and vote on everything to do with the universe. They are the oldest and most powerful of the Dradens, who were created from the broken shards of the falls of creation by Trihonus itself. However, within the Quadrel there is also a hierarchy of Draden, with Life, the original and first being of existence, at the top, and then Society, and finally Faith and Stewardship at the bottom.

Along with the Quadrel, there are their supporters, for among the Dradens there are also political rival groups. The Quadrel lead the main group, whose supporters are known as Gods, while the opposing political group is led by the Quadrats, who in turn are led by Destruction. The followers of the Quadrats are known as Demons. This friction between the two parties influences nearly every major event in the cosmic tree.

The Quadrel and the Quadrats were once, long ago, part of the same council of leading Draden, before an argument between Life and Destruction split the entire universe in two, together they were known as the Octull, the eight original Draden, with Life and Society at the top. The other six were Faith, Stewardship, War, Destruction, Death and Grimmus.

About the Structure of the Universe

The cosmos, as it is seen by the Draden, is that of a great cosmic tree, and so often they show Trihonus as a great tree. Upon the tree, there are eight realms entwined into its branches, roots and trunk, and all beings live in and upon the tree. Through the tree, there runs the river of time. The lifeblood of the tree, that drives all things forward from the spinning of the worlds of the mortal plain, to the simplest action and consequence that allows this whole Cosmos to survive. Time is like a beating heart, and the river is the blood vessel of the tree, without this fourth dimension nothing would be able to happen, and so the tree would wither and die, or become stale and bare of all its leaves and fruit.

At the roots of the tree, tangled among the twisting foundations, is the eighth realm; the dead plane, (not to be confused with the land of the dead) a fallen wasteland and emptiness. Long ago it was cut off from the rest of the cosmos, and there, built on the roots of the tree, was a place terrible and feared by all who know of its existence, the Maze. A place of limbo and dread where the dead go if they are killed. This place is one where none can escape, or that's what was thought anyway. Even Draden have been killed and then have gone to this place.

The realm twisted and held by the trunk of the tree is known as the seventh realm, the Mortal Plane. This is the plane of Worlds and Men, and Life and Death. In this realm lies the Earth, spinning round its start like so many other worlds. Some worlds are life-bearing, but most are barren and desolate. In many the Seed of Life has been planted, and with-it life springs upon that world, mortal life, with mortal animals and peoples, each adapting to live upon their world in the best way they can, till death comes to reap their souls.

In the next realm lies a great meander in the river of time, which runs like a great vein through the tree and before a split in the tree's trunk. This, the sixth realm, is the land of the Dead. Here time stands still, and here Death and his reapers takes all mortal souls once they've died, though they don't stay here. In this place, each soul has the time they need to lay to rest regrets in life, and fulfil things they wish to do, so that they may move on to the next life feeling complete and without regret. Here in the Land of the Dead, there lies a great bridge over a crack in the tree, beyond which the trunk splits into two. It is here mortal souls are judged by the great Judge, and are sorted to either the left or the right.

Upon the left hand of the trunk lies the fifth realm, known to many as Hell, or Hades. Here, the wicked are punished, but there is no fire, nor a devil, though, for a long time, this and the third plane have been the seat of the Demon political group.

Therefore, up the right-hand split is Paradise, known to some as Heaven, though it bears many other names. This is the home of the Quadrel, along with the second realm. The third realm is the kingdom of the Demons high in the canopy of the tree upon the left branch, and is similar to the second realm, with the kingdom of the gods upon the right branch. Here, their branches did once intertwine in friendship, before the Octull divided. But now they span apart, and so there is a great tenseness in the cosmos, a Cold War, as it may be called, though no blood has yet been spilled in nearing sixty-five cosmic years, though it is just a matter of time until blood is once again spilled.

The final realm is a realm that has never been seen. It is the home of Trihonus. It lies both at the very top of the Cosmic tree, and in the space around it. It is the dwelling of Trihonus, and is therefore the dwelling of the Tree itself, yet, as all in existence is the Tree, then it must both be part of the Tree, on the Tree, and yet outside the Tree for the Tree to dwell there. It is a place too great for even the Draden to imagine, and only the greatest minds could ever hope to depict part of it with any close accuracy. Even I cannot say more than this: it is a place inhabited only by Trihonus, who is everything, yet is part of the Cosmic tree, which is Trihonus, and so it may be like the layers of a Russian doll, but is most likely not, for my mind is not great enough to know such a place and how a place can physically be, existing both outside existence and within it, when existence exists inside of it.

The Titan system

Long ago, while life was young, and between the Fey wars, there was a realisation. This may seem simple to us now, but in the history of the Draden it was like the invention of the wheel, or writing, and it was simply the realisation that one man can't do everything. This may seem obvious, but before this time, each Draden had a responsibility, with which it is named after, like Wisdom, in charge of all knowledge, and so is called whatever a particular language's word for knowledge and wisdom is. However, as more and more planets were given the seed of life, the Draden found it increasingly difficult to keep on top of their responsibilities, like collecting all the wisdom in the Cosmos, and so, the Titan System was born. In this system, the Draden with the responsibility becomes a manager of other Draden, and often some mortals who spend their afterlife doing something worthwhile and have a needed skill. This worked wonderfully for the Draden, and before long the Draden were catching up on their workload. However, the backlog had created another problem.

With the Draden busy trying to keep on top of their workload, there had become less time to keep an eye on the life-bearing planets, which had become unruly and less God-fearing. Indeed, when some of the Draden came to some worlds, the inhabitants tried, and sometimes succeeded, in killing them.

Life, in an outrage, destroyed these worlds, (which became the fate of Zamo and Jarik, two of the original worlds). This meant that the Draden needed to do something, and fast, to stop other worlds going in the same direction, and so, Life created the race of the Titans. These are immortal beings that have half as much power as the Draden, yet twice as much power as mortals, making them the perfect guardians of Planets: weak enough so as not to cause a potential challenge to the Draden, yet strong enough to take on any unruly mortals.

On each world, there is a single supreme Titan, for any more than one would lead to the world collapsing from the long-time strain of their power. This Supreme Titan is the parent of all the other Titans on the world, it is also in charge of the other Titans, and it is their responsibility to look after the world. The Supreme Titans are formless, genderless and linked to the very core of the world. They are created upon a world before the Seed of Life is planted there, and live there for a short time after the Seed and the world eventually dies. (The Supreme Titan of Earth is known by many names. Its formal name is Dyeus, taught to the first tribe to commune with it, the Proto-Indo-Europeans. However, it is more frequently known by the name Dei which is derived from, Dyeus)

About Earth

Earth is a small, rocky and old world in the solar system, Sharus, named after the solar system's sun, meaning *rocky-one* in Dradenic. Earth is well-known for many reasons, but not least of all for its age. As life-bearing worlds go, Earth is one of the oldest worlds in the whole Cosmos. It has seen the rise and fall of many great worlds, including famous Maroon, the great Jupiter-sized world in the solar system, Moormas. Indeed, when Maroon was first given life, Earth was already well developed, and when the giant fell, the tyrannosaurus was ruling the world.

To see the age of Earth, you must look at the being that gave it life, known as Life, his invention taking his name. Life may be old and immortal, but he seldom likes to wait many cosmic years for evolution to run its course, so the fact that Earth began with single-celled organisms shows that it was one of the first ever sown.

There were fourteen original worlds given life: Earth, Zamo, Kite, Tigus, K-125, Perat, Xylon, Ashlop, Jarik, Gisma and four others whose names have been long lost to time. From these original worlds, five successfully managed to take the Seed of Life and evolution began; Earth, Zamo, Gisma, Ashlop and Jarik. However, from these first five, now only two remain, Earth and Ashlop. This is partly due to the fact that for much of their history they were completely forgotten by the Draden and left to their own devices, and, due to these two original survivors, there is a blueprint for life on younger and newer worlds, after their existence was remembered of course. So, many worlds are vastly similar, and even familiar to that of Earth and Ashlop, who were almost identical to begin with, being known as the Sister

18

Worlds.

Though Earth spent much of its time forgotten to the wider universe, about 4280 million Earth years ago to 530 million. In newer history however, the Dradens did have an influence on Earth, particularly as the fame of its age quickly became well known by their race about 500 cosmic years ago.

But Earth was set apart from other worlds in the not-too-distant past when the oldest created son of the Draden, Life and Society, Wisdom, came to Earth as he took a holiday away from the kingdom of the gods. It is here that he saw a mortal woman trekking through the ice and snow, having been attacked by a cave bear.

Wisdom immediately took a liking to her and fell deeply in love. Not able to see her die, he took her to a cave and healed her with the Marmin plant that he had brought from another world. Then, out of anger, and to the fury of Earth's Titans, Wisdom killed the cave bear species to take his revenge.

The girl's name was Luna, and the pair stayed together in the cave for all that winter, summer, and winter again, with Wisdom providing all that they needed. Wisdom also, to win the heart of Luna, promised to grant her any wish that she had.

Luna, in the depths of their second winter together, asked that she be made immortal to stay youthful forever, saying that she couldn't bear the thought of growing old and dying while he remains young, his love waning with the smoothness of her skin.

Her wish was answered, but her immortality brought an unintended consequence. Many years ago, and with the cosmic rise of intelligent lifeforms, Wisdom had suggested to the Quadrels that there be put a cap on how intelligent they could become, particularly Hominoids, fearing that if they became too intelligent, they would be capable of challenging the Titans and the gods. However, by giving Luna immortality, he also broke the limit on her intelligence, and she quickly became smarter and smarter by the day until her own wisdom started making Wisdom scared and uncomfortable, for he had loved her in her mortality and her innocence.

By their one-hundredth winter, things had gone too far, and having spent one hundred winters and summers together, they had many children that had spread across the globe.

The last straw for Wisdom came with another wish. Luna wished that her children be given complete knowledge, like herself, freed from the restriction Wisdom had himself put in place long ago.

Having kept his word, Wisdom granted the wish but, soon after, left Earth to the fury of Luna, returning to the kingdom of the Draden to think for a solution to the problem he had made.

Now, more than a thousand Earth years after Wisdom left, Luna, out of spite had made sure to spread her line across the world so that humans freed from Wisdom's restrictions were embedded in every corner of the world; every city, town, village and civilisation. Now almost half the humans on earth were of the line of Luna, and it wouldn't be long before the entire world was free from Wisdom's restrictions.

Finally, Wisdom was forced to return, (mostly by his father, Life) and he formed a cunning plan to solve the problem. He quickly found Luna, and, outsmarting her, he won her love back. Wisdom bided his time, lingering on

Earth for many years, until finally came the day to make his move.

He and Luna were asked to attend a wedding of a Cretan King to a bride from Phrygia, now modern Turkey. At the wedding he was appalled to find that, enslaved to the King, were all manner of other Humanoid beings, Seyters and Centars mostly. For the freedom of Wisdom's restrictions had been kept by humans, giving them an unnatural edge. They were so helpless and desperate, that a centaur, having had to plough a field on the side of a mountain, begged Wisdom and Luna to free and help him.

Luna looked at the creature in disgust, calling it a 'monster, with no right to live on a world with man' before dragging Wisdom away, and back to the festivities.

However, this gave Wisdom an idea. At the end of the evening, Wisdom turned to Luna and asked her if she wishes for man to be rid of the 'lesser beings,' as she called them, and to never see such dark evil again.

Luna agreed and made the wish, and Wisdom, keeping his word from so long ago, granted her third wish and made every Human forget ever seeing any other humanoid, or any other dark thing as soon as it had left their line of sight.

Wisdom left soon after, and the Draden decided to have little to do with Earth ever again, for their problem was solved with Luna's wish. For man can no longer remember the existence of humanoids, like Syters and Centaurs and Cyclopses, besides the myths that have already been collected. But, Wisdom's curse, (so it has been called), also made them blind to the damage they did to themselves, such as not seeing the effects of pollution, deforestation and other world-destroying things that they are doing until it is too late, and so, ensuring their own destruction through their own wisdom and intelligence.

Prologue

Atop a tremendous waterfall stands a tall and magnificent tower, where a mother and her four daughters live. No, not maidens in distress, nor prisoners, nor humans at all, but something much older and more powerful than us. They are not monstrous but beautiful. The mother, so fine and magnificent that beauty itself often gets jealous of her, stands dressed in the finest of her blue silks, on a jut of rock overlooking that tremendous waterfall. As water, with all its might and power, gushes down the rock face, an unhappy, monstrous birth, it roars and falls, and is broken up on the craggy, ever-changing, rock face below. Before flowing away into a shallow but tremendously wide river. With this great beauty, is a warrior of all ages, scarred and battle-worn, with thick blood red hair and an equally thick and red beard. His armour is well used; his war hammer hangs from his wide belt. His long hair blows in the wind of the gods.

"Why did you summon me?" he exclaims in a voice that could only come from one like him, autocratic and battle-hardened to the core.

"Our old friend has escaped," she says in a dull tone, one that hides her real emotional joy, for their old friend is the father of one of her four children. Despite her loyalties to lovers being slim to none, she can't stop the fluttering in her heart, as if their god is leading her down a path she otherwise wouldn't walk.

"The Maze!" he exclaims, surprise in his voice. "Impossible," he says, shrugging away the whole concept, "no soul can ever escape that place, none!"

"Alas, I do not lie, he has indeed escaped Solomon's maze. I saw it in a vision, and you know they are never wrong. He lingers between places, trying to return to us through a suitable host."

"Then we must find this host." The scarred man stands staring out towards the right of the great river. With a sigh, he thinks on the matter for a moment, before the solution pops into his usually more decisive head, "speak to our neutral friend, get him to find this host and report back."

"Are you sure that's wise?" asks the great beauty, with a mind just as enticing and sharp as her looks. She would be the only one, apart from their kings and queens, who would dare to question such a formidable being such as him.

"He cannot take a side in the matter, so he is the best option, besides, I think our friend will be more willing to reveal himself to him, don't you?"

The Beauty gives a sigh, for she must take her orders from him as much as from his masters. She knows he is wise in his decisiveness, for he is one of the oldest amongst them, and she is not. "And what are we to do when we find him?"

"Send him back to the maze! It all ended with him, and it will restart with him. I am not prepared to take that risk!"

She doesn't know why she says what she does, sometimes she just does. Like a puppet whose strings are starting to be pulled, her mind slows and her mouth keeps going, for what she does is not something she would normally do, not to him, anyway. With a mild temper in her tone, she can't stop herself from disagreeing.

"No! I can't accept that! The Maze will have changed him! We have a chance to bring him onside! I could bring him onside. I can't influence us, but, maybe if he's mortal, can I?"

"Maybe? Do you not remember what happened last time? Do you think that's a risk we can afford to take? I will not risk everything on an unproven idea! Not when…"

"Maybe, sounds good enough to me." As the third person to the party arrives, it is now the turn of the warrior to take his orders, as the third person is far more wise, older and stronger than any amongst his company. So much so that, his whole being and presence seems to make the world bow around him. "He found a way out once son, he will find a way out again. We must make sure that he is on our side, not the others'."

Now, he turns to the Beauty, who seems frail and small in his presence, and she feels that way as well. "Do whatever you must, bring our old friend to side, and maybe what we've lost will start to return with him."

It all started just over a year ago. The date was Friday the thirteenth of June, when a terror from the distant past struck again. It started with my Father, Dr Fredrick Smith, in the City of York, remembered to the world as patient 0.2.

It spread like a wildfire across earth. From human to human, human to dog, dog to flea, flea to dog, dog to human. No one was safe.

We'd experienced illness before, from China and the Middle East, but nothing, compares to this. Governments across the world fell into lockdown, but that didn't stop it. It seemed even to spread through cables, radio and social media. I don't know how it got so bad. I don't know why it got out of hand. All I know is that it did.

Governments went dark. Technology went dark. City by city the old women came, brush in hand; no city, town, village or hamlet was safe. Hospitals were overrun. The NHS fell after just two weeks. The rich disappeared and left the poor to suffer. Riots came forth. Robbery and crime festered like a bad wound. We did more damage to ourselves then the plague ever could. We're like rats when faced with death, and it disgusts me to call myself human.

I think other countries went through the same, but we were cut off. No one heard from across the channel, or America. The army rolled in. That was a mistake. They were selfish. They became unruly, trying themselves to survive. They set off the bombs, and so ended our last chance to survive.

The cults came after. Religious fanatics, the lot of 'em! They were worse than the army ever were. The 'Bent Cross', they call themselves; riding horses along the roads and filling the dikes with bones.

They were good to begin with, but I never liked them, and it didn't take long to prove me right. All the ill they found were killed, and all the healthy were drafted to their course, whether they believed or not.

I've always had a religious side. They were no servants of any gods.

I managed to avoid them. I managed to survive by learning quickly how to live off the land, but, then again, I had to. My father died first. Then my sister, and then my mother. That left a bitter taste in my mouth, but now I know, they were the lucky ones. They haven't seen what I have, and haven't had to do what I did.

They were the lucky ones.

After the army came and destroyed, I, like many others, were forced onto the streets to wander aimlessly among the dead and dying. That's when I learnt how to survive. I headed south, along the Ooze to where it forms the Humber. I found my way across, and to the banks of the Trent. The main roads are forever watched by the Bent Cross. So, I followed the Trent, through Lincolnshire, and down into Nottinghamshire.

The Bent Cross is gone now, as is most of humanity it seems.

The more I wander, the more I've started to wonder. The more I see, the more starts to seem strange to me.

I feel like there's something else, something unseen and unknown. It tickles the back of my mind. Something doesn't add up!

I've taken a detour from the Trent, and have headed west into the ancient forest of Sherwood.

I'm writing this so someone knows my story. If I die from

this plague, this Black Death from 1349, then I hope someone else can take on the search; the search for truth. My name is Alex Smith, and this is my story.

This is the truth about everything, the truth that Wisdom never let us know.

Book I

Truth is a Hard Pill to Swallow

Chapter I:
13 Months AP

Alex looked up from his torn and tattered leather diary which he had been keeping with him since day one of the outbreak. The youth, about eighteen years old, was a strong individual. He was healthy, unlike so many around him, which for Alex was more of a curse then a blessing. Seeing the look of the dying, that looks of jealousy and unwarranted hate towards him slowly grinded into his heart and soul, until he hated himself for being so lucky and blessed. He was sat on a log, which was once in the *Sherwood Forest Visitor Centre Car Park,* looking out with deep, blue eyes, hidden by a curtain of blonde, unkept hair.

He was surrounded by men, women and children, most of whom were infected, dead or dying. The few who weren't crying and wailing was doing whatever they could to remove and deal with their dead. Alex rubbed his face and covered his ears; despite all his time, he had never gotten used to the sound of wailing mourners, and that horrible feeling of complete helplessness that strikes into his soul every time he saw someone infected by the disease. He cupped his face in his hands and wept as he always wept; laying on the ground next to his feet was the limp body of an elderly lady called Barbara who had been with him since he had left his home. He had failed to save her. Still he seemed to stay healthy.

"I wish I could grow sick!" Alex screamed at the dead body by his feet. "I wish I could die! I'd rather be dead than see this, this, horror!" With his head in his hands, he sobbed to himself. "I'm sorry. I'm sorry for everything," he wailed, "I'm sorry your son wasn't here. I wish I could have done more... done more to answer your last wish."

He stayed with her for as long as he could, but in the end, he knew there was no point in staying. *There's nothing left to do. I may as well try to be helpful somewhere else,* he thought to himself. So, with a deep and mournful sigh, he staggered to his feet. He took one last sorrowful look back before meandering away, running his hands through his thick locks of hair. He wanders through the people in the car park. Across an old road and through an overgrown cricket pitch. Turning to his left he past the derelict buildings of an arts and crafts centre and visitor centre, before turning and heading towards the forest in an inevitably futile attempt to escape death itself, or find it. Even Alex was not quite sure which.

That is when he saw it by the edge of the forest; a person completely out of place. Alex found himself paralyzed amongst the dying and the dead, staring at this thing that seemed completely out of the world. The person was dressed from head to toe in a golden silk robe, with leather gloves, a mask, and crystal goggles so that none of the person's flesh was visible. Yet, the person seemed, like Alex, to be completely healthy; the only other completely healthy person that Alex had seen since the Bent Cross' disappearance over a month ago.

Perhaps it was Alex's desperation for answers playing a trick on him. Perhaps it was just his imagination, or maybe it was real – impossible, but real. He blinked and rubbed his eyes, as if trying to wake himself up from some dream. Alex watched in awe, paralysed upon the spot as this strange thing walked up to a small child, her back to a tree, and crouched down beside her.

"What the?" Alex began to ask, as he saw the stranger pull out a small crystal bottle, making the young girl drink its contents before holding it up to the light, as if looking at how much was left.

Alex kept watching as the girl coughed and spluttered, but the boils on her neck seemed to shrink before Alex's eyes. He blinked again. "They're! They're gone!" he gasped in shock, "Impossible!"

Before he knew what was happening, he walked right up to the strange being, his mind desperate to grasp beyond a curtain that he didn't yet understand. Desperate for answers, for a purpose, and for an end to all this endless wandering and pointless existence, he saw a small hole in all that he understood, and needed, unable to stop himself, to peek through. "That was a miracle! You- you- you cured her! How?"

The stranger slipped the empty bottle back under its cloak before dusting off its hands.

"Excuse me, did you hear me? How in the world did you do that?" Alex chased the stranger, getting even closer to them, desperate for some answers.

Upon hearing Alex's questions, the stranger turned and the pair exchanged a momentary glance, before the stranger fled into the forest and disappeared among the thick fern beds and trunks of old oak-trees. But Alex still had his health, and was determined to find out the truth, so, without a moment's hesitation, he sped after the stranger and into the dark of

Sherwood.

Alex chased the stranger for what seemed like hours, darting through ancient oak trees and silver birch, gaining on this strange being with every passing moment, getting closer, and closer, and closer. Down old paths, over forgotten fences and across a long clearing, sloping steeply upwards to his right.

Alex ran on until he was covered in sweat on that hot summer's day. The stranger turned back into the wood, running on and on, further and further from the visitor centre and the well-trodden paths around it that had, at one time, attracted many visitors to the old eves of the historical forest.

They were now far away from all of that, and had run across unmapped land, from oak to birch, birch to pine, and back to oak again. All the while, Alex was slowly gaining on his prey. Dressed in their strange attire, they were quickly becoming hot and tired, whereas Alex's clothes were light and torn, and his time in the wild had come with skills of the endurance hunt, which he used in its brilliant simplicity.

Alex is gaining on it. He could just about reach out and grab it now. Closer, and closer, and…

"GONE!" Alex found himself in a clearing deep in the heart of Sherwood, standing before two upright, square standing stones. Alex looked around and scratched his head in confusion, "Where the hell did, he go? I was RIGHT BLOODY BEHIND HIM!"

"I think you mean 'her'!" came a voice from behind Alex. He twirled around to see the most beautiful, glowing, red-haired and green-eyed girl standing before him. Alex's heart instantly began to gallop in his chest, so hard that it felt as if it could burst out of him and run away. "Wh- Wh-, Wh-,

who, are, are, y- you?" he panted, putting his hands on his knees, worse due to his surprise.

"Who am I? No, no! The question is who in the world are you? Chasing me like that! Well, be assured young man, I will not be saving you from the... plague?" The strange girl, not as tired as Alex anticipated, grabbed Alex by the chin and began to inspect him by pulling his head; first to the right, then the left, then up and back to the right. She then pulled his eyelids open to peer into them. "What in the name of Trihonus?" Alex heard her mutter to herself before pulling out a small knife.

Alex instinctively drew back, "Wow, wow! Easy!"

But the strange girl was quick, and grabbed him, pulling him back to her who drew the cold blade along the palm of his hand, creating a small cut. Alex immediately pulled back his hand, clenching it against his chest.

He watched her, becoming more curious by the moment as she inspected the blood drops on the knife. She looked closely at it, and held it to the light of the sun as shattered beams managed to pass through the thick canopy of the trees. "Impossible!" she muttered at last.

"What's impossible?"

"You!" she said, and with that she grabbed Alex's other hand and dragged him towards the pair of standing stones; over-grown and hidden by moss and ivy, they seemed strange and out of place in the dense English woodland.

But Alex planted his feet and stopped the strange girl before she could pull them both in between the two stones. "Where are you taking me?" he asked nervously.

The strange girl came up close to Alex, standing but an

inch or two from him. As she spoke, she slowly began to step back towards the standing stones, taking Alex with her. "Tell me," she said in a soft and almost enchanting voice, "have you ever wondered? Wondered what lays beyond the thin blindfold across your eyes. Of course, you have, you followed me here! You're not like the others. You know there's something, but you've never been able to perceive it. You wouldn't have followed me if that weren't true." She then leaned in even closer, and whispered into his ear, "I offer you truth. I offer you, life, purpose, and a place beyond your dreams. Come!"

She pulled Alex back, and the pair stepped together in between the standing stones.

Chapter II:
Helothom

As soon as Alex passed through the stones, the world before him changed dramatically. The green of the forest immediately gave way to the gold and white of a colossal temple, and the thick, diseased air of Earth lightens into something almost heavenly. Right before Alex's eyes appeared a great marble temple, decorated in gold and surrounded by sheer mountains ahead and a sea bluer than any ocean on Earth behind. The temple was surrounded by a massive garden complex, which seemed to be split into different parts. Each part was scattered with statues of gold and bronze and ended with standing stones, carved with old and ancient runes.

Alex was breathless, his eyes blinded by a light that came from no sun, but fell from the sky like a heavy rain. He blinks as if a blindfold had been lifted from his face, and he sees the world of the first time a new... Questions flooded his mind. A darkness that had hung about him for too long seemed immediately lifted, as if he'd been set free from a curse. He couldn't speak. He looked all about him in childish wonder. All he knew had been shattered and had melted like snow in the spring sun. All around, more of these strange beings, dressed in matching golden robes, went about their daily business. Alex felt like he was in a dream, or had woken up from a nightmare. There was a sound of peace; the gentle patter of trickling water, and the hum of bees. The smell of spring flowers drifted in the light air, and there seemed to be a light and pure taste in the air. Gone was the dark, sick smell and taste on earth as the plague drifted by, and the old woman's shadow looked constantly over. This was bright and fresh and pure.

"Wow!" Alex couldn't help but gasp as he passed through the stones. "Where on Earth are, we? I, I've never seen somewhere so…"

"That's because you're no longer on Earth, human," the strange girl said with an amused giggle, before walking out before him to introduce him to the place. "Welcome to the temple of Helothom, the home of the Draden Health!"

"The home of what?" Alex asked as he nervously took his first few steps in the strange land. He suddenly felt very small and irrelevant, and tried to speak and act in a stronger manner, though, it came across rather arrogant and self-assured.

"You humans have long thought yourselves to know the universe but in fact you know as much as a fly… or rat! Helothom is the home of the Goddess of Health, and we are the Helothom monks, who can cure any ailment or disease known to man, and far more that aren't!"

"Right. And I am supposed to believe that?" Alex replied sharply, though in his mind his thoughts were spinning, *this can't be! How the hell? I shouldn't be here. No. No! Come on Alex, get it together! Act like you belong, or something!*

"Ha!" the girl laughed, before turning around and grabbing Alex by his hands and squeezing them tight, "I like you, earthling, so I'll give you some advice! Forget everything you know, forget science, and forget technology, they're all a lie! This is the real world, boy! And try pegging yourself down a few notches, you aren't fooling any one with that talk. I see the fear in your eyes."

"I have a name! I'm not a boy, and I don't believe a word you say! I hear that the Black Death makes some people hallucinate, and that's all this is, girl!" Alex snapped, but in his mind, his denial was the tip of the iceberg. As he looked around again in wonder, *this can't be real,* he thought to himself, *but if it is, there's no way I can go back. Not now! I need to know.*

"Earthlings, always so eager to learn yet can never accept the truth, always too ignorant, always finding it too easy to turn a blind eye! And my name is Atia!"

Earthlings! Atia thinks to herself, *the bloody! No, no. Calm down,* she thought, stopping herself getting angry. *He's just scared. Of course, he'll be scared. Let him rant. Mother will take the wind out of him.*

"Well, Atia, I'll play along, but I hardly believe that this is the home of a goddess!"

"Well! You better start believing it, Alex!" came a second, female voice from behind him. "Because I can most assuredly say to you, that this is the home of a goddess!"

Alex froze on the spot. A chill ran down his spine at the sound of his own name. "How did you know…?" but before there was an answer to his questions, Atia sprung forth in excitement.

"Destiny!" cried Atia as she embraced the beautiful dark-haired woman in a hug.

This exchange would be enough to blow anyone's mind, but add this third person, and Alex was convinced that he must have fallen into some kind of coma. "Who are you?"

"Oh, my bad!" said Destiny as she turned and greeted Alex with a friendly embrace, her blue, silk gown seeming to glitter in the pure sunless light, "I'm the goddess Destiny, mother of the three fates, or the norms, whichever you prefer. But you must be Alex!"

"Err, yes, but how…" Alex asked as he nervously reached forward, his feigned confidence completely shattered. *Okay,* he thought to himself, *I'm either officially in a dream, or what they say is real. And then what?* But he didn't have to wait long for his unasked question to be answered as Destiny interrupted him.

"No time for questions," she said, turning her attentions to Atia, "your mother will be waiting for you, come along!"

"Wait a second, your mother? This goddess?" Alex asked, becoming more confused every second.

Atia nodded with a smile, before following Destiny through the gardens and towards the main body of the temple, dragging Alex by the sleeve of his shirt behind her.

The great hall of the temple, with a high, barrel-vault ceiling was painted with images of people, most of whom Alex didn't recognise, except for one panel, the first one nearest the door. Here, there were some faces he could put his finger on. Both he and his father had a love of history, and he saw familiar historic faces. "Hippocrates!" he whispered to himself as he was led into the hall, "Alexander Fleming! James Blundell!"

"What are you saying?" hissed Atia, who was walking slowly by his side.

"The people up there. That's their names. "Marie Curie,

Florence Nightingale, Sigmund…"

"Shush!" Atia hissed, "And stay quiet! Unless you want to be sent back to Earth!"

Alex fell into silence after that. The further into this strange place he went, the more intrigued he became, and the less he wanted to go back. So, he began to take in the magnificence of the rest of the hall.

The great hall itself was full of these so-called monks, bustling around a hall that was, apart from the roof above, rather plain, with white-washed walls, pillars, and a white, marble floor. Alex was led through the crowd to a simple white throne at the far end, its only decoration a carving of a salamander, gecko and some kind of honeybee at its base; the animals sacred to this goddess. Yet, above the throne, upon the roof, was another panel with more portraits upon it, like the many panels that lined the roof.

However, in this one there was but two portraits. One was the goddess herself, and the other was the likeness of Atia, by Alex's side. It was there where he was presented to someone who could be none other than the goddess Health, herself. The mistress of all of health and healing, from which she had taken her name, and all medicine across the Cosmic tree was her responsibility. She was the lady of Helothom, the temple, and the monks were all in her service, helping her accomplish her eternal charge.

Alex was placed before the throne and made to kneel, which made him feel incredibly small and insignificant indeed.

"Mother, Goddess Health," Atia spoke, as she strolled confidently up to the throne and stood in front of the kneeling Alex. "I found this boy, Alex, on Earth." Suddenly murmurs travelled through the crowd. "Which, as you know, was the first world to have been attacked by Bubonic, the black son of Death! It is there where I found this, Alex!

"He has Titans' blood, my goddess! And that blood has, I believe been forged by the Black Death to be one of our order, a healer, which is why I have brought him to you!"

"Impossible!" the goddess spoke, and when she did, she did so with the power of an earthquake. "Earth's magic is all but dead! There is no more power there! The Titan kin are all gone from it! Do you not understand what you are saying? Since when has my daughter become such a fool?"

"I know what I said, and that is what I thought too, mother, but it is true! Alex is immune from disease! I know silver blood when I see it, no matter how faint! He does indeed have Titan blood!"

"Your daughter tells the truth!" interrupted Destiny, as she stepped forward before the goddess, out from the crowd of monks. "I have spoken to Life and his son and they have assured me, that there is a little left upon that world, enough for a final son, or daughter, to be born. This boy does indeed have Titans' blood, and it is his fate to join this order, I have written it so. I urge you great goddess, do not cast him out! You'll need his help before the end!"

The goddess sat on her thrown in deep thought for a second, cumulating what she had been told. Finally, she spoke. "This is his destiny. You have no power over me, Destiny. Why should I accept a stranger? With no experience? No history! Just on the whim of a faithless trickster?"

"Call me what you will, Health, but you're the fool if you reject my advice when it comes straight from our masters. Do as you will! But do not blame others for the consequences that will come."

Health became painfully quiet once more as she looked down at Alex, who was at this point completely lost, but terrified of being sent home, having had a taste of what lies beyond. *If this is a dream,* he thought, *then I'm not sure I want to wake up.*

Finally, Health gave a great sigh and a nod. "Very well! Alex shall join our noble rank, under the supervision of my daughter, Atia!"

There was a mixed murmur from the crowd that had gathered. Atia gave a nod and a slight bow, though she hid her true emotions.

The congestion and Goddess then moved on to other matters, while Atia picked Alex up and took him from the hall as Destiny disappeared back into the crowd.

The pair walked down a lit corridor, towards the living quarters within the temple. All the while, Atia spoke to Alex. "You know, earthling, you are extremely lucky. You've been given an opportunity to make a real difference here, you understand?"

Alex nodded. "Yes, I guess so," he replied, still trying to take everything in as everything seemed to have happened in a blur for him.

Atia stopped for a moment before continuing on. "Now, that shall not do at all! I'm supposed to teach you, and I'll tell you now, I'm not very happy with it! I'm not a coach or councillor, and I'm certainly not your babysitter. I expect you to be prompt and on time, and to pay attention! I don't like repeating myself! Understand?" Alex nodded, unable to think of what else to say.

"Good!" Atia said with a smile, lightening up a little. "Then perhaps we'll be able to get on. Be prepared, though, Alex, the cosmos is far bigger and more complex than you can possibly know, and you only are a little person on a little world, after all."

The pair came at last to a small door halfway down a long corridor which was to be Alex's chambers. "Here!" Atia said, gesturing to the open door that led to a simple and small chamber. "These shall be your quarters! You should find your new robes inside, so change and freshen up. I'll give you today to take everything in, and remember, Alex, this isn't a kidnapping! You can come and go as you wish, explore at will if you like. We shall meet in the great hall first thing tomorrow to start your training."

Alex stepped inside, and Atia closed the door behind him, her footsteps echoing in the corridor outside as she strolled back to the main hall.

Alex let out a sigh. He looked around his basic quarters, inspecting the bed and his new golden robes before laying down on the bed. After a while, he began to ponder and come to terms with all that was going on. *What the hell is happening to me? Just this very morning I was in England, surrounded by the sick and dying! Now look at me. In God knows where! I can't do this. And what do they mean? Titan blood? I can't do this! I'm Alex, not some mystic doctor!*

"Hello, Alex!" The voice made Alex leap from the bed in a blind panic as Destiny peeked her head round the door. "Sorry, did I make you jump?"

"No!" Alex said, brushing himself off. "No! Not at all!"

"Oh, good!" Destiny said with a sweet but obviously sly

and sinister smile, before letting herself in and sitting on the bed. "Will you sit and speak with me Alex?"

"Err, yes? Err, sure!" Alex nervously sat back down on the bed next to Destiny, who, to make Alex more nervous and uncomfortable, put her arm round his shoulder and pulled him to her chest.

"I need to talk to you, Alex, it is of the utmost importance, you see! This Bubonic is a threat, if he gets what he desires, well, then he will spread his plague to all life, and it is you who must stop him!"

"Me? What? Him? How? Why?"

"Simple, all you have to do is win Atia's heart, and, when he comes for her, kill him with this!" Destiny produced a long, slender, blade in a snakeskin sheath with a wrapped handle. "For, you see, Alex, you aren't meant to be one of these monks. The All One and the Quadrels have other plans for you!"

"What plans? What are you talking about? Who's Bubonic? Why is he after Atia?" Alex dreaded to ask, but found himself doing it anyway, not wishing to mess with the plans of a Goddess but trying instead to ride the storm the best he can.

Destiny gave a sigh. "Sorry, I forget you don't know much. I feel like you're one of us already!" she said with a smile. "Bubonic is the oldest son of Death. It's him who's the master of this plague. For now, I'm afraid that will have to do. I'll explain more later, for now concentrate on the task at hand." With that, Destiny got up and turned towards the door. "But I still don't understand!" Alex asked. "What is all this, why me? Why have I been brought here, why are you asking me to do this?"

"No! Now, I've said enough already! Heed my advice, and all will become clear in the end. Destiny is about to leave, but as always, she has to have one final word. Oh, and Alex, don't forget, Destiny has her eyes on you!" she whispered with a parting wink of the eye.

Chapter III:
30 Years Before the Plague (BP)

The young man was Fredrick Smith, Freddy for short. Having just been released from the mental institution, this ten, almost eleven-year-old boy had lost all friends. He sat alone amongst the books in the small library of his small village, eating his lunch amongst their towering shelves. Meanwhile all other children of his age, and even many of his teachers, kept him at arms-length. Them who did dare go near him called him names and pushed him around like a rag doll, before running away in pretend fear. The playground was hell for him now. The streets were filled with tormented souls he could see.

The library seemed to be the only place he could get away from those who labelled him 'crazy', and those inside his head. Though even this little refuge at the end of two rows of bookshelves, against a white-washed wall and under a stained-glass window depicting Jesus, was filled with those he could see. Even now, as he munched on his ham and cheese sandwich and looked upon a book about lobotomy, he could hear their echoing screams. Even now, after the asylum, where they had all melted away, he could see and hear them, having flooded back with the free light and free air. *They're not as bad as before*, he reassured himself, *not as bad as before*.

Then the most awful sound filled the library as something came thudding along, half scraping and squeaking along the polished floor. Freddy held his book close to his chest and began to rock back and forth as if in a rocking chair as the noise grew louder. He closed his eyes and hummed to himself to try and drown out the noise to no avail. When he finally had the nerve to open them again, he saw a man who chilled him to the bone. Covered in welts, the monk had skin like snow. One leg dragged behind him as he looked for a book on one of the shelves at the end of the row. He turned his pale head, and stared through eyeless sockets at Freddy, every wooden cross dangling from his neck and weighing him down.

"Release me!" he screamed, turning and beginning to walk towards Freddy, his words a slur. He dropped the ghostly, heavy books that he'd been carrying, making a horrendous racket that only Freddy could hear. "Release me!" he cried again, picking up his pace. Freddy closed his eyes tight and covered his face with his hands, though he could still hear and feel its presence. "RELEASE ME!" it screamed, tripping just before Freddy and falling through the floor.

Freddy did nothing for what seemed like hours, his heart pounding in his chest, his head spinning, making him feel nauseous, his eyes still clamped closed behind his hands as he tried to calm himself. Never had he managed to get used to it, despite this being an almost daily occurrence. "Are you ok?" came a voice, finally breaking his trance. Nervously, Freddy removed the hands from his face and looks up to where before him stood a girl his age, with white hair and ghostly skin. With a breath he nodded his head slowly, still unable to speak.

"Are you the one they call Crazy?"

Freddy nodded sadly again.

"That's a funny name," She replied, holding out a hand, "I'm Daisy!"

Freddy, still rather nervous, took her hand and shook it.

"Nice to meet you!" She said with a charming smile, before she turned to her left. "I hope I'll see you around, Crazy!" She said before she walked away, disappearing through a bookshelf.

Chapter IV:
28 Years BP

"Daisy, come back! I can't keep up!" the now twelve-year-old Freddy cried out as he ran along the quiet village streets after his ghostly friend, running towards their usual hidey hole up in the moorland beyond the small village. The summer sun shone down upon them, and the long summer holidays gave the pair plenty of time to get away from the bullies and explore. Though this day Freddy had strict instructions to be back by ten. He didn't really get why.

Freddy arrived at their little spot high in the moors, warmed by the strong summer sun. Gorse bushes surrounding two sides of the small crater perched on the side of the moor. A stream gushed past the front, and the entrance was blocked by a young willow tree, out of place on the barren moor. Freddy leapt into the crater where Daisy was already laying, arms behind her head and the summer sun on her face, her pale skin and hair seeming to be glowing. The twelve-year-olds came here almost every day, a retreat for them both, where Daisy would pass the time by talking of the most amazing stories from medieval times, something that gave Freddy the deep love of history he would carry with him his whole life. Freddy was amazed by how much she knew. "It's like you lived it!" he had once remarked, to which he had been promptly informed of her father's profession as a historian.

"You're getting slow, Freddy!" she remarked with a giggle.

"Am not! That hill's getting steeper!"

"Hills don't move, stupid!"

"Yes, they do! I read it in a book on geology, the world's constantly moving. It's just doing it so slow you can't see it."

"I don't believe you." Daisy replied.

"Yeah, well, you still think the world's flat!"

"Of course, it is!" she said, sitting up and pointing to the horizon. "If the world was round, then from up here we'd be able to see the curve! The horizon is flat, meaning the world's flat!"

"Fine, have it your way. I know when I can't win!" the response made Daisy chuckle to herself. "Besides, I have to be back by ten!" Freddy adds.

"Okay, what you brought today?" Daisy askes promptly, to which, in response, Freddy pulled out a rather old set of cards and presented them to Daisy.

"My dad taught me how to play. Want to give it a go?" to which Daisy nodded in excitement.

13 months AP, Helothom.

The sun, if it could be called that in this strange place, was shining strong and bright down on the temple gardens the morning following Alex's arrival. Dressed in his most uncomfortable of robes, Alex sat on one of the many scattered stone benches that littered the gardens about the place, scribbling away in his notebook all that he could remember of his father's youth. "There has to be a connection!" he muttered to himself as the monks of the temple came and went through the many stone arches. "I mean, surely it can't be pure coincidence. My father releases this thing onto Earth, and now I'm brought here, the only person who seems immune in England." Alex gave a sigh as he looked about. "Wherever here is?"

With frustration, he stared long and hard at the words he'd scribbled on the page, hoping something would jump out, it did not. He threw his pencil to the floor with a groan and ran his hands through his long, golden hair as he lay back on the bench and let the warm light set his face aglow.

"Here you are," came the voice that Alex was so desperate not to hear. Atia, the one who dragged him into this world and his new mentor (or something like that), was clearly not going to be a pleasant teacher from her reaction to this task yesterday. He could tell she wished for little more than to make his life a nightmare, so, rather foolishly, Alex chose to ignore her instructions to meet her promptly.

"I told you we were to meet at first light at the great hall! Time is ticking here, now get up, you lazy boy. There is a lot to do, and thanks to you, not as much time to do it!"

Alex still ignored her with his eyes locked shut, outstretched on the bench. "Hmm," she said, displaying a sinister simile on her face, "get up, earthling, it's time you knew the truth." Still Alex did nothing. "Very well," she sighed, "if you will not get up of your own accord, I'll just have to do it for you!" And with that, Atia pushed Alex off the bench and into the bush behind it to sit down herself.

Alex let out a yell as he felt himself being scratched and pricked by the bush, leaping to his feet to escape its thorny branches. "Well, look who finally got up!" Atia said with a chuckle and an amused smile. "Are we ready now, or would you like some more time to play in the bush?"

Alex gave her a sarcastic smile, and, scooping up his notebook and pencil, he began to stroll off through the garden, Atia following suit, satisfied with her work.

Moments later, Alex found himself being led through the many narrow sandstone corridors of the great Temple. He couldn't help but to feel overwhelmed and amazed at the expanse of the complex; gardens, halls, corridors, chemist's rooms and places for all kinds of experimentation in the latest of these magical medicines. Atia led Alex deep into the complex, out the far side and up towards the mountains that surrounded the temple like a great wall, closing off three sides of Helothom.

There they come to a set of stairs that winds its way up the side of the mountains like a goat track. Without a moment hesitation Atia begins to climb.

As the pair climbed higher into the wall of rock, Alex couldn't help but ask, "Where are we going?"

"You'll see," Atia called back, her eyes fixated on the narrow goat's track in front of them. "You need some bloody patience, boy!"

Atia didn't speak to Alex again as the pair made their ascent up the mountain along the narrow steps of the path, climbing higher and higher away from the comfortable temple that Alex now strangely longed for. Slowly, the smells, sounds and hubbub of the temple faded away, giving Alex the much-needed time to think upon the past, desperate to try to piece together what happened all those years ago.

Freddy sat silently, bored and waiting in the small waiting room of some random psychiatrist in York, with his mother in her fine clothes, sat on her phone next to him. Freddy never got on too well with his mother, who was constantly fussing over him like he had a severe problem, which, in her eyes, he did. Though Freddy may have been a bit crazy, he was nothing short of a child far more mature than his years. If only she would see it that way. His dad understood, at least. He thought the best way to help Freddy was to treat him like any other kid, let him out on his own, walk to and from school on his own, go out with friends. Yet, if his mother had her way, Freddy would be on a lead like a toddler, so *thank God she doesn't!* he couldn't help but think to himself.

Eventually, a nurse came through and called his name. "He's here!" called his mum, taking his hand and pulling him up before he had the chance to think, and leading him over to the nurse and presenting him like a prize pig.

"Okay, got everything?" she asked him, to which he had little choice but to nod to answer, "Right, yes, we're ready!" The nurse, nothing short of a miracle for Freddy, looked from him and then to his mother and, with a sigh, freed Freddy from her.

"Miss Smith, the doctor needs to speak to Fred alone, please, could you take your seat, and I'll take him through."

"Oh," his mother said, her feelings rather hurt by the nurse. "Very well then, Fred, be good to this kind lady, will you, and remember your manners and…"

"Ma'am," the nurse said, clearly knowing her way around the situation. Freddy couldn't help but breathe a sigh of relief as his mother swallowed her pride and went to sit back down, chuntering to herself as she did.

Leaving the waiting room behind, Freddy was led down the narrow, uneven corridor to a gloomy-looking door at the far end. The nurse politely opened it, pushed Freddy in, and slammed it behind him, abandoning him in the doctor's room.

The room on the other side was not what Freddy had expected at all. In contrast with the dark, gloomy, and rather claustrophobic rooms in the rest of the building, this was a large, airy, space. With large windows, flooding the office with light, a large desk sat at one end, covered in papers and rather messy, and a sofa and rather comfortable armchair sat at the other. The room had a small kitchen area and an old, glowing fireplace at the wall where the door looked onto. The whole room was whitewashed and covered in relaxing, sea-themed pictures. Freddy had to admit, this place was almost as beautiful as his secret spot in the moors, though it did little to stop the butterflies in his belly. Behind the desk, hidden by his rather old-fashioned computer, was the psychiatrist of the establishment.

Freddy did little to draw his attention and it was a moment or two before he stopped typing, grabbed his clipboard from under a pile of papers. The doctor then strolled around to shake Freddy's wobbly hand. "Good day Mr Smith!" he exclaimed as he gestured to the sofa. The man was friendly, Jamaican, with long dreadlocked hair and a smoking problem which Freddy could smell from him, and see by the half-finished cigar in the ash tray on his desk. The man had a kind air about him, calming in the way he spoke. His eyes reflected only care and kindness, and his short beard made him look wise. Overall, he was a man whom one instantly couldn't help but warm to and trust, and Freddy was no different.

"There is no need to be scared Mr Smith, I am only here to help. Would you like a cup of tea before we begin?" he asked, and Freddy replied with a nod of the head. The doctor went to the small kitchenette, and, before Freddy knew it, he appeared back with two cups of tea.

"Milk, two sugar?" he asked to Freddy's amazement; he managed to get it right first guess. "So, Mr Smith, my name is Dr Mikels, I will be your new shrink. I was asked to take over after your last one seemed to disappear. Very strange, isn't it, Mr Smith?" Freddy simply nodded his head. "Okay then, Mr Smith, I am your friend, and you can trust me. I have no intentions to send you back to the mental institution, I simply want to help you. So, anything you say in this room stays in this room. Do you understand, Mr Smith?"

Freddy, again, nodded his head.

"Very well, Mr Smith, it says here you've been seeing things. Things you call... demons? Would you like to elaborate on that Mr Smith?" Freddy didn't answer for a moment, too nervous to say anything, though there was something about this man that made him feel the urge to open up. "It's okay, Mr Smith, take all the time you need."

"I see things," Freddy muttered, "scary things. They think that they're real, but I know they're not. They're old, some are in pieces or fragments, others more whole, but they are all in pain like they're dead and trapped, like ghosts. But they're not ghosts, I know that for sure. They're all in pain, I feel it inside me, and they want something from me, something that seems, well, dark. But I won't do what they want, no matter how hard their pain is, and that pain on me is. They're dark, always surrounded in shadows, always. They seem, well, almost as if they're in hell or something, I don't know…" Freddy paused for a second, unable to stop himself going on, he blurted out, "But one of them is different."

"Different how?" asked a rather intrigued Dr Mikels.

"I know this sounds strange, and I know it's all in my head, but… it's a girl, she seems to have a glow about her, a lightness that keeps the others away. When she's near the others, they just melt away. She's more of a friend than anyone else, I can talk to her, we, well, this sounds stupid, but there's something about her that makes me feel at ease, something that, oh I don't know… makes her seem like a long lost friend. She's the only friend I have, doctor, the only one that really understands me, and I know she's in my head, but I feel I need her."

"To keep the others away?"

Freddy nodded his head.

"Thank you for opening up like this Mr Smith, I understand it can be very hard, but if you don't mind me asking… what is her name?"

"Daisy. Her name is Daisy."

"Tell me more about her, will you? She is rather fascinating." So, it went that the rest of the session was filled with Freddy opening up about his friend until the session came to its end, and the next was booked for a month after. Freddy felt a little lighter as a result.

13 months AP, Helothom,

Alex was finally taken from his thoughts when Atia called out from the winding steps that scaled the shear rock face, one flight above him. "We're here," she called down, "come on, boy! Catch up!"

Alex let out a small sigh as he picked up his pace to get there. "How the hell am I supposed to make someone like her fall in love with me?" he whispered under his voice. "Destiny is such a bloody bitch."

But his complaints were quickly stripped away as he reached the flat stone platform that Atia was waiting on; though it was not the beautiful view of the sea and the temple complex and gardens that took his breath away, not the pure blue of the sea or cloudless sky, nor the sight of the breaking waves down on the pure white sand beach, but what was on the shear mountain side that captured his amazement. Carved in the stone, hidden from the land below, was a seemingly impossible thing. A doorway like no other he'd seen, made of two square pillars of rock, carved straight from the mountain side standing over three men high. Carved into it, as if holding up the mountain top itself, were two trees, decorated and emblazed in gold. "What the..." Alex gasped as he looked upon the sight before him.

Atia looked across at him, a smile coming across her face as she saw the awe in Alex's eyes. She couldn't help but feel a slight warm spot for the boy, to have been through what he has and keep going, she actually found it quite inspiring. She didn't know if she could be as strong as him in his situation.

"Amazing, isn't it?" Atia's tone reflected her growing admiration for the boy, as she used a much sweeter voice. "Come on," she said with a smile, putting a supporting hand on his shoulder. "Let's go, I'll show you the truth of our universe."

Chapter V:
27 Years BP

Snow had been falling heavily all day, but finally, as the sun set behind the moors, it began to ease up, drifting past the window in a gentle and almost orderly fashion. Fred's mother had gone to her work's Christmas Eve dinner, leaving Fred alone with his father, who had his nose deep in a rather thick spy book. Fred was bored by now, having been cooped up inside all day, and with Daisy not calling, he was particularly upset. After all, what's there to stop someone in his head coming to say hi? She did every other day of the year! So, he sat, flicking through the channels of his TV which annoyingly kept losing signal in the snowy weather.

It was at this point, while flicking from 'Dracula' to some war film or other, that there came a knocking at the door. Since his father never looked up to peer out the window on who it may be, there must have been only one person it could be. Like a flash, Fred was up and at the door, opening it, and to his joy finding the young Daisy standing outside. "Come in," he exclaimed in an overly-joyous manner of excitement, "and happy Christmas."

"Who is it?" came his father's voice from the other room, still not lifting his head from his book even as Fred re-entered with Daisy, who his father could obviously not see. "It's Daisy, Dad, you know, my friend."

Fred's father's eyes finally lifted from his book, and he saw only his son standing in the room before him, but, with a smile, he turned and said, "Good evening, Daisy."

"She says 'hi, Mr Smith'." Fred said to his father, his head turned to his right. His Dad followed his eyes to no one. However, he felt that denying her presence might just upset his son, for his idea was, *whilst he's not violent or dangerous, why not let him be?*

Obviously, Fred's mother did not see things in the same way.

"Come on, Freddy, let's go out. The snow's almost stopped now," She said.

Fred turned to leave.

"Where do you think you two are going?"

"Just to play outside."

Fred's father gave a sigh as he put back on his square reading glasses and returned to his book. "Very well, then, but don't go far and make sure you're back before your mother gets home."

"Okay," Fred called back as he slipped on his shoes and big coat, and left with Daisy into the garden.

Daisy brushed the snow off the garden wall and took her perch upon it while Fred trudged up through the snow to meet her. "What are you doing?" he couldn't help but ask.

"Make me a snowman!" she demanded back, "A big one!"

"And would you like to help?" Fred replied sarcastically, "or are you to busy pretending to be a bird." To which Daisy simply shook her head.

"Oh, come on, Freddy, please."

"Fine," he mumbled, trying not to show the grin on his face as he set about his labour, rolling one ball up after the other, in tune to Daisy's instruction. The first ball took up so much snow that the whole of the front garden and drive, be it a meagre little thing, was gone, stripped clean perfectly by her hand, acting through Fred, of course. So, coming down from the wall, they began the second ball on the road outside, clearing everything between their garden's end and their neighbours' next-door, though it was worth noting that the road wasn't a very wide one. Then, for the snowman's head, Fred was forced to scrape up every bit of snow he could from the walls surrounding his home; from atop his father's car, from the leaves of the plants in their garden, the whole lot, and even then, its head was far too small for its huge body. This made it look like a pie on a fork, a garden fork, that is.

All done, Daisy waited with their new creation whilst Freddy nicked his father's old hat, scarf and pipe, dressing their Frankenstein in all the finery the old downstairs cupboard had to offer, before a fruitless attempt to find a carrot for a nose. In the end, they simply used a stick, making it look far too disproportionate to the small head. It was ugly, really, though Daisy never seemed to mind.

"Oh, it's beautiful." She remarked when Fred's job was finally done. "Well done, Freddy," She said with an applause. "Now come on, I've something to show you!" Daisy started to walk off down the road and into the snow that was untouched by Fred's work.

"No, err, my mum will be back soon, and father said I had to be home before her." But it was no good, Daisy had already set off and was still calling him, as if she hadn't heard anything that he just said.

Fred gave a sigh and turned to look towards home, where he saw it – an old woman, her eyes black and her face covered in what could only be described as giant warts standing by the fire, his father reading his book still. Then, he looked down the street, where, from out the gloom, more monsters began to come. A man on a horse came riding through town, his eyes also black holes. Behind him followed more; monks, men, children, women, and upon the wind there was a voice that carried like a whisper, yet to Fred, it was more of a cry. "Free!" it screamed. "Free!"

Across the road lived two brothers, Will, the same age as Fred, and Adam, who was slightly younger. Will was playing a videogame, while Adam was sat at the window, looking out onto the now snowless area before them. "Hey!" he remarks to his older brother, "Crazy's made a snowman!"

"And I care because?" replied the elder of the brothers. Adam kept on watching as Fred turned about like he was on a teacup ride at a theme park, before turning white as a sheep, and sprinting off up the road in pursuit of an unseen, unknown, thing. "Wow, Crazy looks like he's seen a ghost."

"Maybe he has," chuckled Will, "I'm sure that's what he sees all the time... he talks to them in class as well. Drives the teacher insane!"

Chapter VI:
13 Months AP

Alex walked nervously into the temple of the mountain, not quite sure what to expect. It was darker than outside, much more so, with the eerie silence of an old library, making him scared to breathe too loud. The smells of incense and other fragrant oils hung heavy in the air, making it difficult to breathe through the smoke and mist that it created, its taste clinging to Alex's tongue in his dry mouth. As his eyes adjusted to the dark comparison to outside, he was overwhelmed with the sight that he saw. The place was massive, with many levels of balconies above his head leading round the oval-shaped space. Passageways led off deeper into the mountain in every direction, their narrow corridors illuminated with bowls of burning oil. But no fire was needed in the inner space that Alex now found himself.

The space was centred around a great stone tree with upper branches that seemed to hold up the roof, with a great stone man stood entwined within its trunk. Its leaves were made of the finest gold, reflecting the light that passed through a crystal within the roof, shattering the bright light outside into all the colours of the rainbow and painting the white-washed walls with splashes and dots as if it had been painted by a madman.

"What… is this place?" Alex was almost scared to ask and break the complete silence of the place as one or two of the monks made their way around.

"This is our temple," replied Atia, pumping her chest out with a sense of pride like a prize chicken, "and this is just the one for the monks of healing. Here, stored and copied, is all the knowledge that anyone needs."

"But–" Alex was almost scared to ask out of fear of making himself look like a complete fool. "I thought you were the Gods, or Dradens, or whatever you call yourselves. Who do you need to pray to?"

Atia doesn't answer, she simply grins in amusement, grabbed Alex by the hand and, almost tearing it off with the force she takes off at, said, "Follow me, I'll show you."

Atia dragged Alex up the stairs to the topmost balcony, and there, walking round the oval to the furthermost passageway, dove down into the narrow darkness, strolling along it for what, to Alex, felt like quite some distance before the pair emerged at the other side. It was a dark, cold, circular room with a single oil-burning bowl in the middle. A beam of light came from a circular cavity high above in the ceiling. Incense burned in a hanging jar above and filled the chamber with its thick smell. But the walls were what was most intriguing about the small round room, for, they were covered in band after band of carved figures, each delicately painted to look as life-like as possible. The strips of carvings led into yet another room to the side and as Alex's eyes tried to follow them, they vanished into that room beyond.

"What is this place?" he asked, stunned, utterly and completely, as he nervously and delicately traced the carved figures with his fingers. Atia moved around the room to where the bands of carvings start.

"These are the story rooms," she said, looking at the boy's amazement. "They tell the history of who we are, our genesis if you like."

This is when Alex noticed the inscriptions that ran along the base of each of the bands of carvings, though the writing was in a strange and unfamiliar language, one that he had never seen before. Not that he'd seen many different forms of writing in the past; the only real language other than English he knew was a bit of French, though he never really paid much attention in class to that either. "What does it say?"

Atia brought him round the fire and over to where the first of the bands began, which was a simple carving of a man sat doing what looks like some kind of fishing. Atia ran her finger along that inscription so that Alex could follow what it said, then began to read...

"In the beginning there was nothing, nothing but the river of creation, running and winding its way through the blank light that was everything and nothing all at the same time, though there was no time, nor space, nothing, nothing at all, just the river, the light, and a 'Thing'. 'Thing' was everything and nothing; it was the river, it was the light, though at the same time it was none of them and all of them put together in one single humanoid form, a genderless, faceless, nameless form that was everything and nothing at the same time. The 'Thing' sat upon the banks of the river, trying to catch an allusive fish for time that cannot be estimated, for time did not exist at a place that cannot be named, for the place did not exist; it was just the 'Thing' this 'Fisherman' and the River not doing anything but simply existing. Upon a time, unmeasurable, the 'Fisherman' that is everything, yet nothing, decided to get up, fed up at not being able to catch a non-existent fish.

"So, there was nothing further to stand upon as there was nothing for it to see or go to. All that was there was the stagnant waters of the River of Creation, and the light from no source radiating out like a blinding mist, all of which was the 'Fisherman'. Though through some unknown means, means too complicated and great that even the Gods could not understand, the 'Fisherman' that was everything and nothing did walk. The 'Fisherman' walked along the sand at the shore of the river, peering into its stagnant waters, and as the 'Fisherman' stared, everything stared back at it; all the many possibilities, hopes, dreams and chances, and knowledge so great that even the minds of Gods would be unable to handle it, though the 'Fisherman' did.

"The 'Fisherman' that was everything walked along the sandy shores of the stagnant waters for a time and distance that is unmeasurable. Until, eventually, the 'Fisherman' that was everything and nothing came upon the source of the stagnant River. There on a high cliff was a waterfall of frozen light, a waterfall of non-existence. It did not flow, nor roar. Solid in its Sentinel, like a stone guardian it was frozen in place, never before moved yet meant to flow and roar in vibrant colour and great possibility.

"The 'Fisherman' that was everything, including this waterfall, knew that this should be so. The 'Fisherman' that is everything imagined the waters flowing, imagined the worlds that would spring from the gushing roaring falls, and wished that they were so. From the 'Thing's own self, in ways that not even Gods can understand, the 'Fisherman' that is everything fashioned a weapon, a rod, and drove that rod into the heart of the icy falls. The falls shattered in a great bang, and from the explosion the Falls of Creation roared into life, and the solar system and universes came about with it; every planet, every sun, every meteor, every plane of existence from the highest realm of the gods to the lowest circle of hell all came into being.

"And as the Falls flowed, so did the River of Creation that pushed through the universe. As the river flowed, so did the Circle of Time, and so the 'Thing' that is everything became the All Thing for every world, every sun, every plane, every droplet in the river, the river itself, time, everything is the 'Thing', this All One.

"The All One was not satisfied with his creation, for the 'Fisherman' could imagine much more than circles spinning around circles, spinning around circles, the 'Fisherman' imagined more things like itself, things to inhabit and monitor the All One's creation. So, from a broken shard from the frozen falls, the All One fashioned and forged under the Falls themselves; the first Draden.

"This Draden would create something, something that would complete the All One's vision, though the 'Thing's vision was constantly changing and expanding. This thing that it would create would take its name, and its name was Life.

"Life wandered in this empty, desolate universe completely alone for almost five millennia, learning from the all one to become the greatest of all Dradens, until it finally fashioned the first life on a world three planets from the sun. With this creation the All One had created, travelling back to the falls of creation and taking another shard of broken light, made another god. This goddess's name is Society and

Society became the wife of Life. Next, the All One, as Life progressed, produced two more gods, whom Life and Society adopted as their sons.

"The All One kept creating Dradens until they became eight-strong. These eight are the most powerful Dradens ever to live; the Kings and Queens of the universe, and became known over time as the Octull. From these eight, many more Dradens were created at their hands, and so, satisfied with his work for now, the 'Thing' that is everything was able to retire to a realm that he kept all for himself."

"Where does this lead?" Alex asked as he examined the last part of the panel before it disappeared into the next room. The story had led to more questions than answers for him, and now he was even more determined to find out how he was connected to all this and where the plague came from. When Atia didn't answer, Alex turned in surprise to find her shaking her head, her arms crossed over her chest.

"That's enough for today," she replied simply as she began to walk from the room and back towards the main oval sanctum. "You heard what you need, now come on, we've got more to do!"

However, it is not Alex's curiosity that makes Atia fear passing into the other room. Rather, something she'd heard long ago, something that sent shivers down her spine, and what she was reminded of every time she strayed into the second room.

Christmas Eve, 27 Years BP

Freddy wandered up the narrow street, sloping up towards

the white moors, following Daisy's footprints in the snow. "Daisy!" he called out into the darkness.

The only light was that coming from the cottages that were either side of the road, as no streetlights shone in this part of the village, making it difficult for Fred to see where he was going. "Daisy!" he called out again, as her footprints seemed to completely disappear and panic began to seep in.

"Daisy, where are you?" he yelled out, now scared of being left completely alone. Suddenly, from the tree above him, a snowball came flying downwards, hitting him around the head and making his ear cold and numb. "Ow!" he exclaimed, rubbing his head and looking up.

"I'm up here, silly!" Daisy said. She was perched up in the branches of the old oak tree, that marked the end of the houses and the beginning of the wild moor beyond.

"How did you get up there?" Fred muttered as he looked around to find a way to join her.

Finally, after much huffing, puffing and effort on his account, Fred got up to the large, high-up branch where Daisy was sat. Stretching out before them was their small village and the valley in which they call home. Lights twinkled in the dark like so many little candles, and the fresh snow on the moors reflected the moon's icy light, making the whole place seem to glow eerily in the dark. "Wow," Fred couldn't help but gasp at the sight. "It's beautiful."

"I know," Daisy replied, and for the first time she seemed to have a hint of sadness in her voice. "I used to come up here all the time when I was younger, it was a place for me to think."

"Well, I have to say it, Daisy, you're great at finding

these places."

"Thanks!" she said more cheerfully. "And that reminds me, I've got you a little something," she said, pulling out from under her coat a small present, wrapped in plain, brown paper and string. As Fred took it, he can't help but think, and said aloud, "Feels like socks!"

Daisy giggled to herself in amusement. "Don't worry, Freddy, it isn't socks."

"Oh, good, I hate socks," he jested, making them both laugh. "But I'm sorry, Daisy, I didn't get you anything, we never…"

"Forget it, Freddy," she said rather sweetly, "I just wanted to show you mean a lot to me. I don't really have any other friends, most kids just ignore me you know."

"Hmm," Fred sighed. *Can she really not know?* He couldn't help but think to himself.

"Well, thank you Daisy," he said as he went to tear it open.

"What are you doing, it's not Christmas yet! you have to wait 'til tomorrow."

"Fine," he replied in a disappointed tone.

The pair of them sat there for a moment, taking in the beautiful view until Daisy decided it was time to go.

"Well, Freddy, we better be heading off, it's getting late. I'll see you in the morning." Daisy hesitated for a moment while Fred was still looking at the valley beyond. Freddy heard her take a deep breath. She leaned over and kissed him goodnight on the cheek, taking Fred by complete surprise. Then jumped down and disappeared into the street below.

Fred sat for a moment longer, his hand reaching up to his face. "It, it, felt so real," he whispers to himself, "But how is it possible?" his shocked and trembling hand felt his now damp cheek.

Somewhere out in the dark and snow, a car was driving along a windy moor road. Even this gentle snow hit the windscreen like a blizzard, so much so the driver never saw the female deer as it suddenly appeared upon the road, frozen in position until it was too late. The car braked sharply, the thick ice was under its wheels. It skidded, spun and then crashed into the barrier on the moor side. It flipped over and continued down into the valley below, landing in a crumpled heap of metal deep in the snow-filled valley.

The deer was, simply, never really there.

Chapter VII:
13 Months AP, Day 3

The warm light heated up the gardens of the Temple of Healing as the new day dawned upon them. Though despite the quiet peace of the place in the early morning, the warm light and the still-chilly air showed the promise of the hot day ahead, and the smell of the flowers and plants gave the place a relaxing and tranquil feeling. However not all was at such peace.

Atia was storming through the gardens, her red hair flowing behind her like fire, the beauty that usually seemed to radiate about her now devoured by her furiously angry face. She stormed through the gardens in search of Alex, who was supposed to meet her in the hall for breakfast at first light.

Even though Dradens don't have to eat, drink or sleep, they do it anyway, as their powers and strength can weaken if they do not, even though they will never die.

Though this was not what had angered Atia. The truth was that she hated being kept waiting, and she took it as an insult. This was the second time in three days that Alex had not arrived when and where she had told him to. She searched the gardens thoroughly, though, found no one.

As she concluded her search of the gardens, she placed her hands on her hips and let out a very annoyed sigh.

"Where the hell is, he?" she muttered under her breath.

"What's wrong, Atia?" asked the young brunette with a charm like honey, pretty as a rose and had a bit of a reputation amongst the opposite sex for her experience in matters of the bed chamber. She was also Atia's best friend. "No, I'm fine, Emma, thank you."

With Emma, as always, was Atia's other good friend, Reanna; a short, blond-haired, slightly plump girl who was married to one of the sons of the goddess Philia. Philia was the daughter of Life and one of the eight sisters of Love, even though all Philia's children, ironically, were adopted.

"Are you sure you're all right?" asked Reanna.

Atia gave a sigh as she sat down on a stone bench while her friends sat either side of her, while shaking her head and confirming her friend's suspicions.

"Is it about, well, you-know-what?"

"Oh, come on Atia, really, it's not that bad…"

"Oh, shut up Reanna. And no, it's not about that." Atia paused for a second while her friends look at her in disbelief. "Well, yes, it is slightly about that, but no. It's more this earthling. He's just so annoying; I tell him quite simply to meet me at breakfast, yet he can't even do that. It's not hard, is it? I mean, I feel justified to be mad."

Emma looked across Atia to Reanna. "Isn't your husband originally from earth?"

"Yes, err, America. He's a Texan, you see."

Emma looked over with a puzzled expression as if to say *what the hell's a Texan?* Though, of course, Emma had never actually been to earth.

"Was he this bad when you first met?" Atia asked her friend, not quite registering Emma's bewilderment, or, ignoring it.

"Well, on... I mean, when our wedding was arranged, he'd already spent a lifetime in our world, so he understood things better. But I hear that when he first arrived, he was a real nightmare, a real cowboy you see."

"What's a cowboy?" asked Emma, though Atia and Reanna both ignored her question.

"So, they do get better then?"

Reanna took Atia's hands and looked at her with a comforting expression. "Don't worry, girl, he'll get there eventually, just give him a bit of time to adjust. Ease him into how things actually work, you see earthlings are so ignorant, it's ridiculous, but don't worry. He'll get there eventually."

"Anyway," interrupted Emma, "have you checked his chambers? If I were looking for your boy, then that's where I'd have started."

"Why am I not surprised?" Atia and Reanna chuckled. "Anyway," Reanna said, climbing to her feet with Emma, "good luck with your earthling, Atia. I'd love to help, but I've got to go see my own earthling, and Emma's been sent to Zelnon 'cause some of the plague has started there."

"Lucky," Atia said with a sarcastic hiss.

"I know," Emma said, laying it on thick. "I hear that Zelnon has some of the best water to swim in in the universe."

27 Years BP, 28 January

The office of Dr Mikels' was dull that day, as Fred sat solemnly on the sofa, and the good doctor made him a cup of tea. He came to sit down in his chair with Fred sat opposite him, clipboard in hand. The friendly Jamaican man was not so jolly as he usually was.

"I understand it has been a hard month for you, Mr Smith," he said rather dully, yet not heartlessly. "I must assess your mental state following the accident, of course, though I understand this is a delicate matter. So, if at any time you wish to stop that's ok, but know that for many people, talking about it can help relieve some of the pain, put a plaster over it, you could say. So, to start with, just tell me of the events of Christmas Eve."

"I had been with Daisy all night and I was coming home when I heard sirens in the village. I realised they were at my house and I ran over to my father. He didn't say much, just hugged me... that's all. It was a policewoman who told me. She, well, was strange, almost as if she was one of them. But not evil. She said there had been an accident, and that my mother's car had spun on some ice, that it had fallen, and that my mother was gone. My father hasn't spoken about it to me, he just cries a lot."

"And what of the following morning?" asked Dr Mikels. "My father tried to act as if everything was normal, though, in all honesty, we didn't open any presents. It... it just didn't feel right. We went to Grandma and Grandads, they helped comfort us and take our minds off of it. We got home and took everything down and put away the presents."
"What do you mean, took everything down?"

"The Christmas decorations, we got rid of them. Me and Dad agreed that it just wasn't the same. We tried to carry on, but Christmas reminds us of her too much now, is all."

Dr Mikels sat there, contemplating what had been said. Even for him this was a bit depressing.

"I am truly sorry for your loss, Mr Smith, truly, but I'm afraid that there's nothing I can do to bring her back." He took a moment and sighed. "Tell me, Mr Smith, what have your visions been like since your mother's death?"

"Daisy has spent more time with me. A lot more time, she barely leaves my side anymore, and I'm glad of it." Fred stopped for a moment, looking away as if at some unseen thing, but with a sigh he turned back to Dr Mikels to continue. "When she does leave, they are lot worse. They're angry, almost, and with each passing day it becomes even more hellish. I think that they want me to do something, but they're getting more desperate. Obviously, I know they're not real, but it's still scary."

"Aye, Mr Smith, I suppose it is." The doctor jotted something down on his clipboard before turning back to Fred. "Mr Smith, is Daisy with you now? I mean, in this room?" Freddy didn't answer in words, he just nodded his head. Dr Mikels saw him slightly move his hand out along the sofa, as if reaching for something. With a hum, he asked, "I wish to try something Mr Smith, could you ask Daisy to leave us for a moment or two?"

"Go on," Freddy said to this invisible thing, as Dr Mikels curiously watched Fred's eyes as they followed something out the room, before he turned back to Dr Mikels.

"Okay, she's… gone?" Dr Mikels watched as Fred's eyes widened and dilated, fear spreading across his face as his fist squeezed the sofa cushion until his knuckles were white.

"Are you okay, Mr Smith?"

Freddy shook his head in response.

"Do you see one of those things here now?"

Freddy nodded his head.

"Where is it?" asked Dr Mikels.

Freddy, scared, slowly lifted a trembling arm and a trembling hand, extending his finger to point directly at Dr Mikels.

"Interesting," he muttered, scarily not phased. "Very interesting."

13 Months AP, Helothom

Alex gave a sigh as he lay in his small, uncomfortable bed in his cramped quarters of the Temple of Healing. He tapped his pencil on the side of his notebook as he finished writing the last few words. "What the hell does it all mean?" Alex mumbled to himself as he stared off into space, deep in thought; the whole situation was beginning to become rather frustrating indeed. His sources were mixed; his father was hard to get answers from, and everything his mother had ever said seemed to contradict the little from his father and Dr Mikels.

Well, he seemed normal enough to Alex in his childhood. When his father was young, it was easier to piece the information together. His grandfather had been able to tell him quite a lot, though as Fred had gotten older, he had become more secretive. He looked down at his notebook and from it took out a picture of his father as a young man, not long before Alex was born, leaning up against a wall in London, where he had gone to university.

"Who was she?" he asked the picture in the hopes that some hidden thing would jump out at him. "What has Daisy got to do with any of this?"

Alex shook his head with a sigh as he put the picture

back into the notebook, closed it, and placed it on the small table next to his bed. He lay back down, his head in his hands as it ached with confusion. He knew his dad had somehow let this plague loose. He knew that he was looking for her when he did it, but how did he do it? What did a vision have to do with all of this? Surely it couldn't just be coincidence? How was he involved in the situation? How was his father linked to this place? Why did Atia bring him here in the first place? What was so special about him? Why did Destiny need Alex to win over Atia? What wasn't he being told? Why him? What exactly was the plague? These questions were rolling around and around Alex's head, all day and night. It was so bad that he had a constant headache and couldn't put his notebook down for trying to piece all the parts of the puzzle together. He knew his father didn't believe she was real, and yet...

Suddenly, the door to his chambers swung open and a furious Atia strolled in with a face that looked as if she was ready to murder him. In shock, Alex leapt into an upright position, shock and surprise making the blood rush round his body so fast it felt his veins would explode.

"What the... have you never heard of knocking?" Though Alex's anger was far outpaced by that of Atia, who lay into him like a pack of hungry wolves.

"I told you, boy, to meet me at breakfast! That was over an hour ago! I've been looking all over for you, you lazy... idiot! This is two days in a row you've not done what I've told you to. If you won't listen, then I'll send you back to the plague-ridden hole where I found you, you ungrateful little... Do you not see how bloody lucky you are to be here? Are you blind to how blessed you really are? If I had my way, you'd never have stayed. Now, I don't ask a lot! Only that you listen to me and do as you're told! This isn't a vacation or spa or something, and I will not have you lying in bed all day, doing... doing..." but as Atia spoke, a strange sense of curiosity came over her, making her intrigued as what the boy was doing, because she was pretty sure that he wasn't asleep when she stormed in. *No, he's far too awake to have just woken up.* "What the hell were you doing?"

"It doesn't really matter." Alex answered simply as he climbed out of the small bed and made his way to the creaky old wardrobe the get his golden robes, making Atia realise that the boy was wearing nothing but his underwear.

"Oh," she reacted quickly. "I, err..."

She instinctively looked down at the floor, rather embarrassed, yet still very angry with the boy.

"I think it rather does. I want to know what the hell you were doing that was more important than your tutorials?"

Alex gave a sigh, accepting Destiny's job for him. He grabbed his notebook and passed it to Atia, who sneakily peeks at the young man as he did so. "What is it?"

"It's my father's life," he said simply as he puts on his golden robes. "I think that he's linked to the plague in some way, though I'm not quite sure how."

Atia was too distracted to take any care in the words on the page as she pretended to flick through it, though, before too long, Alex was dressed and ready, snatching the notebook back from her and gesturing to the door. "Are we going, then?"

Atia looked Alex up and down before giving a nod of her head. "Err, yes." She coughed to clear her throat. "Come on, then, follow me."

The pair walked through the gardens in silence as the monks left for their tasks. All except Atia and Alex seemed to have left. Even the goddess herself was nowhere to be seen, only Atia and Alex. The pair walked towards the back right corner of the temple, towards a place that Alex had never seen before. Through old arches and open roofed stone corridors they walked, through rockeries and pond systems, environments for all medicinal plants to grow. Finally, at the end of the gardens they passed through a plain stone building, narrow and long like a block of stables. Walking through the large arched doorways at either side, they came out into a large grassy plateau that stretched before to the mountains. Atia leaned up against a post and rail fence at the far side of the building, and peered out as if looking for something in the vast grass expanse. Alex looked out into the grassland but saw nothing except the grass rolling like waves towards the mountains.

"Where are we?" Alex asked, finally breaking the awkward silence that had been lingering over them like a bad smell.

"We've got a job to do. Don't worry, it won't take long." Atia continued to peer out into the grassy expanse, and with a sigh she turned back to Alex. "Ring that bell, will you?"

Alex looked around until he found a cow bell hanging from the post that stood above his head. He took the string and swung it back and forth, making the bell make a sound that echoed out across the field and out towards the mountains. "It's so quiet today, what's going on?" he couldn't help but ask. Atia took her time to respond, sighing before answering.

"There have been reports of the plague spreading beyond Earth. It has us worried. The monks are spreading out, trying to figure out where it's got to," Atia hesitated slightly before continuing, worried about bringing back bad memories and hurting the boy. "But we can't have another Earth on our hands, which is why my mother is traveling to the palace of the gods. She is to speak to the Quadrels about our situation."

"And the Quadrels are?" Alex began to ask, though before the words fully left his tongue, something in the field caught his eye. Appearing upon the grass-covered hill was a beautiful red horse, traveling at a gallop towards the pair at the fence. Its coat shone in the warm light, its mane and tail highlighted white as it blew behind the mare in the wind. The sound of the great horse galloping across the dry, hollow, ground sounded like an approaching thunderstorm in Alex's ears, as the beast covered the large expanse of ground between itself and them in a matter of moments.

It pulled to a halt at the fence and approached Atia with confidence. Alex could see into its eyes, for this was no mindless beast; this horse had an intelligence to rival any other of its kin; a deep and brooding intelligence that burned with loyalty and steadfastness.

Nervously, Alex extended a hand, allowing the horse to sniff it before he continued, waiting for the mare's permission to proceed and gently stroke its nose and head. Alex could feel the power underneath the flesh, the strength and muscle that it held. A feeling that filled him with admiration and fear; to behold such as beast made his heart pound uncontrollably with excitement. Atia stepped away, leaving him alone with the mare, its breath like a hurricane as it snorted and pawed at the ground with its great hooves. "I've never seen a horse like it," he exclaimed, his eyes fixed on that of the mare's. "He's beautiful."

"Yes, she is," Atia remarked with a sarcastic smile as she returned to Alex's side, stroking the horse's neck and running her fingers through its fine mane. "She's a Divine horse, bred in the darkles planes by the Cursed-one. Not all Dradens are lucky enough to have such a creature." She added on rather jealously.

"So, she's not yours then?"

"No. She's mine," came a voice from the small building behind them. The pair quickly turned to face and bow to the goddess Health as she strolled towards them in all her fine glory. "I'd have thought you'd have her ready by now," she remarked to Atia, rather unimpressed.

Atia looked to Alex with a flare of anger in her eyes. "Sorry, Mother. Alex, you can saddle a horse, can't you?"

"Um, yes. My mother used to have one, so I do…"
"Then bloody do it!" Atia snapped, making Alex leap back in surprise. Without another word, Alex went into the little building, and after a good rummage around, returned with a saddle and bridle, and went about tacking up the horse.

"Are you sure you'll be okay on your own?" Health asked, not hiding the worry in her voice.

"Of course, Mother, everything's under control! We can look after the place while you're gone."

"That's my girl." Health wrapped an arm round Atia and pulls her to one side so that Alex couldn't hear them. "And don't spend too much time teaching the boy. Have some fun, I'll be gone about three weeks or so. Besides, he's been in contact lately."

"Mum, you know I won't..."

"NO!" Health looked over her shoulder before hushing her tone, "I won't have it. We've put this off for far too long. You have to do it; can't you see all this is happening because of your unwillingness in the situation. Now, I'm counting on you, daughter, and the longer you wait, the more people will die because of you!"

Atia gave a sad sigh. "At least give me time to train up the earthling, will you. I'd like him to become my replacement." *At his rate that should at least buy me more time.* She thinks.

Health took a moment to think before replying. "I'll think on it, and we'll speak when I get back. Got it?"

"Thank you, mother."

The pair walked back to the field where Alex was finishing tightening the girth of the fine leather saddle. "Is she ready?" asked Health in an uptight tone.

"Yes, ma'am," he replied respectfully, knowing better than to do anything else when around Health.

The goddess inspected his work before giving it her nod of approval and jumping onto the horse as nimbly as a child.

"Remember," she called down to Atia, "have some fun." Before she kicked the horse into a gallop, and to Alex's utter amazement, rather than riding off along the ground the horse rose into the air on fire the colour of freshly grown tree leaves, rising higher and higher into the air until, in a flash of green light, Health and the horse disappeared, as if a wormhole has opened and sucked them in.

"Wow," Alex couldn't help but exclaim in shock.

"I know right, bloody amazing," Atia replied with a smile. "So, we have the place to ourselves. Come! I want to show you something."

Atia led Alex back into the gardens of Helothom and through the great maze of shrubs and healing plants. There was so much wonder still in this place that Alex still couldn't believe at times it was all real, and as they walked, the magic of the gardens seems to grow. They passed through a rockery and bed of shallow water that ran like a stream, filled with small shrubs of healing nature as they headed away from the main complex and towards the mountainous rim wall. They passed deep into the heart of the gardens, through a round space where thousands of bees hummed about their hives, busy at work, filling the place with a magical sound and an even greater smell. But, Atia did not linger long amongst the many hives. She led Alex a little further on, and through a stone arch they emerged into a great place.

It was as if they had been teleported into the midst of a great pine forest, and if it wasn't for the humming of the hives, some of which were scattered under the trees, Alex would have thought he'd passed through another portal.

"Here we are!" she said, leading Alex under the thick pine trees. She stopped where there was a space clear of trees, lit by the great light and nourished by a shallow stream. Here, and indeed all about the pine forest, was a bed of the most amazing red flowers. Atia crouched down by them and gestured for Alex to do the same. Picking one gently she held it up to the light. "This is Marmin," she said, showing Alex the red flower, which looked a similar shape to a daffodil.

Alex took the flower from her and looked at it closely.

"What does it do?"

"It is the most important healing plant in the cosmos. It came from the world of Maroon before its fall long ago. The plant, if aged and prepared correctly, has a chemical in it that speeds up the cell cycle, and so allowing flesh wounds to heal at a much-accelerated rate. The flower must be dried, but not too much, and ground into a paste with honey to make a cream that is then put onto a wound."

"Amazing," Alex said with a smile, "but what if it's prepared incorrectly?"

"Well, if that happens, then the cell cycle shall be too quick, and the cells have a high chance of becoming cancerous. Many a young healer has caused death from a simple flesh wound because of that, which is why I shall have to teach you how to do it properly."

And with that, Atia stood up. "Come on, there's some already dried that we can play with! I've also decided since we're alone to give you a treat by letting you have the afternoon off."

Then the pair left the clearing, heading deeper into the pine forest.

Chapter VIII:
13 Months, 1 Week AP

The light of midday shone down on the shore of the sea as Atia lay, robed and covered, on the soft, sandy beach and listened to the sound of the crashing waves against the shore. She had never been a good swimmer, nor comfortable in water; more like a chick that's fallen from its nest than anything else. No, she preferred just to lay out on the sand and listen to the waves, whereas Alex was the complete opposite. She admired how free he looked in the sea, swimming past the breakers and into the deeper warm waters beyond, something she would never dare to do.

Atia looked out to the blue expanse of sea and smiled as she watched Alex swim. So free, so graceful in the water. She admired it, though had to admit to herself that she was quite jealous of his abilities. *I wish I could swim like that.* She sighed to herself as she watched him, propping herself up by her elbows. "I'd love to be able to swim out there with him, to feel as free in the water as that."

Atia had to admit to herself that she was becoming rather fond of the boy. *I think he's really started to listen to me, and he's company is slowly improving as well.*

Atia lay back in the sand with a smile on her face, feeling the warm light spread through her like a wave. She rolled over to her side, letting the heat warm her entirely, which is when she spied Alex's journal, tucked up in his robes on the sandy beach at her side. A smile overtook her as her curiosity peaked like it had that morning.

"Hmm," she sighed to herself, "he keeps that thing really close. I wonder…"

She peeked over her shoulder to check that Alex was still in the sea, which he was, and quite far out at that. *Perfect!* she thought as she stole a hand under his cloak to pull out the journal and, without a moment's hesitation, flicked through to the last entry to have a read, unable to resist the growing temptation…

'He never spoke of that strange day, not to any one at all, though I knew that it had occurred. I remember one day, a hot summer's eve, my father had gone for a walk and not yet come back, and I myself was out playing with my friends. It was then that I came across that place my father and his vision so dearly loved, there that I heard him talking to someone. Not till much later did I understand completely, but the story I heard seemed, well, almost familiar in many ways, for this is the day, I believe, my father stopped believing in reality and began, well, to think in a different manner.

'To this day, I don't know the whole truth, but I know more than any other, more than my mother even, for it is in me that my father intrusted the secret of his madness. I just hope I can do something with it. I'm convinced that the key to all this, lays in my father's relationship with this Daisy, but it's bigger than that. Maybe I'm just going crazy, I mean, how else I could have found myself in this place, way out of my depth.'

"What are you doing?" came the voice of Alex, making Atia

half jump out of her skin as she shut the notebook and struggled to shove it back under his robes. But it was too late; Alex was already up the beach and standing over her. Having seen what, she had done, he quickly swiped away the book, eyeing Atia with a suspicious anger.

"Alex... I'm, err... so sorry, I didn't..."

"What, mean to read it? You know this is personal. Honestly Atia." Alex slumped down in the sand and threw down the notebook as far from Atia as he could. "I mean, really! Why?"

"I'm sorry, Alex," she replied, finding that for probably the first time since the pair met, it was she who was in the wrong and having to apologise to him. "I really am. It's just you said about your father, and yet, you never really told me anything about him. What was I to do?" She saw that her plea was getting her nowhere, so in desperation to not leave herself looking a complete fool, she crawled across the sand and wrapped her arm around him in a kind of hug that Alex quickly shrugged off. In response, Atia sat up right to face him and looked deep in his eyes, saying, "Alex, please," all the time edging towards him, her arms outstretched in an offering of a hug.

"You made me curious, and it overwhelmed me. I'm really sorry but honestly I couldn't help myself, I just wanted to know." By this point she was almost on top of Alex, her arms resting on his shoulders.

"You want to know about my dad?" Alex finally asked, realising that if he had to listen to Destiny then he couldn't do anything that would upset Atia. "Fine."

He grabbed Atia by the waist and pushed her round, onto the soft sand and onto her back as he leant over, sea water dripping from him and making her robes wet for a moment before sitting back upright. "What do you want to know?"

Atia, rather surprised at the boy's lack of anger at her, was taken back for a moment. She had to admit, after all, that she was quite impressed by his reactions. After sitting up, brushing the sand from her robes, quickly re-positioning her fiery red hair behind her shoulders and giving her time to think, she came up with but one answer. "I want to know the story that only you know, the one that not even your mother knew."

Alex gave a sigh as he looked down at the sand between them. "Oh, that one." After a moment's contemplation wherein, he told himself, *Well, I don't really have a choice. Thanks to Destiny I've kind of got to do whatever she says.*

"Very well, then, I'll tell you about it. It happened about twenty-five years before the Plague…"

25 years BP, Yorkshire

Fred was now fifteen, and, despite all logic, Daisy was also ageing, seemingly keeping his age as her own. Though his mother's death was still a bitter memory on his tongue, it had not been sad for him, as him and Daisy were seemingly growing to be ever closer. On the warm mid-summer's day, things were no different for them. Though Fred was still a bit of a reject at school, he found solace in Daisy, her wondrous ability to keep all other visions away, and her everlasting friendship.

"Come on Fred!" she exclaimed impatiently. "The sun's warm, it's the summer holidays, let's go have some fun!" Daisy was sat on Fred's bed, she had arrived early yet again and Fred knew that he couldn't leave 'til his father had gone to work. Though the sun was beaming in and Fred would have loved nothing more than to get out, he couldn't. His father had changed since his mother's death. Despite having patience for Daisy, he now imposed strict rules on her comings and goings with his son. Clearly not wanting to lose any one else.

"Have some patience, will you, it's not like it's going anywhere," Fred replied as he walked back into his room from downstairs with a bowl of cereal, pulling out his small desk chair and sitting down on it while Daisy stayed on his bed.

"Oh, but please, come on," she moaned, laying back on his bed with a huff of boredom, her pale skin seeming to shine in the sunlight that beams through his window.

"No," Fred said firmly between mouthfuls of Kellogg's. "You know what my father says."

"Fine." she said, crossing her arms in complaint and staring up at his ceiling for a while.

"I have to admit," she said, breaking the awkward silence, "your bed's actually rather comfortable."

"Err, thanks?" Fred was not quite sure how to reply; whilst Daisy had been in the house before, she'd never actually been in his room. It made him feel a bit, well, awkward to say the least. Not that he could exactly throw something out that was in his head. *I mean, really,* he thought to himself, *if she's my mind, then I think I'm kind of stuck with it, or her, or, well, I'm still not entirely sure.*

Daisy couldn't help but giggle to herself in response; everything seemed just so perfect for her, she really couldn't believe that she had found a friend quite like Fred. It almost seemed too unreal to her, a subject that had crossed Daisy's mind a lot over the years; how despite the number of options available to her, chance had given her one so perfect. Always, the feeling of being hidden, unseen, unable to communicate comes to her mind, when she reflects on her time before she knew Fred, and how he had been her liberator. Not that she had ever mentioned anything to him, he would never believe her if she said she felt he were made for her. *Like knives and forks,* she called it, if only to herself.

"What are you thinking about?"

"Oh, not a lot," Daisy said rather dreamily as she rolled onto her side to look at him, a big grin across her face. "Just all the things we could be doing that's better than watching you eat your breakfast."

"Daisy!"

"What?" she jested, "I'm only having a laugh, I know how important your food is to you!"

"And you? I never really see you eat?" as soon as the words left his mouth Fred felt like an idiot. *Why did I say that? What was the point? She's in my head! She's not real! How can she eat anything?*

"I eat," she mumbled back, "I'm just not that hungry is all." It was at this point that a bird flew past the window; an insignificant thing, yet enough to make her notice something she had before overlooked upon the windowsill as she turned to see what had caught her eye. There, amongst some other junk that she didn't really understand, was the small brown parcel she had given him as a Christmas present that dreadful night. Curious, Daisy got up and walked across the room to investigate. Looking at it from its spot, she realised it'd been left unopen.

91

"What's this?" she asked, her voice hurt. "Why didn't you ever open it?"

Immediately, Fred, too scared to upset something in his head, put down his cereal and walked briskly over to see what she had found. Realising what it was, he picked it up, taking a couple of steps back and slumping down on the end of his bed. "I, err," he said, his voice shaky, his grief coming back like a wave. "Well, I've not opened anything from that day. I guess it just never felt right."

Daisy sat down on the bed next to him, her arm wrapping around him in an attempt to provide some sort of comfort to him. "Come on, Freddy, please," she said, trying to sound as sad as he was. "I've not got a lot, I wanted you to have it to show how much of a friend you are to me. Come on, it's a shame to leave it unopened."

Fred looked at her and gave a sigh; he couldn't fight something that was in his head, not really. In all honesty he'd forgotten it was even there, and never really noticed it till she had pointed it out. "Fine."

Daisy gave a little clap and a smile as Fred tore into the brown paper and string to reveal something rather strange indeed.

A hanky? A soft, white, hanky with the letters, 'D H' stitched in red in one corner. Fred was confused to say the least, but, true to form, Daisy took little prompting to explain herself. "It's my favour. A token of how I feel." she said with a smile. "I want you to hold it close, always, and as you do, I'll never be far away," she said with a sweet and pleasant smile. Then she adds "I'd have given you a largess if I'd had something more practical."

"There's no need." Fred replies, "this I love far more."

Within half an hour, Fred and Daisy were climbing up to their favourite spot in the high moors, with the favour tucked firmly in Fred's coat pocket, and Daisy hanging off his arm and every word as if the two were in complete and binding love with one another.

This put Fred in battle with himself, for she felt to him real and all the time Daisy tried to win Fred's heart. But he could never give it to her as he knew that she was no more real than the Dwarfs or Elves from myth. She was just another strange creature that he saw whenever she wasn't around, all the monsters, half-rotten, some far more beast then human. *How could I love her, I mean, even if I do, what's the point...? I'm not an idiot, I know she's not real... I mean, I guess I would if she was, but...*

"Do you believe that there's something greater than us?" asked Daisy seemingly out the blue, interrupting Fred's chain of thought.

"What do you mean, something greater?" Fred asked, rather puzzled.

"I mean, stupid, do you believe in a god or something? Is there something out there that is... well, greater than us?" she replied, pulling on Fred's arm until he started to be dragged to one side of the narrow path.

Fred didn't answer for a good long while. "Well, I don't know. I've never given it much thought, to be fair."

"Well, I do!"

"You do? So, you're telling me that there's some big, bearded man in the sky somewhere who created everything in seven days?"

"Well," Daisy said, rather shocked at the aggressiveness of Fred's comeback, "I wouldn't say it took seven days... besides, there's more out there then just one god."

"So, you're not a Christian then?"

"No, not really."

"Okay," Fred said, thinking that he'd get some ridiculous answer that was rather funny if he delved deeper. "What do you think is out there then?"

"Me!"

"You?" Fred, in shock, pulled Daisy off his arm and took a step back, not sure if he should laugh or run-in fright. "What the hell do you mean you?"

"I mean I'm a goddess!" she replied rather frankly. "A very powerful goddess."

"Yeah, right, and I'm King Solomon!" Fred replied sarcastically.

But before Daisy had chance to answer a great noise came from behind them. "HEY! CRAZY! WHO YOU TALKING TO?" came the cruel and bitter voice of William, from his bike, with his two followers, George and Katy, and his brother, Adam at his back.

The gang rode up to Fred before he had the chance to bolt, circling him in a cage of ill-will and cruelty.

"Probably his little ghost friend!" snorted Katy from her bright pink bike.

"Crazy, is Caspar around?" jested Adam from the back of the pack. "Or is it the grim reaper you're talking to?"

"Come on," Fred said, but it was more hopeful then serious, "what's the point? Can't you just leave me alone? I am not causing you any trouble."

"Oh, come on, Crazy, we're only having some fun with you. It would do you good to get some friends." George called back.

"Yah, what's wrong with a bit of banter?" William said, riding his bike closer, right up to Fred's face as he tried fruitlessly to back away. "We're only having some fun with yah, don't be so boring."

"So, who are you talking to?" Katy said with a smirk as she pinned Fred in from the back.

"Who does it matter? He's crazy, it's not like they're really there!" Adam jested.

"It matters," said William, shutting his little brother up, "I want to know, Crazy, who is it you talk to?"

"You've tried to get me to say for years, why should this time be any different," Fred spat back.

"Come on," Katy encouraged, "how about this, if you tell us who it is you talk to… then we'll stop calling you crazy, how about that?"

"Do you really think I'll believe the likes of you?" Fred spat.

"Ha! He admitted it! He does talk to someone!" Adam cried out, but none of the others were listening to the little cocky thing.

"Crazy, come here," William said in a deep and dreadful voice as he whispered into Fred's ear. "Who do you think you are to talk like that to my girl… now, I don't know what your problem is, we're just trying to have some fun, unlike you, but if you're going to keep talking to her like that, then us two are gonna have a problem, understand?"

Fred quickly nodded his head before turning sharply and deciding it was time to try and walk away – not that that was ever going to happen. Before Fred had taken five steps, the gang was on him like a group of vultures.

"Hey, crazy! Where do you think you're going?" Adam jested.

"Crazy!" called out William, "I ain't done with you yet!"

"Oy, crazy," George rode his bike around him, blocking off Fred's escape route, "did we say you could go yet?"

"Crazy! How dare you turn your back on him?" Katy hissed.

"Crazy! You listen to my girl! Get back here right now!" William called out, dismounting his bike and storming over to Fred with a furious temper.

"Crazy! Get back here!" he commanded, but Fred didn't say a word, he kept his head down and his feet moving. But William was gaining on him.

"This is your last chance, Crazy! Turn around and come back now!" but Fred still didn't listen, trying to keep in mind what the teacher had said at school. *Just walk away, they'll get bored and leave you alone if you just don't react and walk away.* But it wasn't working, it never worked.

Suddenly, Fred found himself flat out on the floor with William towering over him, his hand clenched in a fist. "I told you not to insult my girl," William snarled with a vicious smile as he looked down at the frightened Fred on the floor, admiring his work like some great, renaissance artist. Then, spying something stuffed in Fred's pocket, leant down and swiped out the white handkerchief that was Daisy's favour, holding it up to the sun and inspecting it.

"Hey, Crazy. What's this?" Fred stared up in bewilderment at William. Not only could he see the gift from

Daisy, but he was holding it, as if it were as real as a book, a tree, or Fred himself. *How is this possible!* he thought as his mind raced to find a conclusion, his whole understanding of his predicament and mind thrown into a hurricane of chaos as William asked that question that seemed impossible to come from anyone but himself. So, that Fred found himself asking the question he couldn't help but come to, this, too, shattering all he believed to be real. *Are you just a fragment of my mind?* Though, despite his longing, he could not open his mouth to speak those words out loud..

Fred's shock was nothing to that which besieged William as he took his eyes from the fabric in his hand and back to his gang of friends, and Fred, who was still on the ground.

"What is it?" Fred heard Adam ask his brother, but he did not hear William's reply, for William was staring off into the empty space above Fred, his face as pale as white sheets, his hands shaking and trembling; like there was an earthquake in his body. Fred traced William's line of sight to the empty space behind and above him, where the ghostly vision that was Daisy stepped into, her eyes locked with those of William's. Neither uttered a word, yet Fred could see a thousand running through William's trembling eyes.

"Will, whatever's the matter?" asked Katy, trying to see what he did, though Will didn't respond.

"Will, is everything okay?" George asked, standing in the space behind Daisy, though William seemed not to notice his existence. After a moment, William finally reacted, screwing up the piece of cloth in his hands and throwing it at Fred, before, like a racehorse from the starting gates, he leapt onto his bike and rode away as fast as his legs could turn the peddles, leaving his gang frantically trying to catch up as they darted down the hill. Leaving Fred sat on the floor, bewildered and confused.

Daisy came and kneeled before Fred, a smile across her face which soon turned to concern as she sees the confusion in Fred's eyes. "Freddy, what's wrong?"

Fred didn't reply, instead he fell back onto his back his breathing heavy and frantic.

"What is it?" Daisy said, rather concerned as she moved round and sat beside him, leaning over to look into his eyes.

After what could have been an hour, Fred finally reacted by grabbing Daisy's hand and squeezing it. "Are you real?" he muttered, a trembling fear in his voice.

"Of course, I'm real, silly." she giggled. "I mean, what's that for a question?"

Fred, in disbelief, lifted up his hand to cup her face in it, and feeling the warmth of her body he couldn't help but give a smile. "You're not in my head," he exclaimed with joy, leaping up to give Daisy a hug, "and you really saved me! Thank you, you're... absolutely amazing."

"I know," Daisy said with a smile as she hugged him back, her plan finally coming into action.

Chapter IX:
14 Months AP

Alex looked around. The sun was blinding, the heat incinerating and a cruel breeze moved the stagnant air, giving the hope of relief from the heat but instead gave none. All his senses we're on overload and in pain. Everything was bright, blindingly so, and no matter how much Alex tried to block the sun with his arms, it never seemed to work. As his eyes slowly adjusted to the hell hole that he was in, he found himself stood on a sand bar surrounded by a flat, stagnant sea, so still as to appear as if a great pane of glass has been laid on top of it, reflecting the bright sun up and into Alex's eyes. The white, fine, sand was sharp on his bare feet, and this, too, seemed to glow and shine like the sun above, trapping Alex in the blinding light and heat. *Where am I?* he asked himself in panicky thought as he turned and wheeled about, desperate to escape the cage of light that trapped him and prevented him from seeing.

From this light came a dark silhouette, something that Alex could look at without being blinded. The figure grew in size, as it came closer, and as it did, the light and heat seemed a little less overwhelming and cruel. Slowly the person drew near until *she!* was just standing a few feet away, another stranger in the string of strange people and places Alex had been forced to encounter as of late.

"Hello, Alex, son of the Plague," she said with a sweet and pleasant smile, for she was all Alex could see amongst the burning light, her silk gown blowing in a non-existent wind behind her, *She*, he couldn't help but think, *is beautiful in a ghostly kind of way.*

"Who are you?" Alex asked, no longer as daunted by strange beings as he was just a week ago.

"You know my name," she said in a voice like honey, that echoed with the many voices of the hive, "you just don't know I belong to it!"

"Are you..." Alex began to ask as the one name he could think of popped from some deep and dark memory into his head.

"Yes, my name is Daisy."

"Where am I, where is this place?"

Daisy looked around dismissively. "That doesn't matter, what matters is that you know I've got a job for you."

"What job?" Alex asked warily, slowly starting to back away.

"You'll know soon enough!"

Alex awakened with a terrified jump, leaping out of bed in a cold sweat, his breathing heavy and his mind reeling with fear. "It was just a dream!" he assured himself as he donned his robes and made without haste for the door. "It was just a dream! It was just a dream," he repeated, over and over again as he made his way down the corridor, the light slowly burning off the cold of the night and providing the promise of a warm day ahead. "It was just a dream, nothing more, just a dream, just a dream."

Alex strolled with a quick step as he made his way

through the empty great hall, down another corridor, up a flight of steps and down one last corridor to the door at the end that lay strangely a crack open. Alex could hear voices coming from within, though he was too in shock from the dream to question it. He knocked on the door, awaiting Atia to come from her chambers and join him as she had every day since they were left alone in this place. "It was just a dream, nothing more, just a dream," he told himself one last time, taking a deep breath to calm himself.

"Come in," replied a voice not from Atia that left Alex puzzled. *Atia never lets any one in her chambers?* he thought as he nervously opened the door to step inside.

"Destiny!" Alex exclaimed in shock as he saw the scene before him. Atia's chambers were far bigger and more magnificent than his, with a big bed through an alcove in a roomed-off space in the corner, a large table set in the middle of the room, a fireplace and seats in the far end, with a raised platform in the far left corner consisting of a desk and doors. These led to a balcony outside that was propped open, the wind blowing through silk curtains and freshening the place, spreading the scent of sweet-smelling flowers throughout the room that were in scattered vases.

"Surprise!" Destiny said with a cheerful aura. Her and Atia sat at the large table, and Destiny leapt up and came to give Alex a warm hug before leading him to a chair next to her at the table, opposite Atia, the fine cushions providing a comfort that was as strange to Alex as his dream.

"I heard that you two had been left alone here, so I thought I'd call by to pay a visit, you know." Destiny gave Alex a smile as she sat down herself, passing down a cup filled with wine, another strange luxury for Alex, which, without much prompting, he was happy to accept, but never drank. "We were just talking about you, weren't we Atia?"

Atia, though, wasn't listening, more looking worriedly at Alex. "Are you all right, Alex? You look like you've seen a ghost or something."

"No, I'm fine, thanks," Alex reacted all too suddenly, his mind not having decided whether or not to tell the truth before his mouth spoke a lie. "Just didn't sleep too good last night, was all."

"Bad dream?" Destiny asked, her voice riddled with concern and suspicion as she looks at him in a distrusting way, driving Alex further down the path he had taken.

"No, no, I just didn't sleep well was all."

But Destiny was still not convinced.

The awkward silence that followed was only broken by Atia as she got up and went to leave. "I'll make us all some breakfast, then, if you don't mind being left alone with each other?"

Before Alex had time to respond, Destiny linked her arm with his and jokingly replied, "I promise I won't do anything to your mortal while you're gone, I swear!"

With a smile and a giggle, Atia left the room to head to the kitchen to make some breakfast, leaving Alex and Destiny alone together, and, as soon as Atia was out of earshot, Destiny turned on Alex in complete seriousness. "So, how are things going with you and Atia?" she asked.

"Yeah, not bad, I guess."

"Not bad? I need you to do a lot better than not bad! From what I've heard, all you ever do is sit and work in that journal of yours." Destiny looked into Alex's eyes and could,

102

without a doubt, see what she was saying was true. "Look, you need to spend less time on the past and more on the matter at hand! I need you to do this, or more than Earth will suffer. Don't you see that? This is important."

"Look, I don't see why this is so important in any way!

You're the goddess of Destiny, so..." Alex paused; he knew he should calm his temper but found himself overreaching his mark and not able to stop himself. "Why don't you just do your job, Destiny and make whatever you want to happen, happen! Besides, I refuse to be some pawn in your game. All I want is for everyone to stop lying to me and tell me the truth, all of it, though it seems what I want is irrelevant. If so, I'll just have to find the answers myself."

Destiny stood to her feet, her beauty now a frightful and furious sight that made Alex regret all his words immediately, as the room seemed to darken into an inescapable prison around her, trapping him in it.

"I'd remember who it is you're talking to! I'm not some little creature for your pleasure, and this is not my game, nor yours, yet we must play it whether we like it or not. Now, mark my words, boy, for you're in danger of reaching too far. I could squish you like a bug, make your life hell, and all I'd have to do is blink! I have power greater than you could ever imagine, I'm no mortal." She takes a moment to calm herself, though she does not yet release Alex from her hold, "but the truth is I cannot influence Dradens, but I can you!

"So, you will do as I say, you will win Atia's heart and if you ever wish to live long enough to get the answers you desire, then you will do it as quickly as you can, or I swear I will kill you, and lock your soul up in a prison of my own making for all of eternity! And you will never see the truth!"

Destiny sat down, her expression relaxing a little more as if none of this had ever happened in the first place, and, giving Alex a gentle peck on the cheek, spoke with a sweet smile to the rather shocked and terrified boy.

"Now, why don't you go help Atia with breakfast?"

25 Years BP, two weeks after William saw Daisy

"Good day, Mr Smith," says the presently and forever reassuring voice of the Jamaican therapist, Dr Mikels as he brought Fred a hot cup of tea before taking a seat on his leather armchair, opposite Fred on the sofa. The room seemed to have a particular glow with colour and light. "How have things been this past month for you? Last time we spoke, you told me that you'd been having some problems with some bullies?"

Fred took a sip of his tea; he liked the strange doctor, and thought of him as his only *real* friend. "They're good. Yes, they're definitely not going to be a problem anymore."

"Really!" exclaimed the doctor as he sat back in the armchair, interlocking his fingers in a gesture of inquisitive thought. "How did that come about, if you don't mind me asking?"

"Well," Fred said with a sigh as he sat back on the sofa, running his hands through his hair. "That's an interesting story."

"Go on," beckoned Dr Mikels, not hiding the concern that lingered in his tone.

Fred gave another sigh. "How do I say this without being sent back to the asylum? Because I'm telling you now, it's bloody crazy and I can't believe it myself."

"Mr Smith, I have no plans or desires to send you back to the mental institution, whatever you have to say, say it."

"Okay, if you insist... it was Daisy. Will, well, he got hold of something she had given me, it seemed impossible, but he did... and when he did, he could... well... see her, and I don't know what she did, but he ran for his life, as if he'd been scared half to death by her."

Dr Mikels looks at Fred long and hard, pondering what had been said, before finally, as if he had had to gain the courage to ask, asked, "May I see this thing she gave you?"

Fred looked at him, his mind stalled in nervous confusion for a moment 'til he burst into life. "Err, sure." He scrambled around his pockets until he pulled out the piece of cloth, she had given him, and passed it to the doctor, who hesitantly took it.

As Dr Mikels inspected the cloth, he asked Fred, "Is Daisy here today?"

"No. Why?"

Not taking his eyes off of the cloth in his hands, as if fearful that if he did it would jump up and bite him, he asked, "How does this event make you feel Fred?"

"What, you mean apart from confused, the thought that she might actually be real, or that all the people around me, including, maybe... you, are all in my head and this is just some sick fantasy or something, I don't know. To be fair, I'd much prefer it to be the first of the two." Fred hesitates for a moment as he watched the doctor, inspect the cloth. *How can he see it too?* "What does all this mean?" He was almost too scared to ask.

Finally, Dr Mikels lifted his head from the cloth. "In all honesty, Mr Smith, I don't know, though is there anything else she has said that might give meaning to this?"

"Well," Fred said, thinking back to that strange day. "There is one thing she said, though I thought she was only messing about at the time."

"Go on, what did she say?"

"She said," Fred couldn't believe the words coming out his mouth, "she said that she was a goddess."

"Really?"

Fred nodded his head. "That's what she said, and after the other day I'm almost inclined to believe her."

"Do you mind if I hang onto this for a while?" Dr Mikels asks, holding up the cloth in his hand.

"Err, no, not at all."

"Good…" Dr Mikels paused for a second in contemplation as Fred got up to leave. "Oh, and Mr Smith," he said as he looked up from the cloth to watch him walking from the room. "Don't be going and falling in love or something stupid like that, will you?"

Fred shook his head before leaving Dr Mikels' room. "of course not. Good day, Doctor."

"Good day, Mr Smith!"

Chapter X:
14 Months AP, Temple of Healing

The light shone down strong and hard on the beach as morning slipped away and afternoon arrived. Atia had gone to tend to some of the medicinal plants in the gardens that were beginning to become overgrown, and Destiny had been swimming since breakfast in the sea, who Alex has been told to look after, leaving him, who was currently in no mood to get wet, alone, sat in the fine soft sand, and giving him a chance to scribble in his note book without prying eyes seeing, and Destiny telling him off.

Though as he wrote, and not noted by Alex, Destiny appeared, bobbing like a seal in the small, relatively calm waves, swimming ever closer to shore. She gave out a quiet sigh as she approaches. *I gave him time to do this before he came here, wasn't six months enough?* she couldn't help but question, *I mean, he's proving harder to influence then I imagined. He better come around or where in trouble.*

Destiny kept low in the water and came into the shallows, pushing herself up the surf with her hands. Only when the water was too shallow to lift her from the sand did she stand up and reveal herself.

"And what do you think you're doing?" she said, making Alex jump about six feet into the air in shock as he scrambled, more on instinct than brain, to hide the notebook as if she may not yet have caught him.

"Err," Alex muttered and mumbled, his brain trying to think of a reasonable excuse for the situation, though, not surprisingly, none came to mind. "Well, emm…"

"Oh, stop blubbering, boy!" she said, only now finally leaving the water fully as Alex sat on the sand, still overcoming the shock. His eyes were fixated on her as she rose up from the sea like a flower from the ground, the water running from her thick locks of hair down her body and back into the sea, like a waterfall falling over an opal or diamond. Alex was speechless, partly from fright and partly from his age showing itself, as she slowly walked up the beach towards him. Alex's mind was still in shock, frozen like a statue, his throat dry and his heart pounding so hard it felt it could burst from his chest as the goddess came near. A deep mix of attraction and resentment that came from somewhere he didn't quite know.

A shining glow surrounded her, as if a star was hidden behind her back, the water falling from her waterproof skin, so much so that by the time she reached him, just five or six steps up the beach, she was as dry as if she'd never got wet.

"What is it?" she asked him, an amused smile on her face as she looked into his staring, moon like eyes. Destiny, even for gods' standards, was sex-driven, and she found the boy's reaction more amusing than uncomfortable. "Have you never seen a girl before? I mean, properly, seen one before?"

Alex, still in shock and surprise, was only able to answer with a shake of his head, bringing forth a giggle from Destiny, whose mood seemed to have radically changed since earlier that day. She watched as Alex's eyes followed her as she came to sit on the sand next to him, entwining her arm with his and placing her head on his shoulder. Alex fought to control himself and stop himself from blushing with embarrassment. "Have you done anything with a girl before?" she couldn't help but ask.

Alex took a moment to answer, more to recover himself than anything else, but, finally, with a sigh and another shake of his head, he said, "No, not really."

Destiny looked at him in surprise. "Really, nothing? You haven't even... had a girlfriend or anything?"

"Look," Alex snapped back, though he did not mean to, his heart still pounding as Destiny squeezed his hand. "Can we not talk about this?"

Destiny, on the other hand, had very different plans, completely ignoring Alex's request, and shuffling even closer to the boy, making him really uncomfortable. She said, making him turn his head to look at her, "Well, no wonder you can't get anywhere with Atia!"

Alex looked at her and could immediately see what she was thinking, and he was rather scared of what that might be. "What?" he asked.

Destiny didn't respond. In a split second, she turned on him, locking her legs round his waist and sitting up on his lap, pushing him down onto his back. Running her hand through his thick, long, hair, she leaned in for a kiss, while using one of her hands to move Alex around her.

It was Alex that broke off the kiss, pushing the goddess into the sand in shock as he crawled backwards away. Breathing heavy and in fear of the goddess, he looked at her with an untrusting stare, trying to keep her at arm's length, not sure whether to accept her advance or leave well enough alone.

mortals and gods don't end to well in Myths he thought to himself, before swallowing his own lust and deciding on the latter.

Destiny licked her lips like a lion that's tasted its prey, though, knowing that Alex wouldn't let her close, she swallows her pride and slipped on her silk dress, saying, "Well, at least now you've done something, Alex of Earth."

As she walked around behind him, she leaned down and whispered into his ears a spine chilling prophecy; "I will have you, one day, I will have you," before strolling up the beach and back towards the temple, leaving Alex on the sand alone.

He pondered for a second on whether or not he was right to do what he did, and, realising his rather foolish mistake of denying a goddess what she wants but also succumbing to his own desire, he jumped to his feet and chased after her.

Destiny stopped for a moment as if anticipating his change of mind. She turned to face him with a smile on her face. "Come on, Alex of Earth, I've something to show you." She waited a moment for Alex to catch up before walking on with him, linking her arm with his.

The hot light of the afternoon outside was a stark contrast to the cool and damp of the inside of the cavern temple high up in the mountains. The crystal lighting up Destiny's face in blues, greens and reds. As she walked, her arm still linked with his into the inner sanctum.

"What's this about?" Alex asked, slightly nervous at Destiny's intentions with him. "Where are we going?" Destiny responded with her usual smile and giggle, something that's neither bad, not necessarily good, but always made Alex's spine crawl with nervous fear. She pulled him along up a set of winding stairs.

It was big and cold, a semi-circular room at their top. High and dark, carved out of the black stone of the mountain it lay within. Destiny took a torch from the wall and ignited it in the small incense candle that hung in a glass lantern from the wall, and so igniting the room, though the illumination it created was painfully limited.

"Come," she said, taking Alex by the hand and pulling it under the folds of her blue, silk gown.

"What is this place?" he asked with a shiver. Compared to the rest of the temple, this room was a stark contrast in its neglect and absence of all care, as if its contents were so known to its residents that no one ever had to enter it.

"This," Destiny said in a seductive way into Alex's ear, shining the torch upon the curved wall and illuminating its carved face, "is our family tree!"

Alex let out a gasp as the red-light shined on the raised stone, showing a massive carved tree, its branches spiralling across the walls, fulfilling its entirety. On each leaf of the giant stone tree was the name of a deity and a small carved avatar, often badly depicting them.

"These are all the gods, goddesses and demons of the universe," Destiny said, finally letting Alex go. Like a dog that has been let off its lead, he immediately rushed forth to the wall to investigate it, running his finger across the cold damp stone, mapping the raised branches and leaves with his fingers as he mapped, the best his mind could, the various parts of this giant tree. Studying each name he came across and tracing it's link to the Draden around it. He did this until he found that leaf with the word *Destiny* carved within, and the small figure of a woman that, if the light hit it just right, and one tilted their head and closed one eye, kind of resembled the goddess behind him. From it, sprouted four branches. Alex turned around, the name that he'd found reminding him of who was stood behind him. "Why have you brought me here?" he asked.

Destiny took a step forward, illuminating a different part of the wall as she scanned it in search of a certain name. From the branch of death, she follows it to a leaf, half chiselled from the wall, with the figure that once stood there nothing more than a body and one leg, the rest, long ago having been removed. "You wanted answers Alex," she said, looking up from the wall and holding out her arm for him to take. "Come, I'll give you your answers!"

Alex shuffled, at best, over to Destiny and the part of the wall that has been illuminated by her torch, not sure what to expect. Thoughts like, *This seems too easy!* And *why are they finally giving me answers now?* crossed his mind in the second or two that it took for him to reach the goddess. Her face was impossible to read, her intentions changing like the wind; *One moment she hates you, the next she wishes to sleep with you, then she's all serious with you!* he couldn't help but complain amidst the nervous chatter in his head.

Upon reaching her, Destiny took Alex by the hand and pulled him in close. He could tell that she was hesitant to reveal anything, as if she feared that she was not meant to, held back by the cosmic force that she commanded. As Alex looked at the destroyed carving on the wall, Destiny looked around them, checking that the place was truly empty despite only her and Alex, being present in the temple. "You understand Alex, what I tell you, you must not repeat to any one... not even Atia."

Alex nodded his head in agreement, though, this was not satisfying enough for the goddess. She couldn't risk making a fool of herself within the politics of the gods by telling Alex and him then making it, purposefully or not, common knowledge. "Do you understand? What I'm going to tell you is known to but a handful in the whole universe, you cannot repeat this, no matter how much you wish to!"

"I get it," Alex answered sharply, his eyes flicking from her to the carving on the wall. The answers seemed just inches from his fingertips, and he was now desperate to know the truth. "I get it, just tell me the truth!"

Destiny gave a sigh, drawing out every possible second in hesitation. Throughout the history and immortal lives of the Draden, a lot can come down to just one or two seconds; one or two seconds that can define that deity's next cosmic millennium, and this, for Destiny, was one of her moments, so, she drew out every last second that she could.

"This, Alex, is a demon, a son of death, called Bubonic. He was born in a time when mortals were... well... getting out of hand. His uncle..." Destiny paused, a clog forming in her throat. "His uncle, the Octull, Punishment, also known as Grimmus or Judgment, created one of his cruellest and most destructive weapon to help the situation... the Plague. On Earth, it has been called the Black Death and the bubonic plague, on other worlds it has been called the Jubrakida, the Yoli or the tocktoback."

Destiny sighed; it was difficult for her to form the words, but by some miracle of her own divine power she carried on,

Alex hanging onto and absorbing every syllable of every word. "Punishment gave his weapon to the control of his newly-born nephew, Bubonic. He used the weapon to great and deadly effect, over and over again, world after world and that world again, for the last thousand cosmic years. But then he seemingly just disappeared. 'Til around thirty Earth-years ago, when he reappeared and struck a bargain for Atia's hand in marriage! Since then, the Plague has been spreading like wildfire through the mortal plain. To what end, I'm not yet entirely sure. But I do know that while Health's intentions are good, she is a fool to think Bubonic will keep to his word. The marriage is supposed to stop the plague, that's the deal, but I know it won't."

"Why are you telling me this?" Alex asked, casting his eyes along the wall and the great carved tree.

"Because I want you to know what you're up against."

"But I'm only human!" Alex said, shaking his head in doubt. "How can I kill a Draden! A god! This is out of my league, I mean, I shouldn't even be here!"

"Come now, Alex," Destiny said, leading Alex from the room and into another chamber where the pair could sit on a wooden bench and speak more comfortably in a lighter and warmer atmosphere. When seated next to one another, Destiny puts her hand on Alex and spoke softly to him. "All life has a purpose of some kind or another, and some are greater or smaller than others. It is not up to them what that purpose is, nor how challenging or difficult it may be! All we can do is the best with what we have."

"Then tell me," Alex said, turning to Destiny, "since you are the goddess of all man's fates… why are you playing with me?"

"Playing with you? Come, Alex," Destiny giggles a little to herself, "you overestimate my power. All I do is give a nudge to a mortal now and again in the right direction. I do not write their whole lives, just four or five moments in them. And I certainly have no power over the Draden. Indeed, I picked you for this task, but only because I saw something in you, something different. I mean, you seem well-hidden from the Plague, far more any other Man of Earth. That's certainly not my doing."

"Well, it feels more of a curse then a blessing!" he said grimly. "Having to watch everyone you know die. Your father, mother, sister. Death is by far the worst thing you lot ever created."

Destiny smiled and gave a little snort of amusement as she nodded her head. "Indeed, yet it is more complicated than you think."

"Then tell me."

Destiny gave a sigh. "Very well," she said, glancing up to Alex. "I suppose you should know the story, and it's probably best you hear it from me, for I know it best. It happened a long time ago, when the Octull as a political structure was still young, yet after the creation of the Titan race. The Octull had a problem, you see, for love existed, yet death did not, and so the mortal worlds were becoming dangerously heavy and overcrowded. The Octull called a meeting, and though I was very young at the time, I remember it vividly.

"The main consensus was that breeding should be kept the reserve of the Draden, and so preventing overpopulation of Planets. The Draden would be the sole controllers of new life. But not everyone agreed, in particular was the Octull

115

Life, Grimmus and Destruction, who all said that love is a force too pure and powerful to keep the reserve of the Draden, and so the meeting ended without any real decision. Now, the true reason for their disagreement, or for Grimmus's disagreement anyway, was that he was in love with a girl on a mortal plane, known to all as Otha. Many a long year they spent in each other's arms..."

And in this moment, Alex couldn't help but feel a deep sorrow, and a tear welling behind his eye, but he had no idea why.

"Then, one day they were chasing each other through the meadows when Otha fell, down into a deep pit of vipers. The poison did its work, and Otha fell ill, her body damaged; she was in great pain, yet no relief could Grimmus find. For weeks he tended to her lovingly, but she could not heal, for the damage was too great. In the end, Grimmus took a knife, and with his power, sucked her life force from her body. And so, the first reaping took place."

Destiny sighed. "Otha's ghost appeared before Grimmus, well and healthy, and in that moment, we all knew the solution to our predicament had been found. The Octull agreed that this new duty should be given to Grimmus' brother, Death, and so it was called Death after him. But the process changed Otha, and sickened the world she dwelled in, and so Death created the land of the dead, to take the dead from the mortal realm, for if he did not their lingering soul would rot the planet they dwell upon. Otha, in her anger at being a ghost, disappeared after that, and was not seen again for a very long time.

"Grimmus was heartbroken, and in his pain, he found comfort from his grief in the form of a young Draden. In..."

Destiny pauses for a moment, choking on her words. "In me! Grimmus loved me, and I him," she said, turning with tearful eyes to Alex. "Together we had a daughter. But as the long cosmic years dwindled on, he began to change. He turned dark, and at last we fell out. He hated his creation more than any, for he felt its pain more than most. But that is not the reason he turned dark."

Destiny fell into silent thought, as the rest of the tale was too painful to tell. "Anyway, he died long ago, but his creations didn't go with him. You see, Alex, you're not the only one who's been affected, nor will you be the last. We must stop Bubonic before it's too late." She fell silent again, holding his hand even tighter than before. "Perhaps there's a part of you that reminds me of him, back when he was a good Draden."

Alex sat in silence for a long time, but at last he did break the silence. "If this will end the Plague, then I'll do it. Fail, as I probably will. I guess I must make right what my father let loose onto Earth."

Destiny looks up into Alex's eyes, a fondness in her own that showed once again a change in her mood. "There is truly something special in you." She said, almost in admiration. "Something different." She adds, then a smile comes across her face, as her original purpose and desire comes back into her mind.

Chapter XI

Alex's dreams were haunted by Destiny's story, so much so that it wiped clean the good memories that had been made after. As he tossed and turned in bed that night, his mind exploded with fear as he witnessed a dream far too real to be but a figment of his imagination, almost a memory, though, no memory of his own, as if implanted there by someone outside his mind who took it from someone else. Though its relevance was without doubt, its truth seemed yet to be proven.

Atia returned home, dressed in her fine gold robes after a long absence from the temple. She was glad to be summoned home, relieved even. After all, Kapur, where she had been sent, was about as boring as sitting watching grass grow; there was absolutely nothing to do. *They're all completely healthy, why was I there!* she couldn't help thinking to herself, her heart cold and closed to all but her unending duty to the sick.

But there was a problem. As soon as she was home, she realised that fact. The gardens were empty and void of all people, silent as the grave. In fact, the whole complex was, there seemed not a soul in it. "Something's not right!" she couldn't help but whisper, almost too scared to speak. Her heart was in her throat as she strolled through the great white arches and pillars of the complex, into the temple itself. "There's got to be someone, seriously! What the hell's going on?"

She strolled at a brisk and uneven pace throughout the complex, searching for a sign of life as she headed to the great hall, though all the senses in her body seemed to repel her from it, as if her body knew something she did not, that something bad was lurking behind the doors. Suddenly, she stopped. From a staircase hidden in a small alcove to her right, came a noise of life, though, with no one to be found, the sign was not a welcomed one. Her heart beat faster than she thought possible. Every nerve in her body was suddenly ready to make a run for it. The false sense that she could survive whatever every other in her order had been unable to. Her mind stood there, as frozen as the marble statues that littered the garden outside. The noise came again, and her mouth responded uncontrollably. "Hello? Is someone there?"

The noise came, footsteps rushing to the top of the stares from the beyond. "Atia! There you are! I've been looking all over for you!" a young woman said as she appeared, allowing Atia to breathe a little. The woman from the waterfalls was a relieving sight for Atia, who was now able to relax a little, but the serious look on her concerned face gave little time of relief. "I'm sorry, Atia, I tried to stop her, but she wouldn't have it."

"D- what do you mean?" Atia replied as the woman took her old friend by the hand and dragged her like water back down the stairs. "Who wouldn't have what?" Atia askes as they travel.

"It's your mother, Atia, the plague is flaring up all over again. I tried to talk her out of it… but…" She hesitated for a moment.

"But what? You're scaring me!"

The pair slowed to a walk as they reached the bottom and was presented with the corridor that headed to the great hall. Atia still sensed that something bad was lurking within.

"But your mother thinks the only way to stop it, I mean stop it for good... well, is to give him what he wants."

"What he wants?" Atia said, concern filling her voice and mind. "You mean she's gonna..."

The woman nodded her head solemnly.

"NO!" Atia said, full of panic, taking off like a startled cat, running as fast as she could towards the hall.

"Atia, wait!" the woman called after her friend, trying desperately to keep up, but to little avail.

Atia burst into the almost empty hall, where her mother was stood with a sight that would chill even the fearless to the bone. A monster true to the word in every way, was there waiting for her. "Mother!" she yelled as she pelted into the hall like a racehorse, stampeding to the other end of the room and facing her mother and that thing which was her mother's guest. All the time her friend trailing somewhere behind her.

"Mother! No! Don't do it! How could you?" her breathing was heavy as she came to a halt before her mother's throne.

"Atia!" she said sternly. "Now, I don't care what you think, it's too late, it's already done."

"But how can you! He's a demon! He's a monster! A murderer! He's evil and against everything we've ever stood for! Why?"

"I will not hear it, Atia!" yelled her mother, as Atia's

friend stopped and stood some distance behind her, a small smirk on her face as she watched the events playing out before her. "Now, I don't care and will not hear it! This is Houdoo, he is here to sign the agreement."

"No! I won't do it. How could you even…"

"It's too late, Atia, it's already done! You always said you wished to give everything to help people, well, now's your chance, by marrying him, it will put an end to the plague!"

"No, it won't! How could you even think that?"

"Atia! That's enough!" shouted her mother before turning and storming from the hall. "You will marry him, and that's the end of it!"

Atia turned to the little creature that was her new fiancé's servant. With a smile and a bow, Houdoo extended a hand, saying, "My master can't wait to have you as his bride."

Atia looked down at it in disgust, spitting at the hand before swatting it away. Houdoo, not showing his offence to the matter, simply bowed again and strolled proudly and happily from the room, calling back, "I will be seeing you around, little princess." With that and a brief hiss to Atia's Friend "Warid," he was gone.

Atia was left with her thoughts and her friend to comfort her. She didn't say a word, but simply fell to the floor in a pile, tears streaming from her eyes.

Alex blinked and the dream was gone like smoke blown away in the wind of time, a hazy mirage that disappears as soon as one gets too close, and as the world around him came back into focus, the strange yet tantalisingly more familiar surroundings of the long, sand-bar beach and dazzling sun reappeared, broken only by the dreaded silhouette of Daisy, bringing a foul grunt from Alex as if to say, *What the hell now?*

"Hello, Alex," she said with a sweet smile as she sat down cross-legged on the sand, and invited Alex, with an extended hand, to join her. After a moment of hesitation Alex cautiously sat down in front of her, very suspicious of her intent.

"How are you?"

"What do you care?" he snapped back, cold and harsh. The meddling of one deity was more than enough, but his father's imaginary friend who claims to be another was far too much for him to handle. In all fairness, could he really, trust any of them?

"Tut, tut," she went, her eyes not hiding her hurt and disappointment. "Why so cold, I thought we were friends? Me and Fred…"

"NO! Stop!" Alex said, leaping to his feet and backing off. "Don't bring my father into this! Whatever you two were, that's never going to be us!"

In a blink, Daisy vanished from before him, and Alex's heart was pounding with fear as the sudden feeling of warm air met the cold sweat of fear at the back of his neck. He felt arms reaching round from his back to wrap around his torso.

In a moment of adrenaline and fear, Alex broke free and twisted away from Daisy, only to find that there was no one there.

"What's wrong, dear Alex? You seem as if you've seen a ghost."

Alex spun back around again on his heels to find Daisy sat still cross-legged on the sand at his feet. His heart pounding harder as he searched for an escape, only now realising the truth in the fact that he was nothing more than a bird in a cage. A bird in a cage with a cat sticking its clawed paws through the bars to play with its quarry.

"What is this place?" he asked, scared for his life. "Who are you? What…"

"You know who I am," said Daisy, climbing to her feet and approaching the startled human who instinctively backed away again, though not fast enough. Daisy approached and took Alex by the hand.

As soon as her skin met his, the world around him changed. The bright sun, heat, sea and sand melted away, changing to a place far more familiar and homely than all he'd known from the start of the plague. His home. In that same village and house his father had grown up in, empty and deserted, yet still his home. As if none of it had ever happened, and his father and mother and sister had just gone out. It smelled like home, was warm like home, and all the furniture and pictures were precisely where they were before the plague began. But that's where home ended, for before him, too, stood Daisy. Dressed in clothes like the latest fashions of Earth before it all began, as human as any of us.

"As for this place…" she said with a sweet smile, leaning up to his ear to whisper into his ear. "This is your home!"

Alex let go of Daisy's hands, half expecting the whole place to simply melt away, yet it didn't. Fearful and suspicious yet completely bewildered in his astonishment of where he was, he began wandering through the living room, running his hands along each object as he headed to the fireplace, while

Daisy hung back. His mind was asking questions he would never have thought to ask before, questions like, *who are the gods? And are they really as moral and benevolent as they make out to be? Am I as crazy as my father, this whole thing in my head?* So much so, that the temptation of betrayal began to sneak in like a trickling stream of disruptive water.

"Why am I here?" asked Alex as he picked up a picture; his father, mother, sister, him and Grandfather, stood together at the seaside. The memory opened old wounds, piercing his heart like knives and bringing a tear to his eyes.

Daisy took the opportunity and came up to Alex, walking him to the sofa and sitting him down with her, and for once, he followed without hesitation or complaint, tightly clutching the picture in his hands as Daisy wrapped her arms around him in comfort. She sighed and paused, letting Alex take it all in before she answered his question. "I said I'd have a job for you." she said. "It's time you come back to Earth!"

Alex looked up at her, disgust filling his widening eyes as he leapt up, her spell over him being instantly broken.

"You want me to come back?" he dropped the picture on the floor, smashing the glass in the frame. "You think you can use me? Everyone thinks they can use me! I don't care what you are! You're the same as the bloody rest of them! I MAY BE MORTAL BUT I REFUSE TO BE YOUR PAWN!" he screamed at the top of his voice, his hand curling up into a fist, his knuckles turning white. "You self-centred... I am not my father! I don't know who you are or what you and my father had! I refuse to do anything for you."

Alex took a step forward, his clenched fist shaking at his side. Daisy stood up, and with a wave of her hands, Alex found himself on the floor, the world around him swirling and turning in a blurred vision. Daisy's words were the only clear thing in his confused and angry mind. "You don't have a choice," he heard her say, "you will do my will whether you like it or not!"

Book II

A Long Journey Awaits

Chapter I:
14 Months AP

Alex stirred from his restless and horrid sleep with a sense of an uncomfortable reality about him. He feels as if his mind has been torn in two or three pieces and that a lot had happened, but he has no idea what. It was all too quickly apparent to him that something had changed, but what? In his dazed, sleepy, state Alex sat up, instantly aware that he was no longer in his small quarters of the temple, no longer in his reasonably good bed or, well, anywhere that he recognised at all.

Alex rubbed the sleep from his eyes, his head was spinning like he had never known before and felt sick as if he had a hangover without having anything to drink. His mouth was parched and dry, the lump in his throat prevented him from swallowing, and even clogged up his words. He tried to sit up, taking the weight of his body with his arms but immediately felt his arms shake and collapse under him, sending him falling back down onto the floor. He had never felt this way before, never felt so badly before. Somehow, with blurred vision and unresponsive limbs, Alex managed to crawl, stagger and roll his way to some hard vertical surface that he believed to be a wall.

He sat there in silence for an amount of time that was lost to him, it could have been days for all he knew, but slowly his senses began to return. The ringing in his ears subdued, the spinning of his head and the sick in his gut, the week limbs and the blurred vision, all returned in due course, returning to reveal a sight he did not expect.

Indeed, something had changed, no, everything had changed. Alex was no longer in the temple of healing, that was for sure, though he was not somewhere entirely new either. No, he was home. Back in that place he had left over six months ago, in the place that he thought never to see again. As he surveyed the living room from his sitting position on the floor, he could tell it was not the place he remembered, nor the memory that Daisy had shown him in his dream. This was his home, though not as he remembered it.

Trashed, broken; a complete mess and reflection of the world in which it stood. The windows were cracked and broken, the furniture is scattered about. Anything of practical use seemed to be gone with the wind, and, as Alex staggered clumsily to his feet, he found the rest of the house was the same. The door was hanging off its hinges, the wooden slats that held up the staircase banister had been ripped off, with wood-shavings littering the floor as if they'd been sharpened with a knife. Indeed, the gold and silver of his mother's jewellery had not been touched, but, throughout the house, every scrap of food, anything able to kill and anything for which shelter could be crafted from had vanished. This included large tracks of carpet, the corrugated metal roof panel from the garage and garden shed, the washing line and the wire from the television and walls had been yanked out, yet those items themselves remained.

All the nails and hand-tools from his father's shed had been taken, along with all the soap, plates, bowls and cutlery, particularly the knifes, all were gone. The hands from the clocks were also gone, yet the clocks themselves remained, as had the pens, yet not the pencils, and the clothes, towels, shoes, bed sheets and mattresses, with the frames pulled apart and the unwanted remnants scattered about the bedrooms. Even the old dog food had been taken, though Alex's mother's car remained, though on closer inspection, what remained was merely a shell. The tyres had gone, as was the fuel, and the leaf springs and bolts that held the car together, yet the interior seemed largely untouched. The apple tree in the garden had been chopped down; a pile of twigs left in its place. What hadn't been taken lay scattered about the house, as if blown about by a great hurricane.

Alex made his way back through his old home, back into the living room and, after restoring the cushions to the armchair, slumped back down. He ran his hands through his hair and sighed. *I'm right back where I bloody started!* "How the hell could this happen?" Alex screamed his frustration, picking up the lightbulb of a lamp that'd been discarded, and lobbed it in anger at the fireplace, and, in doing so, knocked over a picture frame that in turn smashed on the floor. With a sigh and a grumble, Alex picked himself up, and in turn picked up the broken picture, the same picture that he had picked up in his dream, so it would appear. Though it was not the picture itself that caught his eye, but something written on the back. He turned it over. *It's a message!* Alex thought, rather shocked. *To me!*

Dear Alex,

I told you that you hadn't a choice in the matter, and that you would do as I asked you to. Now, I see no reason why our relationship can't be a good one, cannot be one of friendship, though, if you feel other than this, know this, you cannot return to the temple of healing before completing the task I need of you. So, I dearly suggest that you do what I want with complete fortitude, so you can return to your new life as promptly as possible. You will be given more information by an old friend, who you are to meet at your father's grave. But, be warned, Alex Smith, be warned, the world is not as you remember it. Older powers have begun to reclaim what was once theirs!

   Daisy

   xxx

Chapter II:
14 Months AP, Temple of Healing

The light emerged on a much different day to the one it had left. Amongst the warm heat, the great temple, the mountains, the sea and the gardens came a colder, darker, air. As if something almost alien had come and the temple itself had reacted badly to it. Atia had been here since she was born; she grew up amongst the temple walls and gardens. She knew the temple almost as if it was her friend. She could instinctively feel when something wasn't right. She woke and quickly dressed, leaving her quarters but not noticing the moved chair and bowl of water behind the door.

Her heart was pounding in her chest as she nervously awaited whatever was wrong. Her hand didn't leave the temple walls as she made her way through it towards Alex's quarters, almost as if the temple itself was leading her there; a living beast that had become distressed and scared overnight.

As she turned the corner, she saw the open doorway of Alex's chambers. She let out a gasp with fear and started to run as fast as she could. "ALEX!" she screamed as she charged down the corridor, fear gripping and holding her as she turned the corner and stormed into the small room.

Destiny woke with a start, sitting up so fast her spine almost cracked like a whip, and the sound of Atia's screams echoing through the temple had disturbed the Goddess from her slumber. She wiped her eyes, not believing what her ears were telling her. Atia's screams came again, the noise sending chills down her spine as she leapt from her borrowed bed and came rushing from the room just down the hall from that of Alex's. Her bare feet were icy cold on the marble flagstone floor. Her light, silk gown blowing behind her as she ran. Her hair was a mess, and her mind was still numb with the dreams of last night's sleep, still unsure what was a dream and what was real, nor what to believe. So much so that she initially ran straight past the open door of Alex's chambers, only being called back by Atia's confused sobs.

"What has happened?" asked Destiny as she came slowly and quietly through the door, though in her mind she already had her suspicions.

Atia was sat on the empty bed, tears staining her face as she grasped tightly a piece of cloth in her hands. Her answer to Destiny's question was a simple shake of her head, her mind unable to form any words to describe what was going on.

Destiny took in a deep breath. She stepped into the room and was instantly hit with a feeling of old, cursed magic, and a deeper feeling that she had not experienced since she was far, far, younger. Pushing through the feeling, she made her way to the bed and, as she had done with Alex over a month earlier, she sat down and put her arm around Atia to comfort her.

"Where's Alex?" she asked, though already knew the answer. "What has happened?"

It was painfully long before Atia gave her answer, taking her, what for her, felt like hours to compose herself and finally form words.

"He's gone!"

"What do you mean gone?"

"I mean gone! Not here! Left!"

"Are you sure?"

Atia nodded her head, though even as she did so she can't help the feeling that all was not as it seemed, as if something didn't quiet add up, though Destiny didn't seem to agree.

"Well," she said with a sigh, "he never did seem to belong here. I mean, he never seemed happy to me… perhaps it's for the best."

Atia looked up at her in appalled disbelief. "For the best?"

Destiny nodded her head a little too enthusiastically.

"For the best! How can you say that! You never even knew him! I can't believe that! You always hated him! I heard you two yesterday morning." Atia shook her head, standing up in protest. Her tears turned to rage as she stormed from the room with Destiny in quick pursuit.

"What are you doing, Atia?" she said, struggling to keep up as she chased her from the temple and into the garden beyond. "Where the hell are you going?"

"Where am I going?" Atia cried back in rage as she turned, sharply, on Destiny, "I'm off to get him back! I mean, don't tell me this all feels right to you!"

"Actually, it does!" Destiny snapped back. "He wasn't happy here, he went home, it's as simple as that!"

Atia turned back around, ignoring Destiny and storming through the gardens to the stone gateway to earth, reading out in the ancient tongue – the incantation to open it in England.

Atia didn't know how she knew, but as if on instinct, she felt as if she knew precisely where he was.

"Atia!" protested Destiny, "this is crazy. You're off out to... the All One knows where, to find someone that clearly wants nothing to do with this place and you! You're willing to go against your mother's command for that! To risk... to risk everything for that! Why?"

Atia sighed, stopping just before passing through the portal. She turned and look at Destiny, all anger melting away as she said her parting words. "I don't know? It just feels as if it's something I need to do." And with that, she passed the cloth in her hand to Destiny before stepping through the portal and vanishing before Destiny's eyes.

As the portal closed behind her friend, leaving her stood alone on the temple, Destiny couldn't help but let a slight smile, appear across her face, as her chess pieces found their places. But then she remembered the piece of cloth in her hand. She looks down and saw the embroidered D H in the corner. "Daisy!" she exclaimed in fear. Her joy turned to ash in her mouth.

Chapter III:
14 Months AP, Yorkshire.

The world is not as you remember it. Are the words that ran through Alex's mind over and over again and Daisy, unfortunately, was not wrong. This was not the world that Alex had left. To say that it was barren and empty would be wrong, but to say that the memory of man was nothing but ruins and old, dead, structures would be an understatement of what Alex saw as he walked out his doorway and into the street where he, and his father before him, had grown up. His eyes were in disbelief of what he was seeing, the hairs on the back of his neck stood up on their ends. It was silent, eerily so. The sky, blue and healed of all the tracks and scars that once decorated it from the planes that once flew above. There was no drone of cars, planes, or any kind of technology once seen and heard. As Alex, holding his head up as high as he could, walked from his home and down the street, he quickly found that his house, in comparison, got off much lighter than most, as nature had already begun to clamber back to what it once was.

The further Alex walked, the stranger things became, so much so that Alex began to wonder if he had been given his father's madness. From trees hung girls, beautiful, scared, and made of flesh and blood, until they pressed themselves to the trees in which they seemed attached and then turned to bark and wood. The moors were covered in far stranger creatures, as Alex stopped behind the very oak tree that Daisy had kissed his father that fatal Christmas eve. He watched as, upon the moors, a ten-foot-tall man herded a flock of sheep with wool of fine golden fleece. The creature turned to look down upon the village and valley and Alex could make out the creature's face, and its large, single, blue eye.

Alex, worried that the creature may see him, instinctively darted down to hide behind the large trunk of the old tree.

"Hey!" came a voice from above, making Alex look up and gasp in shock. "Get off my leg!" a female voice called down as she kicked Alex to the floor, the branch of the tree that Alex had been holding on to turning from wood to soft, pale, skin. Alex looked up in shock, speechless at the sight of the young girl hanging from the tree. Too shocked to speak, he simply jumped up and rushed into the village centre and away from the strange creatures that seemed to litter the countryside and the fringes of society.

"What is this place?" he couldn't help but gasp. "Where am I? This can't be Earth! Surely!"

Alex, unable to do anything else, followed the winding little path up the hill from the high street and to the village graveyard. He knew the path well; he had travelled along it many times in the days and months before complete apocalypse. As if blindfolded, the world around him changed beyond belief. But he was given some solace at least by the sight of the familiar graveyard. This, it seemed, was untouched from the strangeness of the world around him. But that in itself seemed worrying. Alex, too scared to lift his eyes, made his way down the central path of the graveyard, turning right and passing through the graves to that of his father's, Fredrick Smith.

He finds it untouched and clean, as if it has been visited frequently by one left behind. Fresh flowers are in the memorial vase that stands neatly before the black granite headstone, as they are in the graves of Alex's mother and sister by its side. All three are a cold, plain and basic plaque in the ground, under the shade of a willow tree by the stone wall of the perimeter of the crowded graveyard. It is here that Alex finally lifted his head and looked around. It was as much to search for the person he was meant to meet, as to take his eyes from his family before their ghostly memories come flooding back.

His spine froze in the cold and eerie place that he found himself, as far away from the warmth of the temple of healing he felt was possible. Here, amongst the gravestones, he felt an odd feeling, something he hadn't really felt before. He knew the time he'd spent in the realm of the Draden had done something to him, that was for sure, though he couldn't say he was glad to be back. But being back, he couldn't help but let tears fall from his eyes.

Suddenly, the sound of the rusted gate of the graveyard being pushed open came from his back. He swivelled around on his heels to see what was approaching, his heart in his throat, as from behind the graves came a stranger who would seem out of place in this time zone, let alone the apocalyptic world in which he found himself. His fashion was as odd as anything Alex had seen before; top hat, pot-bellied, a stick that looked more like a shepherd's crop, a gammy right leg that made him walk with a terrible limp, a wool fleece-lined coat and a knitted jumper underneath. All this combined with rather large and baggy trousers to hide his odd shoes. He had a pipe in his mouth, an anchor beard and longish, untidy hair. Flowers in hand, the strange man came right up to Alex.

Having placed the flowers on Fred's grave without a word, he turned to Alex, who was far taller than the old, fat man, and removed the pipe from his mouth to finally talk. "You're Alex smith?"

Alex was unsure of the man before him. By now, he was suspicions of the intentions of anyone who wasn't dead. So, answered simply with a nod of his head.

"I trust Daisy told you that I was coming?"

Again, Alex answered simply with a nod.

Taking a puff of smoke and bringing forth a horrid smoker's cough, the old man put his arm round Alex's back, and the smell of his unwashed body hit Alex like an unclean animal barn, making him gag. But, working through it, he followed, or was more dragged by, the small, old man to a bench nearer the entrance of the graveyard and sat him down, continuing to smoke as he talked.

"At least that saves some awkwardness. I trust that she's told you about all this… unusualness, that's going on here?"

"No," Alex said, finally talking to the smelly old thing. "She hasn't told me a thing, only that I'm to meet you at my father's grave."

"Ah!" the old man said, rather unimpressed and unhappy. "Then I guess you must be a bit confused. Have you seen anything off?"

Alex replied with a nod. Despite his first impressions, Alex began to feel that, for once, he'd found someone who would actually give him a straight answer, though he still didn't trust him.

"A… err, Cyclops…"

"Herding a flock of golden sheep?" the old man said, interrupting him. "His name is Eric. You're lucky to see him, he's the last of his kind in England. In fact, you can count his remaining kind on one hand." He extended out his hand. "I'm Jared, by the way, Mr Jared Hacker, though you can call me Jared. I was friends with your father before he died, and I knew Daisy as well. I like to think that I'm the only real person he truly confided in, apart from Daisy of course."

Alex, despite his distrust of the stranger, couldn't help but warm quickly to the pot-bellied old man. Perhaps it was the fact that he'd been the only one to give him a straight answer. After all, Alex was as desperate for the truth as a man in the desert is for water.

"Can you tell me about him?"

"Your father?" Jared asked, taking a puff of smoke. "Oh aye, I'll tell you all about your father, but first…" He let out a spluttering cough into a handkerchief, hiding from Alex the blood that came with it. "But first, you need to know a bit of history. After the god, Life… I trust you know who he is? Well, after he created humans, his first successful species of intelligent life on earth so say, well, in celebration he created many different… fewer effective species of intelligent life. These creatures, the mythical creatures as you might know them as were hated and hunted and persecuted by the self-righteous humans.

"Acts of genocide were common and those who were not killed more often than not became enslaved to the early humans. One such poor soul was a centaur, whose name has been forgotten by time. Enslaved by a king and forced to pull ploughs across his land, given too much food to die, but not enough to survive. In pain and turmoil, he called out to an older, immortal, race of beings... the Titans, whose king granted his wish for relief and killed him. He then turned to the gods for help, and, in their mercy, they hid us from the humans for our own protection. And so, the creatures vanished into myth and legend, and was struck from the memories of man. At least that's one version of the story."

"Wait, what do you mean us?" asked Alex, his voice echoing with surprise.

With a smile of amused joy and a chuckle that echoed around his pot belly like it was a drum, Jared stood up, removing his top hat. He revealed a pair of curled goat's horns, and pulling his feet out of his small shoes, he showed Alex his goat's-hooved feet. "I'm a satyr," he said with a smile. "I'm about as human as the birds in the sky and the worms in the ground, and I'm bloody glad of it. Know this, laddie, and mark my words," he said, pulling off his baggy trousers to show his goat legs. Alex's eyes tried not to stare at the horns or goat legs. "One man's hero is another man's Hitler!"

Chapter IV:
14 Months AP, Sherwood Forest

Atia took in a deep breath as she emerged out the portal and back onto the human world of Earth. The air was fresher than she remembered; the trees greener and the birds louder, as if the whole world was rejoicing that nearly all humans were dead. As birds of prey, worms and all manner of other flesh-eating animals feasted on the littered remains of those left behind by the plague, it couldn't be argued that much hadn't changed since she was last here over a month ago, though one would easily be forgiven for thinking it was far, far, longer.

Though, as Atia made her way through the peaceful quiet of the old English forest, the beauty that was put on display in this place, the blues of young blackberries, the greens of the trees, the faint flicker and flash of brown from the deer who wandered amongst the trees which was more like a painting than the real world, was lost on her. The sounds of the woodland, the fresh, sweet, smells, the taste of the old oak in the air, all were ignored to, for her mission burned a hole in her heart as nothing ever had before. She wished more than anything to find Alex, a need, a burning necessity, as much as finding food, or water, or shelter. More so, even! She simply had to find him; she wouldn't go back till she had. She refused to leave this world until she had. But, for the life of her, Atia had absolutely no clue why.

Driven on by an instinctive desire, Atia made her way without stopping, and without taking as much as a peek back, out of the forest and through the surrounding deserted countryside. She had no idea whatsoever where she was going, she just was. As if following an invisible string, or a scent on the wind, she marched on. She was convinced she had a long way to go. The sun beat down on her as she flew through the Nottinghamshire fields that have been left barren and bare to nature.

Before long she came to a small house left abandoned near the village of Blidworth. *I need to be a little less conspicuous, things are never as empty as they seem.* She thought to herself. Entering the house Atia immediately went to the bedroom and by luck, found some clothes that would fit her. A backless cropped top, a pair of jeans, and a light denim jacket as well as a pair of high boots. Quickly she discarded her golden robes and changed into the salvaged clothes.

Atia didn't stop in the house a moment longer than she had to, so with the change of outfit complete and not wishing to waste any more time in her pursuit of Alex, she took off again, following what she hoped was her instincts and Kimarie leading her towards him. As she did so, Atia was surprised at how comfortable she found her new clothes compared to the heavy golden robes she was used to.

14 Months AP, Yorkshire

Alex was led by the gammy-legged old satyr, up into the moors. Alex would be lying if he said he had no idea where he was going, after all, he'd grown up in these moors and, no matter how much the human world had changed and how unrecognisable his home was, he still knew the moors. Every crag, hill, valley, path, wall and tree. To say that he knew it like the back of his hand wouldn't quite be true, though, Alex knew it better than the back of his hand... by far. It was not the lack of the knowledge of where he was going that made Alex nervous, or, his distrust of Jared, but rather the memory of the rather giant Cyclops that he had seen earlier, who seemed to have been uncomfortably close to where they were heading. Though, for all his worry and fear, of which none he allowed himself to reveal to Jared, he saw absolutely no sign of the beast as the pair, painfully slowly, made their way up, down and through the Yorkshire moors.

Neither spoke as they made their way across the barren moors, travelling deeper and deeper into the wilds of Yorkshire, Jared hobbling along on his stick and gammy leg. It is when, after they had seemed to walk for well over an hour that Alex began to worry about just how far they were going, for they had travelled beyond the moors that Alex knew best and into areas less trodden.

"I don't remember this place," he whispered to himself as the pair walked out from an old patch of trees and onto yet another moor. "No memory at all."

With his distrust peeking, all the bones and muscles in his body were nagging and begging him to turn and flee, though, in his mind he knew, knew that it would be no good, and that he'd just find himself back here eventually, anyway. But there was another thing keeping him from leaving; not fear, but curiosity – curiosity to find out what this Jared knew about Daisy and his father. All Alex really knew was what he'd heard through cracks in walls and from looking through keyholes. Though this, satyr might have actually known the truth, or as near to the truth as any real thing living.

Finally, the pair came to a rocky crag in a shear rock face at the bottom of a steep plummet. "Come on, Alex!" Jared called out from in front. "We're home!"

"Home?" Alex asked, looking the crag up and down. *Surely not?* he couldn't help but think to himself as he cautiously entered the damp, cold and dark beyond.

The cave was long, dark, wet and full of narrow cracks that ran further back into the rock than Alex could tell. The path was narrow, yet well-trodden, merely wide enough to fit a single sheep or goat down. And to make matters worse, the path was incredibly sloppy, slick with the water from the hilltop above, the water trickling further into the darkness of the cave. Alex dared to glance back; the light from the outside little more than a small shaft, dwindling as he moved farther into Hell's mouth, and further from the freedom of the outside. He peered up into the darkness as the path twisted and turned around sharp, jagged rocks on either side. It was too dark for him to see the top, or Jared, who could have been no more than three or four paces in front of him. The cold and damp chilled him to the bone.

"Ow!" he gasped as he slipped on the slick narrow track, his hand cut on the sharp point of a rock to his right.

"Who there?" boomed a voice from beyond and out of sight. Alex was no fool, he knew who and what the voice was.

"Oh, shit!" he gasped under his voice as he froze on the spot, the rock still cutting into his hand, and the blood dripping into the slush below, being taken away down the shallow stream.

"It's okay!" came the voice of Jared from somewhere in the darkness in front of him. "It's only me!"

Alex remained perfectly still, fighting through the pain in his hand. He daren't move, daren't give a single sign of his presence and even his breath sounded far too loud. From the darkness in front, came the echoing sound of a great beast sniffing the air, once, twice, three times.

"I smell blood of human!" Alex heard the beast growl.

"There are no humans here!" Jared's voice echoed from now further down the path, sounding as if he was trying to reassure the beast. Still, Alex stood in the cave, unable to see anything, trying to make as little sound as possible. But that wouldn't make a difference, for, the beast may only have had one eye, but he made up for that with acute vision. Their one big eye was capable in seeing in the lowest of light levels, and at distances that would make an eagle even struggle. Indeed, it was the rock before him that was the only reason the beast hadn't noticed him already.

He heard the beast sniff again. "You lie! I smell human!" the beast roared, his voice like thunder in the narrow confines of the cave. "You brought human here! How... how..."

"Eric! Calm yourself. There are no humans here..."

"But there are! I smell it! I hear its breath! I taste its foul odour on tongue! Human here! Human here! Human here!"

Alex covered his mouth in a flash, but as the beast got worked up in its anger, it began running around whatever space lay beyond, shaking the whole cave. Alex slipped again, clattering to the slick, wet floor and, without meaning to, cried out in pain as his knees collide with the hard rock.

"See!" roared the beast, though Alex could still see nothing of what was going on before him. "HUMAN!"

"Eric! Calm down! He is Freddy's son. You remember Freddy, right?"

Alex heard the beast huff and puff a little before he felt, through the vibrations in the ground, the tremendous weight sitting down.

"Well, why you no say?"

The next thing Alex heard was Jared's wooden stick on the ground as he made his way back up the narrow passageway to where Alex was still laying on the floor. In the darkness, Alex struggled to make out the face of the old Satyr, made even more difficult with the smoke from his pipe that he lit while the cyclops was having its hissy fit.

"Come on then, lad! Let's go!" he said abruptly before turning back and disappearing back into the darkness.

Alex, with his heart in throat, followed the old satyr as the path ahead did a ninety-degree-turn around a thick wall of stone and moss, weaving round to more large, jagged, rocks in a z pattern. When light finally hit Alex again, he had emerged into a world completely different to the one behind him. He had been through portals to different worlds, seen his home change beyond recognition, but none of it compared to the change that occurred between the cold, damp, dark passageway, to the cavern he now found himself in. Large, spacious and light, the walls were lined with a trough of burning oil. A great chandelier hung, lit with hundreds of oil lamps, from above, casting light down in the *home* below.

Carpeted and dry, the walls plastered and lime washed. Apart from the complete lack of windows and doors, the space was no different to that of the home of any man. Lavished with furniture, most of which, like the great armchair in which the giant cyclops was now sat, was huge in size, yet perfectly proportionate in scale. There was a working kitchen in one corner, a table and chairs in another, and Alex could make out, hidden down an offshoot of the cave, bedrooms, with large, normal looking, beds. The only thing missing from this house was electricity, everything else was completely recognisable to the human senses. The smell of the air, the feeling of the warmth, the sounds and sights of the place, the cave was truly a home fit for any human, even a king.

"Forgive my friend," said Jared as he hobbled over to his own armchair, sat down with a groan, placed his gammy leg on a footstool and continued to smoke his pipe, all the time talking to Alex as he wandered round the cave in complete and utter awe. Though he always kept one eye on the giant, one eyed-beast which had become his rather unwilling host, sat in silence, with his arms crossed over his great chest. He looked rather angrily through his one giant, bright blue eye in the middle of his head. Alex could see the muscles under his skin. His head bare of hair shone in the candlelight and the smell of sheep radiated from him.

"May I introduce you to my friend and companion," Jared continued through puffs of smoke and spells of painful coughing. "This is Eric blue-eye, the last cyclops this side of the black sea. Son of Donbar the Brave. Eric, here, is from one of the oldest Cyclops families left in the world..."

"The second," the deep and tremendous voice from Eric said, simple and lacking in words, though for every word he said, it struck more fear and showed more power than any god that Alex had ever seen, each syllable hitting like a recking ball.

"Like I was saying, the second-oldest Cyclops Family, that can trace its line back all the way to Sicily and the time of the Trojan war."

"Nice sheep," Alex exclaimed as he saw Eric's flock of twenty-nine golden-fleeced sheep huddled together in a small pen in the corner of the cave.

"Keep away from sheep!" Eric replied simply and harshly, and Alex followed, moving rather quickly back towards Jared.

"Now, I understand this all must seem a lot to take in?" Jared took a puff of smoke as he got up, and, over a small gas fired cooker, placed a kettle upon the hob. "Tea?" he asked.

"Yes!" came the simple, yet commanding answer from Eric.

"Oh, yes, please," Alex replied, coming over to Jared in the kitchen of the cave. "And honestly, after what I've seen this past month, there's not a lot that's hard to take in anymore."

"Ha," the jolly, fat satyr chuckled, his potbelly juggling like jelly. "I guess not!" he said, a great smile, far too big to look right on his satyr's face, appeared.

"Though I have to ask why it is that Eric is so scared of humans." Alex hushed his tone, but that was pointless for Eric had great hearing.

Jared took a deep breath, his smile turning to grief as he looked up at the boy, his eyes like sad moons on his face. "You see, lad, Eric has more reason than most to hate man. One of the last of his kind and the last of his kin, his father was killed by a gamekeeper two days after he was conceived, shot, right through the eye while collecting wood." Jared sighed, looking up at his friend, his one great blue eye staring off in distant memory. "As a young child, he stood helpless and watched as his mother was killed before him. It was me and your father who saved him, and I've looked after him ever since, raised him as my own son. Like I said, lad, one man's hero is another's Hitler."

Alex stood there for a good long while, looking up at the great beast Eric's blue eye... though to call him such a thing seemed unfair and not right. It was the humans that were beasts, not Eric.

In silence, the kettle boiled, and Jared poured their tea, passing one mug to Alex, and another, larger mug to Eric before sitting back down in his chair. Alex walked slowly over to Jared and, pulling up a wooden chair from the dining table, sat down next to the smelly old Satyr, who continued to smoke his pipe. With a gulp, Alex opened his dry mouth to ask the burning question inside him, though he treaded carefully, scared of asking the wrong thing on such a delicate matter to both Jared and Eric.

"There's one thing in this I don't understand," Alex said, stopping and waiting for Jared's approval before continuing to ask his question. "If humans killed Donbar the brave, then how comes no one knows about it, or that you exist?"

"There, my lad, is the great irony of our existence. Men can't remember us. Aye, there are one or two who have some faint part of blood that allows them to, but most who see us can't remember. All pictures that are taken are blurred... quite simply, the gods will not allow them to know of our existence. The gamekeeper who killed his father... he forgot

151

he ever shot his gun five seconds after he left the crime scene, leaving us to mourn and they to walk around, guilt-free of what they've done. Such is the cruelty of our existence."

Alex took a moment to soak in his words. He felt strange, as if he belonged more with them than he did with the humans, as if he was one of them. *But I'm still a human... right?* "So... when I leave you, I'll have no memory of this at all?"

Jared smiled and chuckled in amusement at the boy's ignorance. "No mere mortal could pass through the gates into the world of the gods, neither us nor human. You may have human in you, but you are not all human. Some part of you is divine, that is for sure!"

Alex hesitated a moment, his mind trying to understand what Jared was suggesting. "So, my father was he this... this demon, Bubonic?"

Jared sighed, taking a long sip of his tea to bide his time, followed by a puff of smoke. "Not that I know of, but Freddy was many things, Alex, that is for sure. After all, he could remember us to."

Chapter V:
14 Months AP, Aszar: The Palace of the Gods

Inside the halls of the Quadrel, before the four mighty thrones. In a room so high the ceiling is the sky, made of precious stones. Destiny presented herself before two of the self-appointed rulers of the gods, the strongest and most powerful of the Draden race, in a meeting so secret that even the other two Quadrels did not know; such were the politics of the gods.

The four Quadrels were the supreme gods, each one not created by some power union, but forged into being by the All One itself, inside the falls of creation. The oldest and strongest of their order, is Life. Alone for four cosmic millenniums before any other gods were formed. His queen, the first goddess and the second being to be created was Society, her Beauty radiating her power, her love and intellect, as well as her capacity for wrath. Each of them is older than many of the stars that light up the mortal plane, but neither looked older than their twenties. Such was the blessing of divine beings, for, they were not only immortal, but also frozen at the prime of their lives, when they were physically the best they could ever be. Young, strong and handsome, forever. Something the Draden call pramic.

The pair, as in love as any mortal, yet as disloyal as any of the deities they ruled, the pair were strangely happy in their love and rule. Sat upon their thrones, they demanded respect from all who saw them and all knew upon sight of them who it truly was that ruled everything. They never showed the full extent of their strength but were humble in their rule, for they had such power and respect that they didn't have to act powerful, nor pretend to be someone they weren't.

Destiny entered the hall to present herself to her Grandparents, though like all gods, she referred to them not as 'my king,' 'my queen,' 'my grace,' or 'your majesty,' but rather as 'Father and Mother,' for that is what they commanded.

"Father," Destiny said as she walked up to the four thrones of the Quadrels, two of which were occupied. "Mother, thank you for seeing me."

"Anytime, Granddaughter," said Society with that sweet, loving, smile that grandparents always reserve for their grandchildren. Though it came from a being that looked barely old enough to be a mother. Despite any appearances, Destiny was their granddaughter, and the love of a grandmother for her granddaughter was the same for them as for any mortal family.

"So, tell me child, what is it you wish to speak to us about?"

Destiny looked over her shoulder to make sure that the great doors to the hall were closed and sealed; after all, in this world, one could never be too careful. "It is about the return of our old enemy."

"Oh," said Life, his voice not hiding his worry like he thought his words did. "And what have you found out?"

"There is a boy, a boy called Alex Smith."

"But I thought you said Fredrik Smith was…" Society said, calm as ever, but confused as hell. "Who is this Alex?"

"Yes, I did, Alex is the son of Fredrik."

"and you now think it's him?"

"without doubt. I have spent much time with him. I see promise in him also, a warmth I have not seen since…"

"Destiny," Life interrupted, though calmly, and not by raising his voice or speaking in anger in any way. "I know you want to be right, I know how you feel about this, but I'm afraid that it will only lead to disappointment."

"I made peace with that a long time ago," Destiny snapped. No matter what the Quadrels were like, Destiny was still emotional; no matter how much she tried to hide her inner feelings about the matter, and how much she told herself that it is over and all right.

"We just don't want to see you get hurt again, is all." replied Society, trying to be as sweet and charming as she could, taking her husband's hand in hers.

"Look," Destiny said with a deep breath, her hand moving cautiously to the cloth in her pocket. "I feel that Alex is the key to unlocking our old enemy, to solving the situation once and for all…" Destiny stopped, choking on her next words. She may have been young at the time, though she remembered perfectly what had happened.

"What is it, Destiny?" Life asked, leaning forwards from his throne with a feeling that the next few moments were going to be extremely bad, and that made even him nervous and uncomfortable.

With a deep breath and a quick movement so as to stop herself stalling again with fear, she simultaneously whisked out the cloth and blurted out, "I think we have to act fast, or we may lose him... Daisy's involved."

Life jumped from his throne in shock, though even with his blood boiling he still managed to speak in a calm and collected manner.

"Are you sure? That sounds...?"

"Impossible," finished Society, rage filling her veins even more than his, though her voice was calm as ever.

"Alex disappeared yesterday," began Destiny, approaching the thrones, her arm extended with the favour on her hand. She passed it to Life before quickly retreating backwards. "We found this. I'm sure it's hers."

"Is it?" Society turned and asked her husband, as Life, still standing tall, inspected the peace of cloth in his hand, feeling it in between his finger and thumb, and tracing the letter D with his index finger before, as if it is some token from a dead friend, he put it to his face and smelled the fabric before dropping it in shock onto the floor.

Life sat back down, his breathing slightly heavier as he nodded to his wife, his neck stiff and his movements slight. "It's hers, all right."

Chapter VI:
14 Months AP, Cave of Eric Blue Eye

Alex and Jared were at the long wooden table in the cave, resting from a large lamb supper, while Eric inspected his flock of twenty-nine golden-fleeced sheep, taking particular care to look over his favourite ewe, Eve, before closing the big boulder to the cave for the night. The last of the day's sun must have disappeared behind the moors and hills by now, not that Alex could see it so deep into the ground. He thought of the day that had come to pass, and while he was beginning to warm to the pair's company, he couldn't help the longing feeling in his gut that, even though here, Yorkshire, was where he was born and raised, it was no longer his home. No longer the place he felt comfortable, safe, and relaxed.

His time in the temple had changed him in such a way that he felt that he wanted to be nowhere else but the realm of the gods. Alas, that was where he was not, and until he did whatever it was, he needed to do to get back there, he guessed he has little choice but to put up with the fairly good company of the old, fat satyr, currently lighting up his well-used pipe once more, and the giant, one eyed, Cyclops who happened to be his host.

"So, tell me, you say you knew my father, how did you meet?"

Jared looked up in surprise from under old eyes, pipe in

mouth and match just lit, clearly not expecting the question. Prioritising the pipe, Jared lit it up and blew out the match before turning to address Alex's question.

"You wish to know how I met your father, do ya lad? Oh aye, that be an interesting tale, and the tale of why I need this," he said, grabbing hold of his crock and holding it out in display to Alex. "Aye, an interesting story indeed!" he said with a puff of smoke.

23 Years BP

The early morning sun had not yet had a chance to warm the cold air as Fred set out from his home in a merry run. The dew on the grass and the smell of the air warmed his already rather cheerful mood, for, Fred had just found out that, after a long two years of fearful distance from Fred, the two bullies across the street were finally going to be gone. His father had told him that very morning over jam on toast and a cup of tea that they had sold up and gone. Of course, Fred had known that the house was up for sale, he wasn't that stupid, though was surprised at quite how quickly after sale the family had gone, it was *almost as if they'd fled overnight.*

He had remarked this to his father between rounds of toast. Not that he was complaining or anything, he hated the pair, obviously, and the feeling was all so clearly mutual. Across the street, Fred could see that already, even so early in the morning, the new neighbours were moving in. Not that he saw anyone, just the boxes piled up in the front garden and an abandoned delivery truck parked outside. Though, too happy about the departure of the old neighbour to seek to meet the new, he ran from his front door and straight down the street where he was to meet Daisy under the eaves of the old Oak tree.

"You seem rather happy!" remarked the pale-skinned girl as Fred approached, dressed in a light summer top and ripped jeans. The self-proclaimed Goddess approached Fred and wrapped her arms around him in a loving embrace.

Even though Fred still was unsure of how real she was, in her company and embrace, all that doubt seemed to melt away and disappear, for, when he was with her it was the world around him that felt false. The longer he stayed with her, the less he felt he wanted to go back. *How can something in my head feel so warm and alive in my arms!* he couldn't help wandering to himself as she pulled back to look up into his eyes. She was more beautiful today than ever, seeming to glow with light as she made his blood pump and his heart melt.

"What is it?" she said with the trusting, loving smile that he'd become so used to seeing. At Seventeen, Fread felt closer to Daisy than anything else in the world, devoting all his time to her like a priest, though, even he had to admit, he would give anything for her to return some of his love. Fred felt as if she saw him as a companion, like a little girl with her doll that she carries everywhere she goes. *Strange,* he had once pondered, *she seemed to love me, and then as soon as I come around to her... it feels like I've been friend zoned.*

"Oh," he said, finally breaking out of his trance. "I'm sorry, I just can't help but see how..." Fred couldn't help but swallow. "How magnificent you look today."

Daisy couldn't help but blush, sending red to her pale

cheeks as she broke eye contact and looked down at her feet.

Breaking the awkwardness, Fred said what he now knew he should have said with in the first place. "And, the boys across the street, Will and Adam, they've moved out."

"Wow!" said Daisy with a beaming smile, taking her hands and holding his, sending an electrical energy through Fred that he found himself being close to addicted to. "That's brilliant!" she said with a cheerful grin, leaning up to peck him on the cheek, teasing him as she always did. "No wonder you're so happy."

Daisy turned in an instant and began to walk off from under their usual oak tree and up towards the moors. "Where are we going?" Fred asked, his right hand still interlocked with hers.

"To celebrate, of course!" she said with that same beaming grin as before.

A half-hour later, and the pair were high in the moors and chasing each other across the hills. Spring was in full swing now, and the moors were covered in the buds of flowers yet to bloom. A world of colour yet to emerge. They ran up into a wooded area high in the moors. As Fred ran after Daisy, he couldn't help but wonder at all that is around him. The trees had the bright-green of fresh leaves, like a great painting that should be hung in the Louvre. The sound of birdsong seemed like they were in a fairy-tale as they paired up and began building their nests, ready for the next generation. The air, still cold from the night, was slowly being beaten back by the strengthening sun, and the smell of fresh growth hung lightly in the air. He watched on as his goddess twisted, turned and danced in a bright, grassy clearing; her beauty more great and divine than he had ever noticed before. As the sun seemed to glisten off her pale skin like she was made of diamonds, frozen, like a statue by her dance, he was nothing but her puppet, her servant to do with as she desired, and he would like it no other way, strangely.

Daisy stopped to look at the boy who was staring at her from the tree line beyond the clearing. Extending her hand and wagging her finger, she summoned her friend to her side. "Come on, Fred, it's not like you've never seen me before, what's up with you today, Freddy?" she said with her sweet and trusting smile that set Fred's heart racing.

The question, however, set Fred a bit on edge. Not quite sure on how to answer it, he kind of just muttered the first thing that came into his mind, something that he had thoughts of before, though, not wishing really to know the answer, stashed it in the back of his mind, only to find himself asking it now anyway.

"No, it's nothing... I just can't work out why it is you chose me."

"Chose you?"

"You know, why did you come to me and not... well... anyone else?"

Daisy didn't try to hide her amusement at his question, as she pulled herself close to him and took his hand in hers, leaning up and whispering into his ear. She said sweetly, "Because you're special, Freddy, I've always tried to show you that."

Fred let out an amused smile, not really believing what she was telling him. "The only thing that makes me special is that I know a goddess," he remarked under his breath, though never actually meant to say it aloud, and immediately, he felt as stupid as a plank of wood.

Daisy took a step back, still with her hand in his. Her cheeks blushed and she looks away to try and hide it; even she couldn't deny that her heart fluttered a little at his words. "Come here," she said, leading Fred into the clearing and dragging him down to kneel next to her by an unopened bud of a daffodil. "I'll show you you're special." Daisy moved around behind him so she could whisper into his ear, resting her chin on his shoulder, one hand gripping his and the other wrapped round his chest. Her hand felt his beating heart under his skin and flesh, and she slowed her breathing to try to harmonise his heart beats with her own. Holding out their arms towards the unopened bud, she began to whisper, her hot breath tickling the inside of his ear. "Look at the flower," she said as sweetly as she could. "Become one with the flower, let your will become its will."

Fred felt her taking in a deep breath and he followed suit. *Seems right?* he justified to himself, his eyes not flickering from the bud.

"Can you feel it? The breeze of the wind on it? The sun warming it? The damp soil on its roots?"

"Err," Fred wasn't sure that that was particularly possible, *but then again, what the hell do I know?*

"I think so?"

Daisy looked at him and smiled in amusement before returning to her initial position, before, rather seductively, whispering into his ear. "Then... will it to open."

Fred willed it, imagined it, urged it with every fibre of his being and... nothing happened. *Of course not!* Fred thought, *honestly what was I expecting?*

Daisy, who felt his will waning, let out a sigh, "come on Freddy, give it another go." Daisy pushed herself closer into Fred, as close as she could. She closed her eyes tight, joining herself to Fred as much as he to the flower. Their breath, heartbeat and all five senses becoming entwined. "Come on Freddy." She whispers even more delicately then before, "I'll help you. Become one with the flower, let your will become its will. Feel the breeze of the wind on it, the sun warming it, the damp soil on its roots. Then will it to open."

Fred tried once more, to feel it, to will it open. Slowly, he and Daisy's entwined hand began to open and it stretched out from a fist, so, made the flower open.

Daisy opened her eyes to see it, her connection with Fred broken. In amused amazement, Daisy rolled back into the damp, newly-grown grass, giggling to herself in joy. "I told you!" she said, sitting up to face the rather amazed and overwhelmed Fred, who was heavily panting, sat cross-legged by the flower.

"I told you, you are special!"

Fred let out an amused and happy smile, feeling like, a little more than Daisy's doll for the first time in a long time. Fred picked the daffodil and, half crawling over to her, took her head in his hand, brushed back her hair, and gently slid the flower behind her ear. She smiled that smile that was uniquely hers and giggled with joy, leaning over to kiss him gently on the cheek – not a peck, but a kiss.

"Thank you," she whispered, making Fred feel more alive than ever before, almost as if he'd awoken from some kind of dream like Sleeping Beauty, but where the prince is the one asleep, and Beauty awake. But it all disappeared all too suddenly as Daisy rolled back in uncontrollable laughter. Between bursts she managed to get out the words, "Freddy... you truly... do... amaze me!"

As if trying to make a snow angel in the grass, she playfully swung out her arms and legs and back together before sitting back up to face Fred. "We'll get you there," she said with a smile.

"Get me where?" he replied, not understanding the question.

Daisy stood up and held out a hand for Fred to help him to his feet. "You'll find out," she said with a sly smile she clicked her fingers and with a twirl, all around her, all the other buds and trees round the clearing came into bloom; the leaves on the trees thickening to full extent and the scent of the blossom that had appeared filled the air and hung thick in Fred's lungs.

"Come on," Daisy smiled, holding out a hand to Fred who was too amazed by the transformation to take it. "Let's not hang around here all day."

With that, she left from the clearing and went deeper into the wooded area atop the hill, leaving Fred stood alone for a moment before bursting to life and pursuing her.

But Fred wasn't the only one to have lay witness to Daisy's miracle, or her diamond-like Beauty in the light of the sun, for a foul, primitive creature had been waiting in the shadows, watching all the time for its chance to strike. The creature saw her in the village and had been stirred by her, and now she was its prey. All it needed was a chance to strike away from her protector. Now it saw it thanks to Fred's bewilderment. It had its chance to strike.

Fred was following Daisy, or at least the trail he thought she had left as he could no longer see her out in front, when suddenly a shriek of terror hit him like a bag of bricks. Immediately, Fred burst into a run, his heart in his mouth, towards the direction of the noise. Instinctively, he grabbed a stick as he ran past a tree, long and reasonably straight, not that that mattered much to Fred right now. He heard another scream, though this time much deeper, more a man's cry than that of his Daisy, coming from the right of the track he had been following. Adrenalin pumping through him, Fred jumped through a thorny bush, scraping and tearing the skin on his arms, but right now his brain didn't register the pain. Over a fallen tree, he leapt and emerged out at the most peculiar scene.

Before him, between three trees and at the top of a sheer sand bank, dropping a good five or six meters, was Daisy. Her hair a mess and her shirt torn and hanging from her arm on the right side, the red marks, the fingers left around her throat. Between her and Fred stood a strange fellow. It looked a year or two older than them at least, with small horns and goat's legs, clutching at his bleeding, broken nose, courtesy of Daisy.

With adrenaline in his blood, and his every muscle and sinew enraged at the act of this, this, thing, almost as if Fred didn't notice the odd creature before him being anything other than scum. Fred didn't think twice, or at all really, before storming up to the Satyr. In his hand he found a long-discarded walking stick that looked more like a shepherd's crook. So much was his fury that Fred didn't even notice himself grabbing it from the fly-tipped pile of rubbish dumped in the undergrowth. Holding the stick so tight his knuckles where white, Fred, smacked the Satyr round the face, thus adding a black eye to his broken nose.

With all his might, and taking the already shocked satyr unaware, Fred took one great swing with his stick and smashed it into his right knee with all the force he could muster. The beast dragged himself back, fear now in his eyes. He didn't see the sheer drop behind him and, in an instant, fell down the bank, landing straight on his right knee and shattering the fractured mess that Fred had made. Tossing the stick over the bank after the thing, Fred finally began to calm down to a point that he could speak and think a little more rationally. Turning to Daisy, he embraced the still-shaking goddess in his arms, for once feeling more in power and appreciated than ever before.

"Thank you," she tried to gasp, though her words couldn't form in her mouth thanks to the shock and fear of the situation. Instead they emerged as a pitiful gasp.

"Are you okay? Did he hurt you? What happened? Why did you wander off? What... what...." Fred's concerned questions came like shots from an automatic gun, though each failed to penetrate Daisy's scared mind.

"I'm, I'm... okay," she managed to get out, "he... didn't... actually... do anything." She gasped for breath, her beating heart finally beginning to slow, though she'd be lying if she said she wasn't still terrified, or, if she wasn't completely blown away by Fred's actions. Something she never imagined from him and was rather impressed by.

"Thank you." She pulled in tighter to his chest, though Fred could feel her trembling with fear. He took a peek over the side of the bank to see the satyr whining and howling at the bottom, his nose bleeding and his leg a twisted mess. "What should we do about him?" asked Fred, now far calmer and less bloodthirsty.

Chapter VII:
23 Years BP, Yorkshire

The cries and sobs of pain from the Satyr echoed throughout the woods and beyond. It clutched its bloody right leg; its knee was blown to pieces and the splintered tibia bone was protruding from his flesh like a miniature craggy ring of mountains. The creature lifted its head the best it could to see the damage that had been done before it rocked back in another bout of yelling. The creature wasn't stupid, it knew that whoever would hear him was more likely to kill him, rather than help him.

It is at this moment, Fred appeared in the corner of the satyr's field of vision. In his hand was the stick he had used before, which he had retrieved before heading round through the trees to the bottom of the bank. With fury in his eyes, he pointed the rod down at the Satyr's left leg.

"What are you? Who are you? And give me a reason why I shouldn't smash your other knee to pieces as well!" Fred's aggressive tone combined with the furious look in his eyes sent the satyr white with fear. Never before had Fred been so aggressive – not that he could ever actually do any of what he was threatening; it was all an act, though a part he was playing extraordinary well, not letting any of his true self through. The creature at Fred's feet refused to answer. He lifted his head, let out a cry of pain, and let it drop back down, onto the hard floor, though no words came from his mouth.

From behind Fred came Daisy with the sweetest smile she could muster, a shell to hide her hatred of the creature. Their plan was good and well-discussed on the way down, and Daisy played her part just as well as Fred. She came around and knelt next to the screaming satyr, taking his head gently and resting it in her hands. Speaking softly into his slightly pointed ears, her words flowed and soothed like honey, and while she spoke, the satyr's screams subsided, though his eyes never stopped nervously flicking back towards Fred.

"Look, we have no quarrel with you. We simply defended ourselves." While she spoke, she gently wiped the blood from his nose while Fred pushed the stick against his left knee to remind him, he was still there. "We want to help you, to forgive you. But we can't help but be scared that you'll attack again, please, just answer his questions. It would be for your own good."

"You're in the middle of nowhere," Fred added in a harsher tone, "no one will find you for weeks, months, even. I'm more than happy to leave you to die! Your scum! Attacking a girl like that, and I have no pity for your kind."

"Oh, shush!" hissed Daisy. She played her part well. "Can't you see you're scaring him?" Daisy turned her attention back to the satyr, a honeyed mask on her face. "Forgive him, he can be defensive, sometimes. Now please answer, he is calm at the moment, but he isn't known for his patience. What is your answer?"

The satyr looked from Daisy to Fred, then back to Daisy again. "I..." the satyr blurted out between screams of pain and gasps for air, the shocking reality of his predicament mixing with his fear of Fred. "I'm... ahh... a... Satyr." The satyr looked Fred over, though for all his confusion and bewilderment, Fred let none of it show. "This... ahhh... is real... I'm not... a... arr... a human." The satyr took a moment, his breathing heavy as he tried to catch his breath. "Name... ahhh... Jared... Jared Hacker."

"And?" Daisy urged him on. "Why did you try to rape me?"

Jared rolled his head to look at her, a guilty grin flashed across his face for a second before it returned back to one of excruciating pain, caused by Fred tapping the extruding bone with the end of his stick, bringing forth a great scream from Jared. "Sorry..." he gasped between yells. "It's in... ahh... my... nature...ahhh!"

"Stop it!" snapped Daisy, slapping Fred's stick from the protruding bone of Jared's leg.

She turned back to Jared and took his head back in her hands. Catching his breath, he managed to mutter out his pitiful excuse. "I know... ahh... I'm an animal... but I saw you... err... and you made my... blood boil... ahh... I'm sorry... help me... ahh... and I will forever... be... in your debt."

Daisy got to her feet, dropping his head back into the hard ground before dragging Fred to one side and out of earshot to discuss what should be done.

"We should help him, he could be useful," argued Fred, now out of character.

"What do you mean useful? It's not like we're at war!" Daisy countered. "He tried to rape me! Does that mean nothing to you? I thought..." Daisy made an effort to get her words stuck in her throat and shed one or two crocodile tears.

Fred gulped with guilt, taking her in his arms and holding her tight as she played out her scene, and Fred's heart, like a puppeteer. But Fred, for once, was having none of it. He felt in his gut he knew what was right, and he felt guilty for being so cruel and heartless. "It doesn't feel right to just leave him. You are my goddess, you know I'm nothing compared to you. That I'd do anything to serve you but," Fred said with a dry mouth, "but it just isn't right to let him die. He's only a young man after all. Surely you can see that he doesn't deserve this!"

Daisy wiped away her crocodile tears and looked up at Fred, swallowing down her hatred for the creature was hard, particularly for one such as her. With a slight and weak nod, she assented with what Fred was saying. "Very well. I'll let him live, though if he ever comes between us, he will die!" And with that, she turned and started walking back to Jared on the floor.

Us? Fred couldn't help but ask himself, a joyful smile creeping to the corner of his mouth and a flush of red in his cheeks. *Wonder what she means by us?*

Jared had been watching the discussion, though heard nothing of what was said. As Daisy came back followed by Fred, and Jared saw the dry tears in Daisy's eyes, he thought it could mean only one thing. The colour draining from his skin, he tried his best to drag himself back, away from the pair, on his elbows. Each jerk and movement sent sheering pain through his body, but, in desperation, he had to try and fight through the pain and screams.

Fred dropped the stick and picked up the pace, as did Daisy. Fred ran around to Jared's head and, with all his strength, held him down at the shoulder. "What are you doing? What are you doing?" Jared screamed over and over again, until Daisy came up and knelt down by Jared's shattered leg.

With a face that was far from character, and a tone that was closer to that that Fred had used earlier, Daisy snarls, "I'll make it so you can walk! Though I curse you that, for your crimes against me, your leg will forever be limp and lame, never fully able to bend and hold your weight, both in body and soul. I curse you never to touch a girl again, for if you do, willing or not, you will die! That is the price that I offer, that and an eternal servitude to the one you tried to corrupt with your lust, me! you will be my servant, lame and loveless. Mine to command. What do you say, creature?"

Jared doesn't speak, he can't and daren't. But he nods his head in consent, his need to survive outweighing the price of his own soul.

Daisy turned to the wound, put her hands on Jared's knee and protruding bone, and, speaking words that Fred was unable to hear over Jared's agonising screams, the bones reassembled and clicked back into place, or at least, almost did.

When she was done, Daisy leaned back to show off her work; a completely healed, leg. Jared sat up in disbelief; never would he have thought something like this would have been possible. He turned to Daisy, only now realising the truth of who she is. "You're one of them, aren't you? A divine being!"

Daisy smiled and nodded. She passed Jared the stick that

had broken his leg from where Fred had dropped it moments ago. He used it to clamber to his feet, quickly realising that, though mended, his right leg still bared a limp. Daisy stood up and, placing her hand on Jared's nose, healed that too. She then gestured for Jared to take the lead, dropping back to take Fred's hand. Her face was no different to any other time, though inside she was over the moon with joy. *Not only have I confirmed my beliefs about Fred, but now I have my own servant to do my bidding! Things are starting to go better than I could have imagined!"*

Chapter VIII:
14 Months AP, Eric Blue Eye's Cave

Alex opens his eyes to the loud, ear-rattling snores of the great Cyclops, laid out on a bed propped up by tree trunks and tucked under blankets made of golden wool, next to his flock of twenty-nine sheep. It was still rather early when he got up out of bed and wandered through the cave. "Hr!" he exclaimed to himself in a harsh whisper. "No Jared?" Wiping the sleep from his eyes, he wandered quietly from the cave in search of the pot-bellied, old thing. Alex had barely slept last night; Jared's stories had kept them from their beds till well gone the turn of the new day. That combined with Eric's unrelenting snoring and the uncomfortable, bed, that he was designated, made for a harsh and brief sleep until he could take it no longer and had to get up.

Alex wandered from the cave and out into the chill of the new day. The sun had yet to fully surpass the horizon, colouring the sky blood-red with its light. The cold, damp touch of the air sent goose bumps up Alex's arms, and the wet grass moistened and chilled his toes. It was a real shock to Alex's system, having lived in the land of the gods, to come back here and feel the Yorkshire chill and wind once more, something he had hoped deep down that he would never feel again. For what was here for him now but death and hopelessness, a feeling he has left behind in Sherewood, but that had come flooding back with Earth's air. At least now it was more a memory than truth.

Out towards the woods that stood atop a hill facing towards the craggy entrance of Eric's cave, Alex spotted Jared walking through the trees in the relative darkness. Alex gave a sigh before setting off after him at a quick pace to try and warm himself up.

"Good morning, lad," Jared said as Alex came up behind him.

"What you doing out here?"

"Eric's snoring woke me," he said with a chuckle and a puff of smoke from his pipe, looking back to the crag in the rock through the trees. "And you?"

"Same," Alex replied.

Jared took a puff of smoke and looked up at the red sky over their heads. "Red sky in the morning! Eric will be grumpy!" He chuckled.

Alex let out a great beaming smile of amusement, getting Jared's joke, but said no more to continue the conversation, rather falling into an awkward silence with the old satyr who was stood looking up at him, leaning on his crock to rest his gammy right leg and smoking his pipe of tobacco.

"Did you want to ask me something, lad?" he questioned, finally breaking the silence.

Alex said nothing, pretending to be relaxed and listening to the sound of the waking birds all about them, and shook his head as an answer.

The satyr, seeming the jolliest Alex had ever seen him this particular morning, let out another chuckle. "There is something." When Alex turns to protest, Jared cuts him off before he could speak. "No! No! Don't deny it. I see it in your eyes, there is something, isn't there?"

Alex let out a sigh, signifying acceptance of his defeat in this pitiful war of wills. "There, may be... something."

"Ha!" celebrated the jolly Jared. "Come on then, lad, let's have it out of you, what is it?"

"Well," Alex said, teetering on the edge between saying and not. "It's just your story that you told last night."

"Go on," encouraged Jared, pushing the hesitant boy.

"Em, well... do you think I can... you know, do some... magic?"

Jared bursted out in a bout of deep laughter and coughing, though not mocking Alex's request as if he were a stupid child who didn't know a cat from a dog, but more being amused at the boy's need to ask in the first place. "Lad," he said as he composes himself into a more serious tone. "Like I said, it's not just any mortal that could pass into the land of the gods, I mean, I couldn't do it. Eric certainly can't, but you can. 'Can I do magic?' You have more abilities than anyone else has currently on this world, I'm sure of that."

"Really?" Alex replied in a scrutinising tone, not of shock and surprise, but a mature, distrusting disbelief.

"Look, lad," said Jared as he hobbled in close and put his arm around the boy's back. "Most mortals can do some form of... well... if you want to call it that, 'magic', if they know how." And with his words, he put up his crock, putting his weight on Alex, and pointed it at a fallen log, which, without a word, he ignited into a blaze.

Alex, though, was less interested in his trick but more on what he had said. "What do you mean by 'if you want to call it Magic'?"

"Well, lad," Jared said, taking a puff of smoke from his pipe. "'Magic' doesn't really exist. What you'd call 'magic' is more influencing science with your mind and soul, which is technically known as Kamari. How it works, lad, is like this. Think of the cosmos as a computer, and science and, more importantly, physics, is the coding. Now what Kamari is, is changing the coding to achieve a desired result. Now, look at that log," he said, gesturing his crock to yet another fallen log near the one he had just set fire to.

"Now, firstly you need to plug your mind into the system. Concentrate and use your will. See the log, become part of the log, feel what's around it, see from its perspective…"

"How can I see through a log? It has no eyes!"

"Humour me!" replied Jared simply and rather unimpressed. "Now, see from the log's perspective, smell the air from over there, hear the sounds that it can, make yourself that log. When your feel you're there, will it to catch fire."

Jared took a hobble back, and Alex concentrated. He stared at the log, trying to run through what Jared had told him, imagining it bit by bit until he felt himself forcing the images into his mind. Slowly they seemed to come more naturally and feel more real. After what felt like a good couple of minutes there was a flicker of a flame at the base of the log, which quickly flickered out.

"brilliant!" Jared smiled and congratulated Alex, who wasn't very impressed with himself.

"That was pitiful!" he remarked.

"You did it, you should be happy with that. When you get to know how the cosmos works, you'll get better and quicker." Jared put his arm around Alex and began to lead him back to the cave. "Now come on, lad, let's get some breakfast."

But Alex wasn't hungry. He created a rather unimpressive flame and wanted to stay until that god-forsaken log was nothing but ash.

"No," he protested, "I want to have another go!"

Jared's smile turned to a frown as he stopped Alex going back. "Lad, look, I like your enthusiasm, but the thing is, to use Kamari is to drain your life. It's like using a battery, the more Kamari you use, the quicker your battery is spent. It's a dangerous game for us mortals, and the addiction has driven many mortals to an early grave. That's the difference between us and the divine beings; their battery is endless, and ours isn't. Now come, I'm starving, and we've got a long day ahead of us."

"Why, what have we got to do?" asked Alex, a bit concerned, not helped of course by the thought that he had just wasted some unknown amount of his life making a flicker that didn't even char that bloody log!

"Daisy gave us a job to do, or don't you remember?"

After a stark, bland and entirely unremarkable breakfast, Alex and Eric began packing up the cave in preparation for what appeared to be an expectedly long journey. They covered the furniture with sheets, packed the blankets and all the food and clothes that they had. All of it went into what could only be described as a sleigh, crossed with a three-year-old's wagon, yet was the size of a horses' cart. Its wheels were close to the ground, and it had shallow sides, fitted with a seat for when Jared's gammy leg could no longer carry him and at the front it had a large handle that Eric could use to drag it along.

The bundles of supplies were quickly loaded onto the cart, wagon, sleigh-thing. Thanks to the combined work of Alex and Eric who, as it turned out, made a pretty good team.

"Another!" cried Eric from inside the cave, lobbing a tied bundle of supplies out, which Alex caught and packed neatly into the cart.

"Next!" Alex shouted back inside.

"Okay! Here comes!"

Alex caught the next, and packed that into the cart too, just as they had been doing for a while.

It was at this point that Jared came down from the moors having collected Eric's twenty-nine gold sheep, after letting them free to graze during breakfast. All twenty-six ewes and three rams where accounted for and gathered into a neat little flock, and, remarkably for the lame old satyr, all without the help of a dog or hound of any kind. *Quite remarkable!* Alex couldn't help but think as he packed another pack into the cart-thing and compressed it down with his weight.

"Sheep ready?" came the voice of Eric, clearly having heard Jared's approach from inside the cave.

"They're all accounted for!" returned Jared as he hobbled up.

From in the cave, Alex could hear Eric scrabbling about for something, throwing bundles about and grumbling to himself.

"AH!" he cried out in excitement. "Here comes Last!" Out the crag flew a bundle of clothes which Alex caught, looking at them and then to Jared, he couldn't help but exclaim.

"You never wore these!"

"No. but your father did when he was your age… I'd say you're about the same size."

Alex looked the clothes over and shook his head. "Well," protested Jared, "you can't be wearing them golden robes much longer, I mean them, err, sandals? Aren't very suitable for walking in. Besides, you'll boil in that lot. That's not if you don't catch the attention of some surviving bandit or something on the way first." But Jared could see the uncertainty in the boy's eyes. "Oh, what are you waiting for, lad? Go change!"

With that, Alex leaves, still not sure on the stile. While he was gone, Eric emerges from the crag. "No took long." He remarks.

"No, only about an English Hour." Jared replies after looking at his pocket watch, using the method of telling time preferred by the cyclops. The English hour used by Eric, consists of fifty-one normal minutes, each resulting in a twenty -eight hour day.

A Few moments later and in a completely different look Alex returns. Jared was right, they did fit. Alex is now dressed in large boots and a long rawhide trench coat with golden woollen lining, covering black jeans and a plain, short-sleeved black top. "I look like a goth," Alex remarked as he approached Jared and Eric, who were now tying down the cart-thing with thick ropes.

"Don't be silly," remarked Jared as he looked Alex up and down. "You look great! Doesn't he, Eric?"

Eric looked up, and, pulling the biggest and cheesiest grin that stretched from ear to ear, gave Alex a giant thumbs up; his one blue eye giving away that his true opinions were in stark contrast to the grin he is forcing upon himself. But in truth, it was not the look that worried Alex, but the feeling that he was drifting further and further away from the realm of the gods, a world he now knew he'd come to love. He felt no longer like a plain, Yorkshire lad, but more a monk of healing, more a student of Atia. This wasn't the world he wanted to be a part of, not anymore, and with every change he made to himself here, he felt further from it. His clothes being changed made him feel human when, for a while, he was able to forget the apocalyptic world he'd left behind, the world he had, despite all his efforts, found he was back in. For the first real time he couldn't help but think, *I wonder how Atia took my disappearance, I mean, will she ever accept me back, especially like this?*

But there was little time for Alex to ponder, for, before long, Eric had finished tying down the cart, had slipped the leather brace over his shoulders that attached to the cart and, taking the handle in his hand, began to pull it away, with Jared herding the sheep alongside, with Eve sticking particularly close to her giant master. Alex walked behind. He took one last look back at the crag, that symbol of Yorkshire he was leaving behind, and every step, his feet felt like lead. His heart was heavy with sorrow, as every step made him feel as if he was getting further and further from the temple of healing, and from Atia, whom he now missed more than ever.

Chapter IX:
23 Years BP, Yorkshire

"Evening, Jared," said Fred as he came from his home and out into the street where Jared was waiting, rucksack on his back and crutches in hand. The warm evening of late summer after college bringing a smile to Fred's face.

"Happy birthday!" Jared replies. Stood outside with Jared was the beautiful Daisy, who had been waiting with Jared while Fred changed. She stuck out her arm and linked it with his before leading him off, up to their usual spot up in the moors, with Jared following on behind them. From his new house across the street, his father shouted from the bedroom window to stay safe and hidden.

The world was not kind to those like Jared and the young orphaned cyclops who walked by his side. But, even in his unspoken servitude, Jared felt freer than he had in, well, all his life. *For what could be freer?* he asked himself, the wind off the moors blowing through his hair as he walked behind Daisy and Fred. *Than to be in the freedom of the isolated moors with friends, no matter who they are?*

Above them, the sky was red with fire, streaking across the evening sky like an angry dragon falling from the dying sun, the clouds illuminated in purples and blue. "What a beautiful night," said Daisy, linking her arm with Fred who no longer felt like the crazy kid that he was once labelled to be. Far from his year in the Asylum, he had dawned on the simple truth of the life he led. That, just because he saw those who are not really there, does not mean that they aren't there, only that those around him were simply too ignorant to see the truth.

"How are you two doing back there?" he called back, taking a quick glance back to the satyr and young, orphan cyclops that were trailing behind. The rattle of the camping gear that was slung over the already seven-foot Cyclops' back sounded like an unorganised band marching through the streets. "We're doing just fine," Jared gave a cheesy grin, "Don't worry about us," he said, not in a sarcastic, attention-seeking way, but rather in a manner so as to allow Fred the peace of mind to focus on the pretty girl at his side.

An hour later, and in a sheltered little crag at the bottom of a hill crowned with trees, the group set out four small tents and stood around a yet unlit fire. Jared prepared to cook some supper of bacon and sausages as the young Eric approached, holding two tree trunks, one under each arm. He laid them down into position as two benches, one either side of the fire and as he did so, it fell on either Fred or Daisy to start the fire.

"Do you want to do it?" asked Fred, gesturing to the unlit logs and kindling.

Daisy looked from the logs to Fred and shook her head with that heart-pumping, head-spinning smile of hers that made Fred feel as if he'd do anything for her. "You can light a little fire, can't you?" she said, putting her arm around his back in a seductive way. "Besides, I always thought anything to do with fire was more a..." She took a moment to change her tone. "Man's jurisdiction."

Fred gave in with a sigh of acceptance. *She knows just how to talk to me!* he half grumbled in his head, and turned to look long and hard at the kindling shoved crudely under the sticks and logs. He took a breath, concentrated, followed all the steps and… was shaken completely and utterly from his concentration by the sly and tender running of Daisy's fingers down Fred's spine. She leaned towards him, her hot breath kissing the inside of his ear as she whispered to him, something Jared couldn't quite make out.

Fred looked back to the fire and, to his surprise, the kindling, sticks and logs had burst into flames. He looked back to Daisy, who was leaning away from him on their trunk bench, giggling to herself in amusement, knowing her words had caught Fred off guard.

"Do you mean…" Fred asked in a harsh whisper, cut off by Daisy's answer, nodding her head as she laughed, leaning in close to Fred and resting her head on his shoulder.

Jared looked from one to the other and back again, seeing in their eyes the quiet words that had passed between them. He hid his jealous smirk with a joyous declaration, his trunk-bench shaking as Eric sat down. "Right! Who wants some sausage then?" he chuckled as he placed a frying pan full of Yorkshire sausages and bacon over the fire.

After the food had cooked and had been devoured, mostly on the part of Eric, and the moon in all its crescent glory was shining its light down upon the friends, Jared broke out the marshmallows, and placed them on sticks. He passed them around the fire till everyone had marshmallows caramelising and melting over the roaring fire. As owls sung their lullaby, Daisy rapped a woollen blanket about her and

Fred's shoulders and as the smell of burning sugar filled the night air it became time for the stories.

"Who wants to go first?" asked Daisy, her eyes fixed quite firmly on Eric and Jared.

"You go, I tell bad story!" Eric replied in his usual, simple style of talking, something that had not changed, matured or gotten better between his youth and his time with Alex yet to come.

Jared looked at Fred and then to Daisy, a sly smile appearing at the corner of his mouth. "Should I tell them about the story of the Jabbering?" he asked Eric, all the while his sly smile was growing across his face.

Fred looked to Daisy, his eyes asking, *What the hell's a Jabbering?* To which Daisy shook her head. Neither were versed in the tale that seemed quite well known to those creatures opposite them.

Eric returned Jared's sly smile, which quickly turned into a frown, then a scream. "NO! NO! NO!" the cyclops exploded, jumping up to his feet and jumping up and down on the spot like a child in protest, all the while blowing on his stick with far too many marshmallows on it. Holding the blackened sugary blobs that now hung from the stick like slime, to all those present, and with a gloomy frown, he said, "I burnt marshmallows!" and, throwing the stick away. Again, looking like an upset child, he sat back down, his arms crossed over his chest. "Go on," he mumbled in his gloom. "Tell 'em story."

"Okay," Jared turned back to his friends across the fire, wrapped in their blanket, and, in traditional campfire fashion, placed a torch under his pointy chin, though it was so close to his chin that all it served to do was light up his neck. "The story of the Jabbering, is, a traditional scary story for us... though, it might be less so for you, I guess. Anyway, the story started with a little lullaby." Jared cleared his throat, and, realising the torch wasn't doing much, simply tossed it away.

"Sleep, little baby, sleep, my son, be good or the
Jabbering will come, my son.
Don't stay out too long, nor up too late, or the Jabbering
will come, my son.
If you speak out, or if you kill, the Jabbering will come,
my son.
If you show yourself to men, you will come to regret it,
for the Jabbering will come, my son.
He comes at night, hidden in the dark, and will take the
gift of the gods, my son.
Listen out for his boots scraping along the floor, listen
out for the scraping on the bedroom door.
Beware where you tread, who you anger or mislead, for
he may just be the Jabbering, you see.
So, before you lay your head in rest, my son, send a
prayer that the Jabbering don't find you, my son."

"Nice little lullaby," remarked Daisy, "but I'm not really scared, I'll admit."

Jared put up his index finger to ask for her patience as he continued with his story. "You see, that's the traditional lullaby for us creatures... the story goes that the Jabbering was a man... once. But not just any man, no! He was a man, taller than any other, stronger than any other, with arrows made of the deadliest poison in the world, so much so that it is said that even the gods feared it. To men, he was called a different name, but to our ancestors, he was called the Jabbering. He lived before the gods hid us from humans, in an age of tyrants and enslavers, and this Jabbering was one of the worsts.

"It is said that he once killed a whole tribe of Centaurs for daring to speak up when he stole their wine. He killed the Giant king and all his kin and, if you believe the stories, even returned from the land of the dead. They say he was so blood-thirsty that when there was no one for him to kill... he killed his own wife and children... with his bare hands! Smashed and mushed their brains into the floor of his home. He was so crazy, so blood-thirsty, and so vicious and brutal that it was said he could only ever be killed by one as great as him. But there was no one as great as he in our ranks, none who could challenge him and win, though many tried. In the end, it was one who was as great as him, strong as him, brutal and blood-thirsty as him who ended his life..."

"Who?" asked Fred in awe, hanging on to Jared's every word, though, not out of fear, but a deep pride of his kinsman. *In the films,* he couldn't help but think, *we are always the weak ones, we never think that humans might actually be the strongest, most advanced things.*

"Go on," urged Daisy, ending Jared's attempted dramatic pause. "Who killed Jabbering?"

"Himself!" Jared replied at long last. "Climbed onto his own funeral fire and stood there while the flames consumed him. Though this isn't the worst part, as Jabbering was so strong, that not even death could hold him. Instead, when he encountered death, he wrestled him to the ground. Jabbering didn't stay dead, but came back, twisted, deformed and yet stronger than ever before. It is said that his ghost, his spirit refuses to move on 'til all of us are dead, and humans are all that remain on this world. He hunts down the non-humans, finds us through our naughty deeds, and shoots us with one of his poisoned arrows.

"It is said, that if you're shot by one, your powers to him become useless and all humans can see you and kill you; tear you to pieces as a result. They say on cold and windy nights you can hear him, scratching at walls and windows and drifting along, his feet scraping on the floor, looking for his next victim." Fred looked to Daisy and her to him, a chill running down both their spines. Though none seemed more scared than Eric, who was rocking back and forth on his log, hands clasped firmly together and over his eye as he hummed the lullaby to himself.

"Are you all right there?" asked Fred, rather concerned, though he got no response.

"He'll be fine," remarked Jared as he placed a comforting arm over his back and spoke to him gently till, he calmed down.

"Perhaps a happier story," suggested Fred as he looked to Daisy to tell the next story.

"Aye, probably right, don't want him to be up all night," replied Jared.

Daisy waited while Eric came back around completely, sitting back up and shaking off their stares, remarking, "indigestion! Me scared? No!" even though his one great, blue eye wasn't telling any lies.

With a sigh of disbelief and over the crackling of the warm fire between them, Daisy looked to her friends to give her an idea of the sort of story she should tell.

"Well, a goddess like you should have loads of stories from over the years," suggested Fred.

"Aye." Jared looked from Fred to Daisy, and that sly smile crept back into the corner of his mouth again. "Let's have a story about love, shall we? Surely a goddess like yourself must have some of them."

"What's that supposed to mean?" Daisy asked, her eyes squinted in suspicion and warning that reached right into Jared's bones.

"Well, I just meant, well, because you're rather, err, attractive is all," Jared said, thinking on his feet and realising it was probably best to keep his mouth firmly shut for a while.

Making sure that she had firmly put Jared in his place before moving on, she asked her question again. "So, what kind of story should I tell?"

Daisy looked to Fred who gave a gesture as if to say, *Jared's idea sounds great,* and, giving up rather easily, with nothing but a mutter and sigh in protest she concedes. "Fine, fine. If you want a love story, I'll give you a love story." She gives a brief pause "The only one I got," she muttered, her voice dropping to a whisper and a clog of sorrow blocking her throat. "Though, I have to warn you, it isn't happy.

"It all happened long, long ago… before humans or satyrs or cyclops were even a flicker of a thought on this world. I was young, very young, and foolish. You see, I fell in love with a god, far more powerful than me. I was a nobody, a toy, to him. Yet, I had the delusion of youth, and he raised me up from a dark time, so I thought we'd be together forever… and for a time we were, and it was good… but as it turned out, he was married."

"You didn't know?" came the interrupting, simple voice of Eric as he built up the fire with some more logs.

"No, as it turns out. He tricked me. But what was far worse is that he tricked me further. He said things like, 'I love you more', 'I'll leave her for you', 'she's meaningless'." Fred put his arm around her as her eyes began to flicker with tears and her cheeks moistened. "He said he'd run away with me and we'd be together forever, and the worst part was that I was so deeply in love with him that I actually believed him, and I thought he felt the same. So, I was fool enough to stay his mistress. He gave me gifts and favour yes. But all meaningless and when it became clear, once again, that he was lying, that he'd never leave her, I confronted him." Daisy's words clog in her throat. "He stood over me and watched, did nothing as the other gods gathered round, started calling me a whore and an evil that had to be gotten rid of! They cast me from the realm of the gods and laughed at me, and still he did nothing. He said nothing, he just stood there and watched as I, heartbroken and humiliated, was left in the dust to cry. His eyes never even got wet, like I was nothing but an amusement to him, to have his way with and discard! The dammed Devils. War and Destruction, they chained me and threw away the key, and still he did nothing. I saw in his eyes then, it was him! He ordered that upon me. He claimed me, to be his greatest love! Who else could it have been but the king of the gods, Life? You wanted to know a love story, there you go, that's my love story."

The camp fell into a tearful silence as no one amongst them had any inclination whatsoever as to what to say, each in their sad and gloomy expressions trying to give condolences with a smile. Apart from Eric, of course, who was never one for comforting gestures, but instead in his heart of hearts, he felt the sting of disgust.

With a nod of her head and shoving a sad marshmallow in her mouth, it was Daisy who broke the silence. "You wanted a love story, that's all I got," she said, chewing through the sugary treat.

"Well," Jared said with a cough, "I'm sure you'll find someone better."

Daisy looked to Fred with a smile. "I'm sure I already have." Daisy cuddled up to Fred and gave Jared a look as if to say, *Now piss off, then!*

Reading the message loud and clear, and, of course, bound to serve her every whim, Jared yawned and stretched before announcing to all present, "Time to call it a night, I think." He stood from his log and turned to walk towards his little tent. Though before entering, he called back to the fire, "I think it's time you call it a night too, don't you think, Eric?"

"But not tired!" Eric protested like any child not wishing to miss out, a large beaming grin across his face.

"Okay," Fred remarked, climbing to his feet. "But I'm going to call it a night as well, so you'll be left out here all alone... with the Jabbering," Fred said with a smile in the direction of Daisy, making her smirk.

Eric needed no further persuasion, and quickly trudged unhappily off to his tent, chuntering to Jared as he went in. "Not gonna sleep wink, now, thanks you," he snarled, before being scared enough to scurry quickly into his tent like a mouse at the sound of an owl landing in a nearby tree. The three remaining friends laughed to one another for a moment before Jared went into his tent, leaving only Daisy and Fred left by the burning fire.

Neither did anything until they heard the zip of the two tents be firmly closed by their occupants, sure that they were indeed alone. In the awkward silence that followed, Fred began to shuffle back to his tent, unsure what to do. "Well, err, good night I…"

"Aren't the stars just magnificent?" Daisy cut Fred off, looking up into the darkness of space, a longing, pining, look in her eyes, hidden from Fred's view. "Come back, will you, Freddy." she commanded, patting the place he had been sat moments before with her hand.

Fred followed her command and sat back down as she cuddled in next to him. "I loved someone once," she said in his ear, "but he never loved me back. I know I can be cold towards you at times… but I have to ask you, would you stay loyal to me?"

Fred's mouth became dry and cloggy; he knew the answer, but it took some time for him to be able to say it. "You know my goddess, I'm loyal."

"And what if I wasn't, what if I were just a normal girl, then what?" she said, turning to look deep into Fred's eyes.

"I think you know the answer," Fred whispered, taking a deep breath as he leaned towards her, and her to him. In that moment, there was no question in Fred's mind what was real and what, if anything, was in his head, for that was a question he no longer cared to ask.

With a sudden movement like a cat pouncing on its prey, Daisy knocked Fred and herself onto the floor. Throwing aside their blanket, she sat upright on top of him and smiled a lustful grin.

"Go on Freddy," she said, moving her hair behind her shoulders. "Ask me what I know you've been dying to."

Fred swallowed hard, his blood boiling and his heart pounding as Daisy sat over him, his goddess, his best friend, his vision of craziness now feeling more real than ever as she placed his hands on her hips.

"Will you go out with me?" he managed to blurt out, not able to say anymore.

Daisy grinned and laughed in amusement, as she said, "I'll do more than that! I think it's time for your birthday present, isn't it?"

Chapter X:
14 Months, 2 Weeks AP, Somewhere in France

Atia had been traveling, searching in desperate need for days, with no sign of Alex. She was following her gut instinct in her relentless hunt for her friend. Trying to use her kimarie to find him. She was still unable to believe that he would just leave her like that, she just couldn't bring herself to do it, like she was bound to him and him to her in some way she simply couldn't understand.

Her day's journey ended with her pulling up outside an old, French hotel by a rather beautiful lake. The hotel looked to have a large number of rooms, with the upper floors having balconies that overlooked the lake. A road separated the hotel from a small, wooded area, set in the backdrop of forgotten fields. Atia had crossed the channel into France days ago. There was no doubt in her mind that she was heading in the right direction. "By the All One," she prayed, the same prayer that she said each and every morning and night. "I will not rest, not stop 'til I find him. Not go back to the temple or be distracted by my duty until I achieve my goal, I swear!"

Atia broke down the old door of the hotel, taking a key from the wall behind the small reception desk and going to the room on its tag.

The old-fashioned French hotel was cosy yet stripped

bare, the wooden finish, the food and knifes in the kitchen, carpet from the floor and the floorboards all gone, much like Alex's home.

Atia opened the door of the room, and found this too bare, so she went back and got another key, and another, and another, until on the fifth attempt she found a room that was relatively untouched. It was missing carpet and curtains, but at least it had a complete bed. She shook the sheets free of their dust and closed and locked the door behind her. *Never can be too safe!* she thought to herself, putting the key on the hook behind the door. Then she walked to the balcony that looked out across the large lake behind the hotel and sat, looking up to the newly woken stars and felt very small indeed. "Oh, Alex," she said up to the early wakening stars that had started to twinkle as the sun died. "Where the hell, are you?"

Before dropping her head down for her long and deep slumber, she casted up one last prayer to her god, the great All One who binds the cosmos as one. Returning inside and kneeling down before the base of the bed, she stripped off her clothes, down to her bare form, to show her humbleness before her god. Closing her eyes, Atia does her best to connect herself with her surroundings before saying her prayer in the traditional language of the Draden. "Of key, of cross. vo jusch quoto ov soulus Alex. Lemu vo figurt cha!" Atia took a deep breath; it was not too often that she prayed, yet recently she had done it more than ever before, her desperation taking her over completely. As she climbed into the stiff, old, uncomfortable bed she couldn't help but think, *I don't know why I feel so protective over the boy. I've never been like this before. What's happening to me?*

She closed her eyes and fell into a deep and exhausted sleep. In her slumber a voice came to her mind, a voice she had never heard before, but one strangely familiar. It loomed out of the darkness of her mind like a great star, and it's words become etched into her memory.

Thy shall not find Alex, nor shall you ever marry him. Yet thy souls are the entwined branches of two trees. Thy shall be his rising and his downfall, though, thy shall not find him, thy shall be there when Mr. Smith falls!

Atia's eyes snapped open, the words of the voice still echoing around her mind. Her vision was blurry as she woke, feeling the sun pouring in through the doors to the balcony. The voice was deep and eternal, genderless and kinless. A sound that was sound itself, not deep, but powerful, not forceful nor weak. Not slurred or flawed, but far from perfect, neither old nor young, yet wisdom held within its sound. The sound, once clear and strong, faded away. *Was that fall? Does he mean he's to die? Or worse?* But as the voice faded and she became more awake, she found she had a more urgent problem on her hands.

"Bonjour, belle." The voice was harsh and cold, with a Desperate yet forceful tone. The thing it belonged to was by far worse. Small and bald with a tufty bit of hair on his chin for a beard, his head was egg-shaped and there came a stench of body odour and wine that made Atia want to throw up. Scrawny as a twig and with four missing teeth in the front of his mouth. A crude knife in his hand, with spots of rust on the blade, was stabbed into the wooden panel at the base of the bed. Atia instinctively scuttled back, unable to speak with the dry fear in her mouth, pulling up the bed sheets to her chin thinking it would protect her. The Frenchman tutted as he shuffled his way up the bed to maintain the same distance, topless, his chest hair hung in a great knot and his nipples seem to sag with loose skin as if he was once much plumper. The tell-tale signs of the plague were under his arms, revealing themselves as he reached back to place his hand on his knife. "Ne pas avoir peur princesse," he said.

Atia knew precisely what he was saying, of course she did; she was, after all, a Divine being, though she refused to lower herself to his level, and thought that perhaps the best way to do that was to refuse to even show him the courtesy of speaking his language. "Don't call me princess," she snarled like a lioness trapped in her cage.

"Vous anglais!" the Frenchman said with a smile. "I... can speak English too," he blurted out rather shakily, but truthfully. Though Atia stayed quiet, under the sheets she searched for something, anything that she could use to defend herself.

"My... name, Leo Bonhomme... I... own this hotel." He said, pulling out the knife and waving it about to show he owned everything around them.

"Well," Atia said, shuffling uncomfortably. "It's a very... nice hotel." She didn't really think she could simply talk her way out of the situation. Not given the look in the Frenchman's eyes, *but it's got to be worth a shot!*

"Merci." He said with a smile, sitting back a little and letting Atia have a moment to breathe, but it wouldn't last as his smile turned to greed. "It, err... very expensive hotel."

"You want payment?" Atia said, turning white, already knowing what was going to happen next. "I'm afraid I don't have anything of value."

"Oui," he said with a grin and a nod, "Though, err, I think you do have something," he said, licking his chapped lips and coming in close to Atia again. He sniffed the air in front of her face and touched her hair with his knife as she tried desperately to escape, only to be trapped by the headboard behind her. "Hum, you are very... belle. I could make belle... happy, very happy."

Atia could feel the innards of her stomach climbing her throat as the Frenchmen's stench filled her lungs and she felt the jerky pulling of the bedsheets from her. As she gripped them, her nails went into the palms of her hands in desperation to stop him.

"Now, now, Belle... I will not bite!" he said, his tongue coming from his mouth, the knife still pressed against the side of Atia's head. He leaned forward to try to kiss her, nicking off a lock of her red hair with his knife at the same time.

Atia was scared, desperate to escape this nightmare. It was not the knife that scared her. That crude thing would do nothing against her, she just needed to find a way to get from under his scrawny but surprisingly strong frame. *Think, Atia, think!* she screamed to herself, turning her head and trying not to throw up.

Then an idea came to her. With a firm upward thrust of her right knee from under the sheets and into his groin, the scrawny Frenchman rolled off the bed and into a crumpled heap on the floor. Climbing from the bed, hair dropping down her shoulders, victory filled in her eyes. Dressed in nothing but her underwear, Atia stood over the crying, bawling man whose hands were fast around his bruised manhood. In that moment, Atia's eyes shone with the true power of a goddess, not that the Frenchman saw it.

Atia spit at the man on the floor before turning to walk from the room in disgust, but she was too keen to get out, merely grabbing her clothes in a bundle under her arm.

"Oh, Belle!" came the skin-crawling voice of the Frenchman as Atia reached for the door, only to find it was locked. She turned in horror to find Leo dangling the key before her, before dropping it down his trousers. "We not done yet," He said, knife out and a horrid grin across his face.

Atia shook her head at the Frenchman, so lustful as to not be put off by the clearest evidence of her divinity. "Let me go," Atia snarled.

"Belle… you know the… price. But," he said with a calm shrug of his shoulders, "as long as you're warm… Je me fiche que tu es vivant!" he exclaimed with a smile that made Atia's skin crawl and her spine turn cold.

"Evil bastard!" she snarled, anger filling her from head to toe as she acted in a fury she hadn't shown before. So disgusted by the Frenchman, combined with the effect her desperate and endless searching of Alex had on her mind, she burst into action and charged Leo. In one swift move, she threw him back towards the balcony and he was only stopped from falling by the railing. Atia staggered back around towards the bed, an unbelievably excruciating pain emanating from her chest and filling her entirety, something else she had never felt before. Looking down, wedged firmly just above her bra near the base of her neck was the rusted knife of the Frenchman. So furious was Atia that not even this pain woke her. In a swift motion, she pulled out the knife, with it coming a single drop of her silver blood. At the millisecond the knife left her skin, there was no sign of a wound ever being there at all. So fast was the healing that it would appear as if the scene had been played in reverse, so fast that the mortal eye could not register that it was happening, only that it had.

"Qu' est-ce que vous? Démons!" Leo screamed, turning as pale as a sheep as he made a bolt from the balcony to the door, rummaging around for the key he had hidden earlier, now regretting that he had ever looked upon the strange woman at all. Finally, he pulled out the key, and, with trembling hands, looked back over his shoulder while trying desperately to open the door; what Atia had been waiting for. As soon as he took his eyes off her, she was on him like a hawk, and, in one swift movement, took the knife from right to left across his neck, splitting open his arteries and painting the white door red with his blood, his limp body, hand still holding the key, fell face-down on the floor.

In the blink of an eye, it was all over, and Atia stood over a dead body, adrenaline leaving her as quickly as it had come. She fell, hands on knees, coughing and belching at the sight of it, but not because of the smell, but rather because of the fact she herself had done it. Not some evil entity, nor some sick-minded mortal, but her. She had seen her fair share of dead bodies, after all it was kind of an occupational inevitability, though for it to be a body she herself had plucked the life from in anger, was way more than she could cope with.

After an hour of trying to compose herself, praying for forgiveness and getting dressed, Atia decided it was best to leave as quickly as possible, before Death arrived and told her mother what she had done. Then, she would be in real trouble. Killing a mortal wasn't much of a big deal for most of the gods, but for a monk of healing, it was a tremendous no. Though, for Atia, as she stormed quickly from the room, knife tooled under her belt, *just in case!* it was a case of out of the frying pan and into the fire.

Atia had barely taken three steps outside and had tidied her now uneven hair, before she was in conflict again. From the sky and following the road running past the hotel, came the thudding of air being pushed down by blades, and the rumble of heavy vehicles on the road. First came the five rocketing, booming jets, bellowing smoke across the sky like the claw marks of a lion. Then came the entourage, the caravan of metal monsters and armed men, shadowed by helicopters and accompanied by building-crushing, tree-uprooting tanks, their long metal barrels and muzzles glinting in the sun.

"Oh, shit!" Atia exclaimed, freezing on the spot as the helicopters were upon her before she had a chance to hide. Armed men pointed their machine guns at the lone woman on the floor. Army trucks quickly pulled up on the road, and armed men dressed in cavalier vests and wearing masks and gloves to protect themselves from the plague dismounted their vehicles.

"Freeze!" one cried, pointing his semi-automatic at her as he approached, and his comrades formed a line behind him. "Get on your knees! Keep your hands up!" he commanded. Atia, looking all around her, decided it was better to do as they say. *Best not to create too much work for Death,* she thought to herself as the men closed in around her.

"She's one of them!" cried another man as he circled to her back. "Sir, what do we do?"

"Shoot!" he cried.

Chapter XI:
14 Months AP, England

The trio crossed the one great bridge spanning the Humber, the toll booths empty and the barriers smashed. Its twin concrete towers were left unmanaged, the steel rusting in the sun. Heading south- east, they took different roads to the ones that Alex had taken when he first headed south after the plague, a much more open path to his surprise. Across the flats of Lincolnshire; Eric was so tall and had such amazing vision with his one blue eye that he could see at times right across the county, with no hill nor hump in sight. They bypassed the Wolds, sticking to the flatter landscape till they hit Rutland after turning southwest.

They passed through the tiny county in less than a day, turning south at Barrow, they headed into the county of Northamptonshire where their paths kept left, past Corby then cutting cross-county to Wellingborough, and then, keeping south, past into Buckinghamshire. They marched on through the hilly, wooded, landscape, not wavering for a second from their purpose. Buckinghamshire was a county that Alex found far better than he expected, and a place where Eric seemed more at ease than the flatter landscape they'd come through. Though they did not stop here, for their intention was to make for Dover and from there to France. Though, after a long evening of debate, they decided it would be best to give London a very wide birth. So, they changed their path to the southwest once more, passing into Oxfordshire, a place Alex had always wanted to visit, and indeed, had originally intended to go to before he had met Atia.

It was striking to him that even with Jared's bad leg the three of them were traveling much faster than Alex had done on his previous expedition, wherein he'd merely got to Sherwood Forest, *but then again,* he had once thought to himself, *this time I have a reason to walk. For the faster I get to where Jared is leading, the faster I can return to Atia.*

The three passed in a straight line, overcoming any obstacle in their path. *Amazing what you can do with a cyclops!* Alex couldn't help thinking, as they passed from Wheattey to Sutton Courtenan, then on to Steventon and Grove before dropping into Wiltshire, spending perhaps too little time in Oxfordshire. They kept their course to Avebury and then turning back to their south course till they reach Wilton. Then, turning to a steadier course, was able to briefly take in the beautiful countryside as they went. It turns out nothing could distract Alex from that, who had his father's passion for history, he persuaded Jared to take a detour to the white horse and another to spend a night camped out in the middle of Stonehenge.

From Wiltshire, the three went southeast through Hampshire, correcting their course to an almost direct east root. They passed through Hampshire to west Sussex, passing from South Harling and hitting the south coast at Shoreham-by-sea. They follow the south coast from there across East Sussex and into Kent and to Dover.

It was afternoon when the three arrived at the great white cliffs, too late, in Jared's opinion to make the crossing, so, with cart being pulled behind him and twenty-nine sheep by his side, Eric followed Alex and Jared up to Dover castle where they planned to spend the night.

While Eric was settling in his sheep within the walls, Alex couldn't help but go exploring. He walked along the old, abandoned walls and towers of the once great military base, which protected England for over half a millennium. Looking out from the walls, he looked out across the English Channel and across to France, which was nothing but a haze on the distant horizon, like a mirage in the hot of the afternoon sun.

"There it is!" said Jared, and he hobbled over along the walls, to Alex, who is leaning against a merlon that has half crumbled away, "France, the next step on our journey. It seems so close, doesn't it?"

"Have you noticed," says Alex, as if he hadn't heard what Jared just said, as the old satyr came up to him and lit up his pipe. "This castle took so long to build that new innovations in building techniques made parts of this castle old fashioned before it was completed, look," Alex pointed out towards the outer wall, there the towers were square in shape, and then nearby, to where the tower was cylindrical and round. "It was found that round towers were better at resisting undermining and deflecting bombardment then square ones, so, some towers are square and other's round."

"Fascinating," smiled Jared, clearly more interested in the smoke in his pipe then Alex's knowledge. "Really!" exclaimed Eric from below them, having heard the little fact whilst going about his business, "That amazing!" he chuckled, before going back to gathering up his golden sheep, all of whom have stood with their master along the long journey.

"Where are we actually going?" Alex asked Jared as he smokes his pipe, the satyr having been rather cold and stark on facts of their destination until this point.

"To France," he replied simply.

"Yes, I get that, but where, then? What is our actual final destination?"

Jared gave a sigh. *Suppose I've kept this quite long enough!*

"Daisy wants you to find something, you know that. Your father was looking for it before the plague, as was I, but we never found it, though we figured out where it is, we narrowed it down to the south Peloponnese. That is where we're heading!"

"The Peloponnese?" Alex muttered to himself. "You mean… Greece!"

Jared nodded with a chuckle and a smile. "That is where we're heading!"

"Okay?" Alex said, daunted by the journey ahead of him. *I'll never get back to Atia!* With a sigh he added "So, what's the plan?"

"Well, tomorrow morning, we'll charter a boat…"

"Charter!" roared Eric in hysteric laughter. "Charter!" he repeated, cutting off Jared's voice. "Steal, you mean!"

Eric wandered off, deeper into the castle complex, his laughter still booming around the castle long after he'd gone.

"Charter! funny," he boomed.

Chapter XII:
23 Years BP

Fred sat, tea in hand, on the sofa in Dr Mikels' office while he fetched Fred's folder from a filing cabinet in the corner, his cigar hanging from the corner of his mouth and surrounding his head in a helmet of smoke. His dreadlocks hung low behind his shoulders, his suede suit dusted with ash from the cigar's end. "Now, then, Mr Smith," he said, taking his folder and placing it on the coffee table between him and Fred. From it, he took some note paper and pulled out a pen from his jacket pocket, before taking it off and slinging it onto the back of his chair. "How have things been?" he scanned the notes quickly from the last session. "You said last we spoke, that you'd booked in your driving test, passed?"

Fred nodded his head, placing the mug of tea on the table. "Just scraped through!"

Dr Mikels smiled and chuckled. "Well done, Mr Smith, you must be pleased. Did you drive here today then?"

"Aye, my dad got me a car for my birthday."

"Ah yes," said Dr Mikels, jumping to his feet and strolling to his desk. "It was your eighteenth last week, wasn't it?" Fred nodded his head, watching Dr Mikels cautiously as he sipped his tea. Dr Mikels retrieved from behind his desk a brown paper bag with '*Mr. Smith*' written in black sharpie pen on one side in big letters. He walked back to his armchair and passed Fred the brown paper bag.

"Happy birthday Mr Smith, it's only once that someone turns eighteen, now isn't it. A big number deserves a gift!" he said, grinning. Fred nervously looked into a bag and was surprised at what he saw.

Pulling out from the bag was a little rectangular box, which he opened, his eyes flickering back and forth from Dr Mikels to the box and back again. Opening the clip on the front, he pulled open the stiff hinges. The inner of the box was lined with felt and the groove in the middle was home to a long, fine, fountain pen, entwined with decorative metal. Fred gently took the pen from the box and held it up like a trophy to Dr Mikels, yet his eyes showed his confusion. "A pen?"

"You never know when you may need a good pen, Mr Smith, you're an adult now. That pen should last a lifetime, and will make you look the part."

"Thanks," said the unappreciative Fred as he placed it back in the box, and the box in the bag.

"So, Mr Smith," said Dr Mikels after Fred had placed the bag to one side and sat back on the sofa. "Did you do anything particular for your birthday?"

"Yes, actually," Fred lightened his mood a little, moving forward from the unappreciated gift from Dr Mikels. "I went camping with some friends."

"Oh, yes, your new neighbour, Mr Hacker. And what about Daisy, did she go with you on your trip?"

"Yes!" replied Fred, fearlessly confident, and so infatuated with Daisy that he didn't even notice anymore how insane he sounded when talking about her. So, in love with her that he no longer believed that she was not real, for, to him, she was as real as you or me, despite, apparently, for some strange reason, her only being visible to himself, Jared and Eric. "Yes, she came as well."

"And, err," Dr Mikels leaned forward slightly in his arm chair as he asked his next question, determined not to miss a single syllable of what Fred has to say. "What do your friends make of Daisy, Mr Smith?"

"What do you mean?" began Fred, a little confused. "They're fine with her, they all seem to get along to me."

"Hum," sighed Dr Mikels as he took the cigar from his mouth and put it out, swallowing as he sees the truth in the lad's eyes. He knew that he'd played with this for far too long, in a desperate attempt to achieve a motive hidden from even god. "I think I want to try to give you something a little different, just to try for a little while, okay Mr Smith?"

"What something?" Fred eyed Dr Mikels suspiciously as he got to his feet and took a small box of tablets from his desk draw, returned to the armchair, and passed them to Fred, who took them unwillingly. He looked down at them in his hand as if they were the murder weapon, he'd just used to kill someone. He couldn't help the shaking in his hands as he stared long and hard at the box, fear gripping him, the sense of death lingering nearby. "I don't want them!" Fred exclaimed, trying to pass them back.

"Now, now, Mr Smith," Dr Mikels quickly realised that this was going to be a game of wits, something that he was particularly good at. Thinking on his feet so fast that his words flowed like a river from his mouth, continued and unbroken, he said, "You've turned eighteen now, they're simply the adult version of the pills you've been taking.

There's no need to get defensive." Of course, a sly lie.

Fred took them, still unsure. *Well, I suppose it makes sense,* he pointed out in his head. *Though, why did he only mention these now?*

But before Fred had time to talk himself out of it and protest once more, Dr Mikels intervened and brought the session to a hasty and sudden end.

"I think that is all today, Mr Smith. We'll see how you get on with those tablets, but we might have to alter them by our next meeting." Getting up, he showed Fred to the door and almost pushed him through it. The best Fred could do to round things up was call back from down the corridor; "Oh, thanks for the pen," as the door was slammed shut behind him.

Meanwhile, in the small and stuffy waiting room of the psychiatrist, Jared and Daisy were waiting unnoticed, having agreed to accompany Fred. They had been sat awkwardly and silent for a good half-hour or so before Jared at last found something to say.

"You like Fred, don't you?" being the only question that came to mind at that particular moment. *Stupid question!* he thought to himself, though only after the words had left his mouth. Daisy turned with a smile, that smile that she seemed always to give, and giggled a little in amusement.

"What's that for a question, of course I like him." Daisy took a moment before saying her next words, her mind and heart at odds inside her. "I do believe I love him." Admitting the words seemed to trigger something within, as her cheeks flushed red and she looked away, a bit embarrassed.

Jared took a breath, having thought of something else to keep the conversation going; a hidden truth he'd seen in her eyes and heard under the tones of her voice, a subconscious admittance that something else may have been at work. "Why is it you came, honestly? Goddesses don't just appear because they *like* someone. There must be a reason, something that allows Fred to see us and you, when most other humans cannot. What is it, I mean, really, that drove you here?"

"Fred is special," she answered quickly and to the point, addressing one point. Though the other, as to why she really came, that she found was a bit more difficult to answer. She had to think long and hard on what to say, but finally came up with the truth of the matter, though, admittedly, her heart did the talking, not the brain.

"You're right. I didn't come because I liked Fred, I came because I need him…" Daisy paused, checking on her words, for she had never told a mortal what she was telling Jared now, her servant on this world.

"Need him, for what?" Jared pushed, a spark of curiosity being ignited to a flaming, burning, all-devouring beast in his mind.

"Well," Daisy said, forcing the words from her mouth. "You know how I told you of the story of my love, the god who betrayed me. Well, he bound me in more than just bonds. It is true that I want revenge on him, but there is some part of me that still in some small and hidden way, still… loves him. I need to free myself; Fred is the one who will help me do that. I came to earth to get him to free me. But now find myself bound in ways that I could not have comprehended. It is true that Fred is a means to an end, and, in my heart, I know it will not last the test of time, but, for this brief moment I do, honestly… love him." Then she lets out a sigh of relief under her breath.

Chapter XIII:
15 Months AP, Dover

It was a cold, windy morning as the three made their way down to the sea. They went from the castle, via Castle Hill road, leaving the once magnificent fort not by the gate, but a crumbled gap in the outer wall. For, much as England itself, Dover had begun to crumble and fall, fall back into the white cliffs and sea, for it had stood resolute for hundreds of years, but now, mis kept and abandoned, standing alone atop its white thrown, the great gate of England was brought low, home to nought but bats and seagulls and spiders occupying its once great halls.

As Alex stepped over the rubble and out onto Castle Hill road, he looked back and, under his breath, muttered, "Such a pity the old girl's all but gone. Just another casualty of this... plague."

Though there was little time to mourn, as Jared led on down Castle Hill road and towards the harbour, for the wind was in their favour that morning, and Jared was in little mood to waste it as if the hunters' hounds were nipping at his ankles. They went onto Madison Dieu road, from there winding to Town wall street and finally to the harbour via Marine Parade.

The great harbour was surprisingly abundant, though not with the usual ferries and cruise ships that anchored up, nor with containers, but surprisingly with small boats and yachts. Moored up and abandoned, their owners no doubt fleeing from the continent and France, back across to cold, wet England in hope of safe refuge and the protection of England's NHS. For they had all been such heroes all those years ago when coronavirus attacked these shores. Though the Plague, as it would appear, was indeed a different beast all together, and one that ate heroes more readily than anything else.

"This one will do!" exclaimed Jared, breaking Alex from his train of thought as he approached a big, luxury, yacht, badly tied and abandoned upon the north Pier where the metal rails had been bent, broken and lost to the sea. Alex, Eric, the cart-thing and twenty-nine golden sheep made their way onto the yacht, where, after checking the fuel tank and ordering Alex to nick some from the surrounding boats 'til it was full, Jared hot-wired the boat and the long dead engine roar to life on a battery that was on its last legs.

"We've got power!" yelled Jared in a great fit of triumph coughing after a long hour of preparations, and, came to steer the boat. Her name was almost gone, battered off by the scraping of its hull against the pier. What was left, ironically spelled, F... R... ED.

Out the Fred and its crew of three and cargo of twenty-nine went from the Admiralty Harbour at Dover and out onto the choppy English Channel. While Eric's attention was consumed by the seasick sheep, Eve, and Jared had his eyes fixed firmly on the faint glimmer of France ahead and the map before him at the wheel, only Alex did the courtesy of looking back upon the rolling hills and country in which he had been born. Only Alex fought back the tears as, from the stern of the yacht, he waved goodbye, not for the first time, to beloved England; the great, white cliffs of home that appeared to cry farewell back as the choppy water sprayed their faces. It may not have been the first time Alex had to say farewell, but in his heart, Alex felt it may be his last.

They were over halfway across the Dover straights and heading straight for the coast of northern France before Alex tore himself away from the sight of England, which was slowly disappearing into the haze, and made his way past Eric, who was cuddling one of his rams, and up to the boat's captain at the wheel.

"Upsetting ya lad?" Jared said, a skipper's cap that he'd found atop his head and his lit pipe in his mouth, making him look the part – except for the goat part of him, anyway. "Don't want to leave her?"

"Who?" Alex asked, trying not to sound upset as he looked back quickly to the white cliffs.

"Our good lady, Britannia!"

Alex nodded slightly in agreement, though said nothing else on the matter. "So, what is it exactly we are looking for? You keep telling me of this thing, but I don't actually know what it is?"

Jared looked at the lad from under his cap, smoke rising to cover his face. After a while of giving a menacing stare, to which Alex refused to move an inch. Jared gave a sigh. "Very well, lad, but I'll answer with a story."

23 years BP, waiting room

The young Jared and Daisy, having spoken of Daisy's relationship with Fred, are still in the waiting room as they awaited Fred's imminent return. Jared returned to his seat after fetching Daisy a plastic cup of water from a cooler in the corner to quench her thirst, while she composed herself after her deep and emotional confession to Jared a minute or two earlier.

"Thank you," she said surprisingly weakly for one such as her. A weakness that sent more fear into Jared than any show of strength or power she could muster. Interlocking his fingers and leaning forward, he gave Daisy time to drink before speaking to her again, though his spine was icy after her words.

"So," he began, though, realising quickly that that is the wrong way to do so, he paused a little while to think of a better approach to the matter.

"Daisy, look," he restarted, squeezing his hands together so hard that his knuckles and finger joints turned white.

"Yes?" she asked Jared, prompting him on after he stalled for the second time, which was starting to bug her a little.

Jared took in a breath. "You say you needed Fred to set you free, I mean, I want that for you... after all, I am pledge to you... so, if there is anything I can..."

"Well, there is. I mean, if you're asking," Daisy interrupted Jared. "You can recover something for me."

"And what is this... something?"

"Well, when I was bound and cast from the gods, the key to my... chains, was split into seven pieces. The keys pieces were then shared out by the seven who bound me. I need them back. I know for sure that one is on Earth, and I'm convinced that it's somewhere in Europe... or Asia Minor... or maybe North Africa I suppose... truth is, I'm not sure, I can't find it. Nor can I touch it... or you for that matter. But Fred can, he can find it and touch it. So, if you could retrieve it then that would be brill."

Jared nodded his head in agreement, of course, what he agreed to now he could never know, would take him the rest of his life to try to complete. Right up to twenty-four years and five months later to be precise, when, he would find out that it was Fredrik's son, not Fred, who was at his and Eric's side when they leave from dover in a last attempt to find the key piece. "But- err, what does it look like?"

"A stick?" Alex exclaimed in disbelief. "That's it?"

"Ha!" chuckled Jared, taking his pipe from his mouth to allow his words to flow more freely. "Indeed, that is it, a stick, a silver stick, to be precise, wrapped in burgundy red leather from the immortal cows of Heffa, Goddess of cows and daughter of the cursed one... before he became cursed, of course."

Alex nodded, amused. "A bloody stick!" he chuckled to himself, rubbing his forehead with his hand. "A bloody stick."

"No, lad, a silver stick, wrapped..."

"In the burgundy red leather from the immortal cows of Heffa, I got it."

"Now lad, don't be getting cheeky, I'll have none of that on my ship!"

Alex took a deep, rather annoyed breath; *have I really been dragged from Helothom and Atia, brought all the way back home and dumped with an old satyr and a, well,* Alex couldn't say anything other than, *an all-right Cyclops to find a stick!* In truth, Eric had made their journey actually bearable...

"Okay," Alex said, trying to stay calm after his internal rant. "And how did you figure out that it was in Greece?"

"Well, from what we, that being me and your father, could figure, an object with divine origin must have left some historical trace. So, we looked to the great ancient civilisation. We believe that it started somewhere in the new world. Now, I have no clue how it got there but we think it then went to Japan, then China. From there it may have found its way to Egypt, where I believe it stayed for some time, then going to... and this will make you laugh, your father believed it went to Atlantis, being smuggled from the city before it vanished and was taken to Athens. Then, I believe... and of course no one in the historical community ever believed us about that stick, it was given to Leonidas when he fought at the hot gates, believing that with it he could somehow defeat a great army with three hundred men. From there, we believed it must have been taken back to Sparta where it remained until the Romans took it from the city... or so we presumed, though, having begged Rome to let us, well, look in the Vatican, and being refused, I... may have snuck in."

"And?"

"It wasn't there. The trail went cold, your father turned to searching for... other things, while I kept looking. The thing is, it doesn't really matter how, but I found something that makes me think that the Stick never left Sparta at all... or, if it had left, it was returned, taken back when its... darker... secret was revealed."

What secret? Alex was about to ask before being cut off by Jared's celebratory cries of success, as at long last, and after being blown a tad off course to the north-east by a easterly wind (which had dramatically changed since they had set off earlier that morning), the yacht and all its passengers and sheep arrived safely at the long beach that stretched the north of France at the most infamous of places, Dunkirk. Eve quickly recovered from her sickness, now back on solid ground. The feeling of history weighed heavy on Alex as he climbed off the yacht that had been parked in the mariner just behind the beach amongst yet more abandoned boats, and there helped Eric unload his golden sheep.

Chapter XIV:
23 Years BP

Fred woke from a strange dream, a very strange dream indeed. He had been stood in the entrance of a deep cave, half way down a deep, sheer shaft hidden in darkness that he could not see the bottom of.

There was a narrow path and a breach descending below him, and a stone bridge crossing the shaft to a small, flat, outcrop of rock below. On the outcrop, dressed in white, dulled and stained by dust and time to a grey colour, and chained to the wall by silvery cuffs, was Daisy, screaming in the light of a single torch. Fred tried to go to her, yet found his path blocked by a hidden force he could not see. He screamed to her, but she didn't hear him. He tried to push and break against the invisible wall to get to her, but the more he tried, the more Daisy below began turning to stone, stiffening and hardening, starting at her feet and toes. In horror at the realisation of what he had done, he stepped back, yet the damage was done.

She continued to turn to stone, though finally her screams broke through the invisible wall. She screamed his name, looking straight at him in horror as she was consumed as if by fire, her head, finally, being taken as well and she stood there, stiff as a statue, lifeless in her damnation. Slowly, the cold stone turned to pure white crystal, her features, delicate and beautiful, were captured in its delicate grains. Fred screamed in horror, an ear-splitting scream of pain, hate filling his entirety. It was now that he noticed, stood in the shadows of the breach, two cloaked figures who only revealed themselves when they turned to look at him. Turning their attentions back to Daisy and again becoming hidden in the dark.

The sounds of their chants now echoed up to him at the cave's mouth. He saw, in his great fear, cracks appear across her crystal form. One moment she was stood there, the next, she shattered into a hundred and two crystal doves, her inner light illuminating the cave in its entirety, her light seeming, somehow, to enter the cloaked figures stood on the bridge below. The doves flapped and flew all about the cave, round in a great column like a twister over the bridge. Then, all of a sudden, the doves flapped and flew their way onto the wall between the two silver shackles that moments before had held Daisy. Interlocking their wings, beaks, feet and feathers, formed a crystal door, that stood open, and behind it where once there was solid rock, now a great portal swirled.

The two figures brought forth a strange object that Fred couldn't really see and walked to the open crystal door and slammed it shut, the blinding light that radiated from the other side being shut away. They placed the object on the keyhole and with a great clink it locked, then they pulled the shackles across it and locked them together for extra security. From behind the door, Fred saw a hand slam on the door, trying with all its might to open it, but that was not what drew his attention, but rather the fluttering, floating, handkerchief that, from high above Fred's head, fell into Fred's hand, the embroidered D H on its corner labelling the item's owner. Suddenly, Fred felt a hand on his shoulder.

Fred woke with a start; it was a beautiful day and the sun streamed through the curtains and the sounds of the chirping birds filled the room; a beautiful day. But Fred was still in the consuming throes of his dream. In a cold sweat, he looked down to find, to his disappointment, not Daisy's handkerchief in his hand, but only the sheets of his bed. He looked to the side of him to find, to his surprise, that Daisy had gone. Fred got up, still rather shaken, and began wandering the room. He took the second of his new pills to calm himself, but it didn't work. He swung open the door and ran down the stairs, going from room to room, yet in each one he found no sign of her.

"What's up, son?" asked his father from the kitchen table, putting his paper down and taking a sip from his coffee.

"Nothing!" exclaimed Fred, trying to stay calm and showing as little of his distress as he could.

His father sighed, he knew he couldn't get anything from his son which he didn't want to show, though equally knew that something was wrong. "Very well, you better get dressed, or you'll be late for college."

"Err, yes, right," Fred said, a little flustered before turning to go up the stairs.

"Oh, and Fredrick."

"Yes, Dad?" asked Fred, walking back from the hall to the kitchen.

"Don't forget, I'm off to look at a building site in Oxford, so I'll be gone for a couple of days."

"Yeah, I know, Dad," Fred said impatiently, trying to get away.

"There's plenty of food in the fridge…"

"And no house parties, I know Dad, you tell me every time."

Fred's father smiled in amusement. "Just checking,"

One hour later.

"What do you mean… gone?" asked Jared, hidden and disguised, sat at the desk with Fred in a classroom; his father was determined for him to get some kind of education, despite that he'd never get a qualification, nor be remembered by his teachers nor anyone else after each lesson had finished.

"That's what I'm saying… gone, vanished, and disappeared off the face of the earth," replied Fred with a sigh, sat awaiting history class to begin, and the teacher was yet to arrive, as were many of the others in their class. "And what of this dream? Do you think that might have had something to do with it?"

Fred simply shrugged, saying nothing more but sitting, his head resting on his propped-up arms on the desk, just trying not to cry.

Jared shook his head in disbelief, not that Fred could see him, anyway. "I can't believe it, and I know how she feels about you… it, just…"

"Well, she is a goddess, I doubt it was ever really real for her."

"Don't be so daft!" Jared exclaimed a little too loudly, before lowering his voice so as not to draw too much attention. "She, she, she told me." Jared stopped, his mouth dry.

"She told you what?"

Jared swallowed, finding the words hard to say. "Well, she told me she loved you! I don't believe that she'd just disappear."

"Well, she has!" Fred moaned, turning and looking through the classroom window to his right, where, on a lawn under a young oak tree outside, a grey, eyeless and mouthless man was raking leaves from the grass. He took a deep breath to calm himself, fighting his every instinct to run and hide in fear. "That's not the worst bit. With Daisy, I-I couldn't see them. Now she's gone." Fred paused. He'd seen one or two when she wasn't about, but just this morning he'd seen more than he had the last two years. It was a shock, a scary, tremendous shock. He almost crashed his car three times already because of them, and facing a lonely, empty house was just a thought that was enough to drive him mad.

"Who's 'them'?" pushed Jared, a mistake that sent the already rather stressed-out Fred over the edge.

He jumped to his feet in anger and stormed from the room just as the teacher arrived. "You know who they are!" he hissed viciously back to Jared before he finally went, leaving a confused history teacher stood in the doorway.

After briskly making his way towards the bathroom, keeping his head firmly focused on the floor and splashing some cold water on his face to try to calm himself. Fred looked up and into the mirror, desperate to have Daisy back even after her disappearing for as short a time as she had. His thoughts were suddenly broken by a murmur in a cubical behind him, the door a crack open, the noise sent icy chills down his spine. Fred shook his head. "It's not real!" he whispered to himself, now desperate for Daisy to be with him. "It's not real, it's not real!"

The noise came again, this time louder and this time more distinguishable as a muffled voice.

"It's not real!" Fred told himself over and over again. "It's not real!"

The voice came again, muffled to the point that Fred couldn't understand what it is saying, but as it spoke louder, the thing it belonged to became more distressed and sounded to be rocking as if against restraints in the cubical, banging and clattering against the walls as its distressed voice became louder and slightly clearer. Fred, now unable to ignore it, his hands tight over his ears, desperately wanted to run, but some part of him, for whatever reason, wouldn't allow it. "It's not real!" he yelled to himself again. The noise and muffled voice, though, became louder and stronger in his mind until it was him with the muffled voice.

Slowly, he found himself shuffling to the cubical, ears still covered by his hand. Slowly, he nudged the cubical door open and was terrified by the sight he saw. Bound like a mummy in tight linen from head to toe, its mouth gagged by the cloth, it was eyeless, and its skin was melted and grey, its hair gone and the protruding hands from the cloth were armed with long, black, finger nails, packed tightly with dirt as if it had been digging. Sat on the toilet, its feet lopped off at the ankles, the thing was not human but more monster, though, now in a distressed yell, the muffled words that poured over and over again from its mouth became clear as the sky after a storm. Fred was drawn in, pulled by a rope in his mind, too close. The creature grabbed him by the collar of his shirt and there, into his face, from under linen and from a tongue-less, toothless, mouth, it yelled once more. "FREE

ME!"

Fred twisted and turned, breaking free of its grasp, its claws cutting at his collarbone. He fell back from the effort, and spun and caught himself on the sink. He pulled himself up.

Fred's eyes widened at the sight before him. The mirror was no longer there, just a hole where it used to be, a hole that looked out onto a stormy scene, where a dead army marched through planes of purple grass and hills, where winged men fought from the sky and green asteroids plummeted onto the battle and drew swords against the marching army. A great battle of blood and gore. A black dragon and its master sent fire down from the sky. On the opposite side of the field the ground lifted up like a gate, and out of it an opposing army emerged, them also looking dead. All this surrounding a jutting out piece of stone, where, upon its top, three men were stood. Two were fighting, one took a blow to the stomach. The third approached behind him, holding a curved piece of metal in his hand, and took the injured man is if he were his friend, helping him back to his feet. The injured one gained his strength, and while the newcomer engaged the third man, the injured man staggered to the edge of the outcrop and there raised his arms, and the land around exploded.

Fred was trapped, looking into the hole which had now changed. Seven men walked out onto a battlefield, no, five men and two girls. One was Daisy! Two men were with her, one much bigger than her or the other, and three men and a girl opposite her, preparing for a fight.

"Are you all right?" asked Jared as he came into the room, breaking Fred's hold on the mirror. Fred blinked once, twice, three times and nodded his head. He turned to the toilet where the bound creature had sat – it was gone – then back to the mirror.

"Just a mirror," he whispered to himself, "it was all in my head." He breathed a sigh of relief. "None of it was real."

Chapter XV:
15 Months AP

The trio made their way south from Dunkirk towards Amiens over the course of three days with relative ease, before changing their course towards Leon, making sure to give cities and towns particularly wide births. France, as it turned out, was no different to the UK, with bodies piled high in the streets and fields filled with crops, self-set after last years were failed to be harvested. There was no sign of intelligent life, human or other, apart from the odd abandoned campfire scattered here and there. Something had definitely survived the plague so far, but what exactly it was, or how many was impossible to tell.

The camps were cold and their inhabitants had long gone, for all of human knowledge and intellect and all for all the isolation and health care and tried cures, it was impossible to survive such an indestructible thing as this, something from another realm, made and sent by immortals to punish the living world. Though there was one thing that struck Alex more than any other; the damage that humanity had done to this world seemed, quite simply, to be irreversible. There were few animals seen as the three made their way south, few birds in the skies, as if the plague came simply too late to save the world from man, if indeed that was its purpose as Jared seemed to believe. However, Alex knew better. From his conversations with Destiny and the stories he'd heard, it seemed obvious to him that this was just a skirmish in a much larger war that was brewing over the cosmos.

It was not until about a day and a half into their trek from Amiens to Leon, that the trio encountered their first real sign of life.

"Do you think it's safe?" asked Alex, hidden up in a tree overlooking the silent road, peering out to the large, luxurious hotel that stood on the banks of a glistening lake before them.

"Eye, I think so, we haven't seen any humans thus far, why should we see any now lad?" replied Jared from behind his bush at the base of the tree.

"Nice place!" remarked Eric blue-eye as he came from out of the wood behind them with a tremendous crash and racket, to come and stand, hands on hips, on the road beyond the trees, in full view of the total of zero onlookers. His head was still a couple of inches taller than Alex, despite being hidden up the tree.

"Lake look pretty!" he said, pointing to the glimmering water behind the hotel. "Look! Fish in lake!" he said, using his great vision to peer into the murky water even from this distance. "I miss fish! Want fish?" he asked Jared, who, with a sigh of annoyance at Eric's inability to hide, came out from behind his bush.

"Aye, Eric," he said, chuckling to himself as he began to walk towards the hotel. "We'll have some fish for supper."

The hotel was rather luxurious, taking Eric quite by surprise as they approached, with Jared manning the sheep and herding them to the grassy bank of the lake round the other side. "King live here?" asked Eric as he looked up at the towering hotel before him.

Alex chuckled to himself in amusement. "France has no king!" he said. "This is a hotel, Eric, humans used to sleep here when they were traveling or on holiday."

Eric gave a smile and nod of understanding. "Now cyclops sleep here. Better have big bed!" he exclaimed jokingly to Alex.

"I'll have a look," Alex sarcastically joked back, "now go catch some supper if you want fish!"

Eric nodded with agreement and strolled up to the lake and, without a moment's hesitation, waded straight into it to hunt down something to eat. Alex shook his head in amusement before heading inside.

As he wandered the corridors and staircases, making sure that the hotel was clear of human presence, he was struck quite unexpectedly by a stomach-churning stench drifting from one of the rooms on the upper floor. Instinctively, he grabbed the first thing he could, in this case a small wooden side table, and, holding it by its legs to use as a weapon and pulling his shirt up over his mouth and nose to protect against the stench, cautiously made his way into the room.

"Holy shit!" he exclaimed, gagging on the stench and dropping the table. He covered his mouth and nose with his hand as an extra layer of protection against the stench of rotten flesh, as, before him was a small dead man. His clothes hardened by dry blood and his skin white-as-snow, stiff-as-a-stick and beginning to decompose. It was the first reasonably fresh corpse that he'd seen since Sherwood Forest. He was used to the sight of death, but its pungent smell was something that always got him. The man's swollen tong protruded from his mouth, his purple lips and staring eyes were enough to give Alex nightmares, but it was what the corpse was holding in its hand that drew Alex's attention. Not removing his hand from his face, with the other he reached down and plucked it from the man's stiff, cold fingers.

Quickly, he darted from the room and the stench to look at his find in the window at the end of the corridor more closely. "Impossible!" he gasped to himself, the overwhelming feeling of hope filling him, though quickly being replaced by dread, fear and guilt. "Atia!" He tried his best to hold back tears as he looked at the lock of hair in his hand. Instantly, he recognised it as hers.

Somewhere, in the back of a lorry

Atia had been bound, gagged and blindfolded for days, weeks, maybe, she couldn't tell anymore. Chained to the back of the lorries, she had been jolted and battered about on bad roads for far too long, though, despite all her struggles, she found herself unable to break free. She couldn't understand it! She had divine blood in her veins, but still, she couldn't free herself. *How! It should be impossible for mortals to restrain me!* She kept revisiting to herself the first words in her dream. *'Thy shall not find Alex, nor shall you ever marry him.'* She had long and hard thought on it and on its meaning. After all, she had nothing else to do. She had thought long and hard at first, simply on whether or not it was a dream at all. *I will never marry him?* That had been the part that stuck with her the longest. *I have no feelings for him? Why would that be part of the prophecy?*

She knew it must, if it was real, come from the All One, as, though Destiny could manipulate Alex as a mortal, there was no way her power could work on Atia, *could it?* Atia, in blind hope more than anything had thought, *perhaps 'him' doesn't refer to Alex at all? Perhaps... no, no it must be talking about Alex!* But the part of the dream that she had locked deep, deep inside her was, *'thy shall be there when Mr. Smith falls!' at least by the sounds of it I'll see him again? Right? But I can't help but fear that I am intended to cause the fall?* She shook it from her mind, denying that the dream was nothing more than that at all. *Come on Atia! How could I ever do anything to hurt him? It must be a stupid dream! Created out of my fears, nothing more!*

Suddenly, Atia felt the lorry stop, and couldn't help but feel her heart begin to pound in her chest. Outside she could hear some muffled voices, one spoke with an Italian accent, but as soon as she heard, then the conversation was over. She then heard the door creak open and the helicopters fly overhead, the noise of soldiers moving echoed through the metal space. Suddenly, her dark world was filled with light. For a moment or two, she was blinded, until her eyes adjusted, and the doors were slammed shut, once again bringing darkness back on her. Then the light came back, dimmer and more fake than before. A desk lamp had been turned on, the only source of light now. The lorry was empty bar two beds, one on each side, one vacant, one occupied with a man, taken with a terrible fever and sodden with sweat as he frothed from the mouth and jolted, the only visible wound being a small cut on his arm. The doctor sat by the bed was fighting terribly to save his life.

There were two more men in the room, one sat on a chair by the desk lamp, armed with a gun; he was the captain who shot at her outside the hotel. The other man was a young man, only a few years or so older than Alex. He had hair so short he looked almost bald, and was dressed in camo apart from an American flag sown onto his sleeve. The other man was by far more terrifying; taller, strong and fiftyish, his hair was grey, and each strand seemed to stand to attention on his head like hundreds of tiny soldiers. An army man through and through, square jaw and a horseshoe moustache decorated his face. An American through and through; he had seen combat across the world and was now in charge of this not-so-merry band, never seen without his bowie knife, M9 pistol and a bottle of beer on his person. Large boots clunked like hooves on the floor, camo uniform covering his person entirely, with black leather gloves completing the look.

"Now, little missy!" he said with a cruel grin, untethering her from the side of the lorry, taking out her gag and throwing her, her arms still bound, onto the vacant bed. "You're gonna tell me what I want to know, or… or I'll let my men have you one by one 'til you talk." He leaned forward until he was but an inch from her head. "And I'll make sure it hurts, got it?"

Atia nodded. It didn't look like she had a choice, and there was something about the man that truly terrified her.

The general smiled. "Good," he declared much more happily, in his strong, southern accent. He put an arm behind him, and Lieutenant Gabbles passed him the chair, which he took and sat down on facing Atia, his legs splayed either side of its back.

"The name's Major General Francis fucking Howard, I've led ten tours of duty, got fifty-four confirmed kills and seen the darkest fucking evil that He has spat up to this god-forsaken world, and never, I say never, have I seen something like you. So, where the fuck are you from, how the fuck are you able to resist bullets? And what the fuck did you do to him?" he said, pointing a finger at the man laid on the bed behind him.

Atia said nothing at first, but soon began to giggle to herself, not a sweet giggle but one with malice in its tone. She was cut off quickly as General Howard took her by the throat and began to squeeze. Of course, he could squeeze as long as he liked, it wouldn't kill her, but it still hurt. "And what do you find so fucking funny, missy?"

Howard let go to let Atia speak, leaving red finger marks round her neck. "Is 'fucking' really your middle name?" she said, still laughing as if none of this was serious to her, for the general had awoken in Atia some deeper, more violent, part of herself. *After all, what can a mortal really do?*

Howard took a swig of his beer before spitting some over Atia. "You better fucking start talking! I brought my men across the Atlantic, sailed all the way to Scotland and picked up some nice supplies from a base there, including a Dr Bryon Mcherring, who is particularly good at making much stronger men than you talk, so let's make this easy, shall we missy?"

Atia, taking a leaf out of Destiny's book, leaned forward at just the right angle, giving a wink and a nibble of her lip, said as seductively as she could, "I don't think we need Bryon, I much prefer your company." She could see

231

Lieutenant Gabbles shuffle uncomfortably behind Howard.

"How about you tell me your first name… and I'll tell you what's up with your man."

Howard looked at her up and down and glanced back at Lieutenant Gabbles, who was looking at his General for guidance and shuffled his hold on his rifle. Howard turned and pushed Atia down with surprising strength onto her back on the bed. With a sigh and a nod, he answered. "That's first lieutenant John Terrence Gabbles, now, missy, what the fuck's up with my man?"

Atia gave a smile, casting her mind back to the day she was captured; the man on the bed had shot her in the back of the head, the others shot after. She took the knife and slashed out at him, cutting deep – that's when the net had been thrown over her. "Your man was cut by my knife… that knife also cut me, it's stained with my blood." She added, remembering the small drop that had come out as she ranched the knife from her chest.

"Go on!" Howard urged.

"My blood is poison to your kind; he will die a painful death. He might have a day or so left at most. He will die," she said, beginning to laugh again like an old witch. "And there's no cure. He'll die and there's nothing you can do about it."

General Howard turned red, with anger or embarrassment at being made to look weak Atia was not sure. Either way, he stood up and struck her, knocking her back onto the bed and barking orders at Lieutenant Gabbles. Her ears rung and her vision blurred; the last thing Atia remembered was the shooting of guns outside.

The hotel, between Amiens and Leon

As the sun set over France, decorating the sky with red and maroon. Alex, Jared and Eric sat down before a campfire, the twenty-nine golden sheep eating peacefully behind them as they tuck into a supper of fish and chips. Crunching the golden batter and swallowing fish like chips, Eric smiled and hummed to himself. "Good fish!" he boomed with a smile, though Alex wasn't listening. He stared into the fire, barely touching his dinner, and his mind thought of Atia. *If she's really in France then I've got to find her! I can't leave her alone out here! But how do I do it? She could be anywhere, and Jared has us on such a route march! What to do? What to do? Perhaps... perhaps... perhaps I should go!*

Chapter XVI:
15 Months AP

Jared woke and left his uncomfortable bed, strolling out in his sleepy daze along the corridor towards the door, seeing on his way that Alex's door was open also. "Last up!" he muttered to himself. "Odd?"

Wiping clear his sleepy Daze, he wandered towards the pond, the sun still dazed, hanging low in the sky and had yet to embark on its daily mission across the sky. Ghosts of the recently departed night raised from the placid lake and towards the red heavens above, while the grassy bank was gowned in morning dew. The sheep were grazing greedily by their shepherd, who was scribbling a drawing in the ash from last night's fire with the end of a charred stick.

"Morning!" announced Jared as he approached the great cyclops, shivering in the cold morning air. He hobbled over to a picnic bench that overlooked the lake, leaning back against the eating surface and began to clean out and refill his pipe. He looked around. *No Alex?* he asked himself, a puzzled expression forming on his brow. "Where's Alex?"

"Gone!" replied Eric in his usual fashion, his eye not moving from his scribbling, a sheep, which looked remarkably good.

"Gone?" Jared said, becoming rather cross. "What the hell do you mean 'gone'?"

"He say," began Eric, still not looking from his work, "dead man mean danger, gone look at road ahead, make sure safe for Eve." Eric pointed his stick to his favourite golden sheep, the fat little ewe munching on grass almost in the lake.

"Gone scouting?" Jared said angrily. *I need that bloody boy!* he thought to himself.

Eric at long last looked up, but didn't pick up Jared's anger. "That what he said."

Alex, a stick slung over his shoulder, strolled along the road, striding out in his black boots and jacket. This felt good, this felt right. He was back to what he was used to; he survived alone for six months, and he could make his way across France just fine. He had found a knife outside the hotel, blunt, but stained with silver blood. Tucked in his belt besides the knife given to him by Destiny, he couldn't help but smile to himself, not looking back to Jared and Eric. "This feels right!" he exclaimed to himself. "Atia, I'm coming!" He casted up a prayer.

The back of the Lorry

Atia never heard it, gagged, bound and blindfolded. The caravan had come to its destination early that morning, two, maybe three a.m., as much as Atia could tell. She had been moved from the lorry and into a half-demolished building. In the corner of a wall. A sheet had been stretched across the roofless top as a cover and wooden planks had been used to cap off the two sides the crumbling wall did not cover to make, as Lieutenant Gabbles called it, her little bird cage. The night had been cold and damp, the floor was nothing but dirt with one lone fallen stone protruding from the floor as a seat.

At the very least, in the cage, Howard had deemed it safe enough to take off her blindfold and gag, though she was still chained like a dog on a leash within the cage. Just enough links to let her reach the wooden planks, though too short for her to reach the door on the fourth side, its hinges were hammered into the falling stones to give it extra strength. Opposite her the crumbling wall continued with a little bit of the corner remaining, though not enough as to present a full back to the house, but enough to provide at least some shelter for the medic bed in which the dying soldier lay, coughing up his last in this ancient place. As for the wall that once bared the door of the house, that had, too, long since gone.

All night the caravan settled, floodlights and watch towers built up, the tanks parked and the helicopters landed, with the jets coming to rest on a makeshift runway to the north of the camp, cleared away by the well-organised battalion. It was dawn before Atia, in her bird cage, finally began to realise that she was no longer in France – far from it, actually. Above, the sound of troops, guns and tanks roaring came the deafening chorus of cicadas, hidden amongst the trees and ruined buildings. It too became clear, as the temperature began to soar, that this place had long been absent of human occupation. *This place can't have been lived in for over a thousand years*, was the conclusion that she came to.

It was not until the midday heat broke the ruins that Atia's solitude was finally broken as Lieutenant Gabbles opened the rusted, makeshift door, and lead General Howard inside. "Good day missy!" he said with a grin, taking a swig of beer before visually spitting it at her. "Fancy talking today?"

Atia returned his question by spitting back. "Whatever it is you're looking for, you'll not get it! Your man is dead, there's no cure! It's just a matter of time."

General Howard tutted to Atia, smiling with malicious intent. "Who says I give a shit about one man? I'm looking at the bigger fucking picture here!" He turned to Lieutenant Gabbles. "Bring her!" he snarled.

The Lieutenant did as his general commanded and grabbed the end of the chain from the wall, before dragging her from the wall and pulling her from her cage and through the camp.

She was led through the hissing crowds of soldiers, through an olive-tree-blanketed hill and up to a ruined acropolis at the top, overlooking the great mass of ruined city, some parts ancient but most far more modern, and camp below. Here, in between the trees at the top, she was pulled harshly by John to a stop. Howard walked to the edge of what used to be the acropolis and stood upon what was left of an old wall, though now was nothing more than long foundations protruding a little from the ground, where, overlooking the camp, he addressed his men.

"We've arrived!" he boomed, his voice echoing across the ruins below. "The journey is over! We've come across the pond, travelled through England, Germany and France. Italy, Slovenia, Croatia, Albania and to Greece. We shall save the human race! We, these men amongst us, shall be heroes! We shall claim back our world from the monsters that now inhabit it!" Every time the General took a breath, his men cheered, cried and shot into the air with their guns raised above their heads. "And we have them scared!" he screamed. "Look! Look! The greatest of their ranks has come forth to stop us!" Howard held out his hand in a gesture to call up Atia,

Gabbles threw across the chain and Howard began to pull her up until she was stood next to him, looking out across the camp. The view was breath-taking, the ruins and camp protected by a river bending round to the east before her, creating a 'c' shape boundary capped off behind her with mountains. "Look at the monster!" he cried at his men who booed and cursed Atia, who found she had no time to look at the view. "Look! Disguising her vicious, monstrous nature in a shell of beauty! She is so deadly that even her blood is poison! But now she is our prisoner!"

Howard smiled a little, saying his next words more quietly as he gently pushed her hair behind her shoulders. "Ours to do with as we like!" Then, he turned back to address his men, though his words had done their damage, sending chills down her spine. "LOOK! She looks like us, sounds like us! Dresses like us! But do not be fooled! This is no human!" he said, pulling away her dignity and leaving her bare for the men to see and they gasped in shock at the sight. Howard pulled her hair harder as he screamed, pulling her head back to show his dominance to his men. "This is what victory looks like! This is a taste of the future!"

Atia could do nothing but cry as she was dragged, insulted and despised, back down the hill and back to her dirty little cage amongst the ruins. She was spat at, tormented and teased, sworn at, pulled and punched and had all manner of objects thrown at her, from stones and sticks to mud and filth.

Such is the darkness in all men's hearts, she tried to comfort herself, *to hate and kill that which they don't understand.*

But it didn't stop with her being thrown back into her little cage; the tormenting continued all afternoon and well into the night, all of Howard's men seeming to have their turn, while Lieutenant Gabbles did nothing but sit in the back and watch, expressionless, feeling neither pity nor content at her torture.

It was pitch-black night when her torment finally ended. Atia was curled in the furthest corner she could find, shivering from fright as much as cold. The night wasn't too chilly, but it was getting colder and she found she had nothing to protect herself from it. The songs of the cicadas had ceased, the only sound was the occasional passing of guards and the snores of Lieutenant Gabbles, her guard, sat in his chair before the cage, and, of course, the dying moans of the man who was destined to die, the sounds that, as the night drew ever colder and darker, slowly died before they ceased altogether.

Like a whisper echoing about the camp, too quiet for mortal ears to detect, was a breeze so slight, too slight for mortals to feel, but Atia was no mortal. As a shadow crept into the ruined house, too slight for mortals to see, Atia perked up and rushed to the wooden bars of her cage. As the last breath left her second victim, she called out, to desperate to care for the consequences, in a whisper to the hidden figure who lurked in the darkness, out of the detection of all humans. "Death," she hissed into the glume.

At once, the shadows that she could not see through seemed to come alive, as the dark angel looked up from his work and towards the cage, though still it remained hidden.

"Atia?" came the whispered, cold voice in return.

"You come quickly."

"Did you have a hand in this?" it returned, the only sign it was there were the small embers before its face, yet not too much as to reveal the face of death, still hidden in the shadows. "Your mother will not be pleased."

"Yes, yes, I know!" she hissed, keeping one eye on Lieutenant Gabbles all the time. "Come on, Death, please, free me!"

Death gave a sigh, or what Atia thought was a sigh, and not just some trick of the wind. "You know I can't, I must remain neutral, I cannot influence gods or man in any way, you know this!"

"Yes, yes, but please!" she begged in a harsh whisper, falling to her knees inside the cage.

"There is something about this General I do not like; I sense something's wrong with him. He knows too much." Death whispered with the unmistakable sound of fear. "I dare not free you, it would be too obvious… the Quadrels would know."

"What if there's something you could do where they wouldn't know?"

"Like what?" he sounded hopeful. Atia knew Death and the binds that held him. They had met once or twice before when she had lost an ill patient and it was him who came, rather than one of his servants. She also knew, under his hard exterior, he was a kind and gentle soul, who would help, if he could.

"Could you get a message to someone on paper? And don't go yourself, get a mortal animal to take it, perhaps then they wouldn't know!"

"Perhaps," Death replied, a tad of excitement underneath his tone. "Who is it you want this message to reach?"

Atia let out a sigh of relief and smiled. *Hope! Hope at last!*

Death went on to finish his work, and as he did so, an otter ran from the shadows, an otter with a piece of paper in a small, plastic zip-lock bag tied to his leg. "Run, my friend," Atia smiled, "find Alex."

Chapter XVII:
23 Years BP

Fred stormed along the corridor, his hand shakily holding the box of pills. It had been a month and he simply couldn't take it any longer. As he headed for Dr Mikels office, his head echoed with the sounds of his screaming visions. It was too much, too much for the poor man to take, too much for him to bear. The truth was, he couldn't stand life without Daisy, and he needed her more than anything else in his world. His eyes were baggy and his body weak, he had barely slept or eaten in weeks. He was dehydrated and hungry and on the utter verge of passing out cold in the hall outside Dr Mikels' office. Anger filled his veins. He took a moment to clear his mind, taking deep breaths in a futile attempt to calm himself.

His mind echoed with great beasts taller than trees, on spider-like legs, human bodies, and heads that looks more like that of an octopus than anything else. Or the red-eyed foul things that lived in the dark of his cupboards and wardrobes of the home, with beards made of worms, red eyes, sharp teeth and metal hands. Or worse still, the looming beasts that haunted the skies above him, monsters bigger than the moon descending overhead. But, by far the worse were the people, rotten and dead, the lot of them, crying out in pain for release. It was true, he couldn't stand it any longer. He took a deep breath before barging into Dr Mikels' room and, in an outburst of rage that just proved that all his deep breaths were utter useless as a means of calming oneself, verbally attacked the Jamaican, who was caught quite off guard.

"What the hell are these?" he cried, waving the empty box of pills in the air. "What did you do to me?"

"Now, now, Mr Smith, calm yourself a bit. Please, sit and talk. Shouting will do you no good!" replied Dr Mikels, surprisingly calm in the circumstances. "Please, sit," he said again, gesturing to the sofa in such a way as to simultaneously comfort and intimidate Fred so he would not take this any further in such a manner. Fred felt little choice but to calm down and sit down, suddenly terrified by something in the doctor he couldn't quite put his finger on. Fred never quite figured out how Dr Mikels managed to do both contrasting things at once, but, nevertheless, he did. "Good," continued the doctor once Fred had been firmly seated. "Now, how about a hot, sweet tea to calm you?"

Fred nodded his head in approval. "Tea would be good," he said, though it came out much more of a whisper than intended. It was amazing how Dr Mikels could move someone's mood to the complete polar opposite without so much as a glare, nor raise of his voice.

A few moments later, and Dr Mikels returned from the little kitchenette with two decently-sized mugs of tea, giving one to Fred and keeping the other for himself.

"Now tell me," began the good doctor, after allowing Fred a moment to drink, "what is the matter, Mr Smith?"

Fred said nothing for a good long moment, too shaken to form the words, and when, at least, they did finally emerge, they came out as more of a shallow whisper, like a gentle summer's breeze through willow trees, though far less

243

pleasant. "I- it- it's the tablets... they aren't helping... I can't see Daisy anymore."

Dr Mikels gave the boy a puzzled look, one that was wary that the lad he'd known since he was a boy had suddenly lapsed to a state closer to that of when he was put in the asylum, many years ago. Though Mikels could tell, nonetheless, that the memory of that place still haunted the lad and scared him to the bone. It had not been easy for the Doctor to keep him from that place, and now he was worried there was no stopping it at all. "Then surely, they must be working, Mr Smith?" He watched Fred like a hawk, recording every twitch and facial expression produced.

Fred shook his head in disagreement. "She was not the problem," he replied, rather defensively, requiring a gesture from Dr Mikels to stop him getting worked up again. "While she was here, they weren't."

"Who are they?" Dr Mikels couldn't hide the worry in his voice. He remembered perfectly well who 'they' were, but he wanted to hear it from Fred himself. *Better to be sure!* he thought to himself.

"The... the..." Fred could barely say the word, as if by saying their name he would somehow bring about their summoning, nor could he bear to look upon Dr Mikels face. "Things... in my head!"

Dr Mikels gave a sigh. "I suppose that you will refuse to take any more of the new pills then, Mr Smith?"

Fred shook his head; he feared more the pills than the asylum, at this point. His mind was being crushed by the things he saw, unable to escape them at night nor day. It was overwhelming and he needed relief, he needed Daisy.

Dr Mikels thought long and hard on the matter, and

neither speak a word while he did. So long did he think on it, that his tea became well and truly cold, and his cigar, which was only one a third-gone at the time of the beginning of the session, had disintegrated into a pile of ash in the glass ash tray.

Finally, he looked up, taking Fred well and truly by surprise, as if he had come out from a vision or something. He sighed more than once, obviously unhappy with whatever it was he had decided on. There was a grim look in his eyes, though Fred had no clue as to why.

"Very well," he said finally, slowly nodding his head in a gesture of his submission to Fred's will. "Very well," he said again, and at least once more before saying anything else. "I will not prescribe you the pills again… though, I do ask that you go back to the ones you were taking before. I do not believe that one vision of madness gets rid of another." Dr Mikels reluctantly signed a little green slip and passed it to Fred. The pair sat in silence for another moment or so, before Fred took Dr Mikels' silence as a sign that it was time to go. So, after bidding the doctor a 'thank you,' Fred made for the door and was just about to walk through it when Dr Mikels called him back.

"Fred, here!" he said, throwing Fred the handkerchief that Daisy had given him for Christmas all those years ago. It hit the back of his head when Fred failed to react fast enough, though he managed to scoop it up before it hit the floor. The feeling of the soft cloth in his hand made him feel something strange, as if he was holding Daisy herself in his hands. Fred didn't speak, he simply smiled, nodded and left the room, closing the door rather loudly behind him before running along the hall.

It was when Fred was long gone that Dr Mikels gave another sigh, this one gloomier than before. He went to his desk and there took out another cigar and lit it up, taking in deep breaths of smoke to calm himself. He sighed and looked at the phone on his desk. He regretted immediately what he had done, but he had no other choice. In a sudden dart of energy, he picked up the phone, dialled a number, and pressed the phone to his ear under his dreadlocks.

"Yes, it's me," he said to an unheard voice at the other end.

"No. It's much worse than I thought... it won't be long now, not long at all," he continued.

"I'm afraid not! I think our best strategy is to move to plan B," he recommended.

"Aye, it failed... I fear to push on will make matters much worse!" he sighed.

"Okay, sir, as you wish, sir." And with that, Dr Mikels put down the phone and dropped his head into his hands. *What have I done!*

Fred smiled and laughed to himself as he drove home from Dr Mikels. "Well, that went better than I thought!" he said with a beaming smile to Daisy's handkerchief, that was folded neatly on the passenger-side seat. "It will all be over soon!" he cheered. But it was safe to say that Fred may have spoken a tad too soon.

All was quiet as he drove from Dr Mikels' practice, out onto the A59 towards Harrogate and on, back towards his little village. Indeed, the journey home was very uneventful, almost all the way home. It was only when he left the A59 that things began to turn sour. It started with a bat, a big, black bat made of smoke, flying over the hills a mile or so from the road he was driving on. Fred quickly blinked it away, though became suddenly nervous and looked down to Daisy's handkerchief. "Come on, Daisy," he begged, his eyes flicking from the piece of cloth to the winding road. "Where are you?"

Next came a vision a bit closer, down in a little village tucked between the moors about three miles from his own. He saw, chained at the neck and hands, many rotten men and women and children, being led by monstrous beasts made of mummified flesh on their bones with big heads. Light from their burning brains shone like torches through their empty eye sockets, down on their prisoners who were much shorter than them. Fred peered down at them from the road above that wound around the moors; their shrieks were deafening, their smell drifted up and churned his stomach; the smell of rotten flesh. By far, though, the most haunting sight was that of his own father being led along by these things and towards the gaping, all-swallowing mouth of a great cave that he had never seen before.

In a cold sweat, he sped up, his foot hitting the floor as he pushed his car to the limit to try to flee from what he saw. He passed an old lady that looks more like a demon, with an old broom in her hand, making her look like a witch about to take flight, wandering along the road he was driving along.

By now, he was more terrified than ever, unable to think, one hand clutching Daisy's handkerchief as he prayed. "Come, Daisy, please!" he begged. "Come back to me, please! I'll never do anything to offend you again!" His eyes flicked up. There, in the middle of the road, stood a female deer. Fred swerved to avoid it, smashing into a tree by the side of the road at such speed that the tree found itself on Fred's lap before the car stopped. In his mind, Fred could hear something, someone that sounded a lot like a laughing Dr Mikels. But his mind turned dark instantly, and it appeared to be yet another figment of his mad mind. But one thing he knew, in the dark, he felt something soft brush against his face, sending warmth down his spine.

Of course, the Deer, was simply, never really there.

Chapter XVIII:
16 Months AP

It had been two weeks since Alex had left Jared and Eric, and he hadn't seen them since. Nor for that matter, had he seen any other intelligent life, human or otherwise. Sadly, that also means he had not seen Atia either. Still, he searched \for her tirelessly, heading along the pre-planned route from Amiens to Leon via Chaumont, and from Chaumont to Jussey and finally to Menouille, just west of the Swiss border. Alex was loving his time alone. It felt right to him, it felt natural to him, and this was what he should be doing; living in the wilds, fending for himself with nothing but that tatty old knife for aid. With a sharpened stick in his hand, he felt dominant. Watching his own back came easy to him, as did hunting and lighting fires and mending his clothes.

After all, he had spent six months fending for himself before he met Atia. Back then he really did have to watch his back, for there were a lot more people than there were now. His time in the temple of healing had only bolstered that. Now, he knew of healing plants and herbs, keeping his wits sharp and his heart pumping. Alex would go as far as to say he even loved it, for it brought back memories of his youth, when his mother would encourage outdoor activities, almost as if she was training him. The only sign he wasn't alone was the occasional distant glow of Eric and Jared's campfire at night on the horizon, though even this seemed too close for his comfort, for never had he given up in his search and his new and primary aim... to find Atia. Even when he had seen no sign since the hotel, his heart told him he was heading in the right direction.

But this was not what occupied his focus that very moment. Just outside the village of Menouille, to the south, Alex was sneaking up on a great stag, its head heavy with its large antlers. The stag was lying half-dead and sodden with sweat on the ground. Alex tightened his grip on his sharp stick. This was endurance hunting. One of the oldest types of hunting known to man. Alex had learnt of it as a child and found that he was rather good at it. The hunt was simple; chase your prey down until either you or it died of exhaustion. The stag was big, but so too were its antlers, their weight holding it down and making it hard to run.

The stag, too, had wounds from a fight, maybe a week old at most, making it slow and easy for Alex to keep up. The stag looked old to Alex's eyes, not that he really knew the difference, but this one's best days were definitely long behind it. This was why Alex had picked it, yet despite this, as the dawn sun struck the old field where it lay dying, it had still taken more than six hours to run the poor beast down. Alex hadn't slept that night; he started the chase late into the evening, making sure the cool air would help him stay fresh, yet still he streamed with sweat after the long pursuit. Alex was sure it was over now, as the beast was too tired to even lift its head as Alex approached. Its heavy breathing quickened a little as he stood over it, before the stag finally rolled back his head in acceptance of his defeat.

"Thank you, my friend. Now go, dine with the gods,"

Alex whispered, heaving for he, too, had heavy breath, before bringing down his stick and ending the beast as mercifully as he could.

There was no time to waste; within an hour the old stag had been gutted, skinned and butchered into portions and was cooking over a fire he'd built right there in the field. Alex left nothing for the crows, something else he had learnt from his days before Atia. The antlers were sharp at the points, good for pegs and tips for his spears. The fur was warm and made a thick blanket. The bones he put on the fire to burn, the smoke from the bone-fire, as it was called, helped deter the mosquitos and other biting insects that would, no doubt, be attracted to Alex by the smell of his sweat. The blood, rich in iron and vitamins, made a safe drink when much of the water now was unclean and contaminated by disease. Alex was a good survivor; how else could he have lasted so long? Soon, the meat from the stag was cooked enough to be wrapped up and put in his deerskin bag, sown together with a small piece of Antler for a needle, and dried Omentum from around the stomach as thread. Though it was hardly the best in the world, it was the best that Alex could think of, and it looked kind of like thread when all the webbing was taken apart, so he did the job the best he could with it. It is surprising how innovative one can be when all one has to work with is what naturally occurs inside a deer, disgusting, even Alex would admit that, but innovative.

It was just when Alex was packing the now-cooked and cooled meat into his deer-skin bag that something rather strange caught his eye. "What the?" he asked himself, and he found himself being stared down by an otter. Not a very big otter, nor one with any feature that would make it stand out particularly to the human eye, but nonetheless a little European Otter was staring him down from the far side of the now, almost-gone-out fire.

Neither moved for a good while, Alex out of surprise, the otter, out of whatever had driven the normally shy little thing to become so bold and cocky. In truth, of course, it was a servant of Death. Much like the crow or vulture, the otter was a sacred animal to Death and, in some cultures , was seen as a symbol or harbinger of death, for this was a mammal that could easily move from water to land, and thus warranting it that mythical ability to travel from the land of the living to the land of the dead with the same ease. Of course, it was nonsense, but the idea stuck with Death, who subsequently became so fond of the little creatures that they'd been serving him ever since. Although Alex, of course, knew none of this; he liked history, but he didn't know that much.

It was only when Alex saw a little something attached to the Otter's leg that he finally twigged of the cocky little thing's origins. "You're from the gods?" he asked the otter, who of course could only answer with its characteristic whistle. "Well, I don't know of any water around here, so I guess I'll take that as a yes!"

The little otter whispered again, and bobbed its head in a gesture that Alex could only take as meaning "Follow me!"

Alex gave a sigh and climbed to his feet. "Lead on, then," he said, surprisingly acute to what the otter wanted. It was a funny thing that the land of the gods did to Alex. It gave him a sixth sense, a connection to the mortal realm around him by his Kamari. Alex could sense that the otter was after him, and not just any other animal. In the back of his mind he did hope, perhaps wrongly, that Atia may have been controlling it or something.

Still, he set off after the little otter as it scurried away across the field and north, towards the village. The otter, whistling all the way, led Alex right to the other side of the Menouille, up the hills that surrounded it and through the woods that blanketed it in thick green trees. Finally, the pair emerged out onto a flat clearing, clear of trees with the ground burnt and thick with ash. Alex gasped at the sight he saw. The sight sent chills and fear through him, the smell making him feel almost sick.

The otter whistled again, drawing Alex's attention from the sight. The little otter was gone, and a piece of paper had been left on the floor in a plastic zip-lock bag in its wake. Alex bent down and scooped it up, his eyes flicking from the horror before him to the rolled-up paper in his hand. He opened it and hesitantly his emotions were mixed like a vat of cake-mix. For, his fear and horror were offset with hope. Finally, he had found a sign of Atia, as the message on the paper read,

'Go to Sparta'

About two hours later, Alex was back. In this one morning Alex's whole world had been changed, again. He had decided it best to return to Jared and Eric. After all, it turned out that they were heading to Atia anyway. So, what was the point in looking anywhere else. Alex did, maybe rather strangely, trust the little otter and its message. But he couldn't just leave what he found alone. He thought it best to go fetch Jared and show him this, though made sure that Eric didn't come, not until he had shown Jared anyway, out of fear for his reaction.

"So, what the hell is it, lad?" asked Jared for about the hundredth time since setting off from where Alex had found him. The heat was roasting and beating down on the old, crippled satyr as he climbed the steep slope up to the place the little otter had shown Alex.

"We're almost there, just wait," replied Alex for at least the fifth time.

"You said that half an hour ago, lad! Now ya better start explaining yourself soon, cos… it's ridiculous, disappearing like that then just turning up out of nowhere! Did your father never teach you anything respectable?" Jared had grown rather grumpy since starting on this unexpected expedition, even more so with the prospect of climbing such a steep hill, which he found difficult at the best of times, but in a day such as this, which was particularly hot, it was just outrageous to him.

"Sorry," said Alex as they neared the top, and he stopped for breath. "But I thought it best that Eric didn't know."

"Didn't know what?" puffed the old satyr as he too neared the top. "He's a grown up, not some kid, lad! If I can know…"

Jared's words left him all in a sudden as he reached the top and saw the same sight that had so terrified Alex before. All the colour washed from his red and out of breath face, his stomach turned sour at the sight before him.

"Aye lad," he said, the only words he was able to utter. "You were right to leave Eric behind."

The sight that greeted them was one of utter horror. A holocaust in an age that ought to be beyond genocide. The sign that showed humans have not moved on since the stone age. An atrocity that was horrific and devilish, darker than sin and yet carried out without a second thought. For them who committed it have done more than killed, they'd mutilated and burned.

Blackened and rotten, a decoration on a pole, the flag of the New World Order, there, crowning the hill, king over the landscape, were four cyclops' heads, burnt and on spikes, their eyes taken by crows to feed their chicks and their hair singed and gone. But it did not stop there.

The cyclops were not the only ones to fall foul of this slaughter; burnt on their own sticks and covering the land on the hill behind them, like a forest of impaled dead, were Blemmyes, Satyrs, Dog-Headed men, Elves, Goblins, Lamassu, Monopods, and all manner of beast that neither Alex or Jared could name, burnt to a crisp, impaled, beheaded, decorating the land in the pride of man. Even the local Dryads had been staked to death, their bodies hanging from their own dead trees.

Jared could neither bear the sight, smell, or taste in the air nor feeling in his gut that surrounded that horrid palace. He felt the urge to run and scream, cry and bury himself in the ground. The non-humans were all but extinct before, but now there could only be a handful left, if that, hidden in the small corners of the world. They were truly doomed, and all in his lifetime. He could hardly bear it, the thought that he may be the last of his kind left on the earth, all others dead.

He wept, his tears soaking the ashy, burnt ground at his feet. But it was not for him he wept, but for Eric. "Aye, lad," he muttered again, between sobs of sorrow, the words finally returning to him. "you were right not to bring Eric." He pointed up to the centrepiece of this hideous gallery of death; the four Cyclops heads on spikes before them.

"For there were four great Cyclops families left..." he

muttered. "They must have thought, with most humans dead, that it was safe to come together for the first time in generations."

Alex's mind rolled and he sat down in the dirt by Jared, placing a comforting arm round the smelly old goat, for at this moment, all thoughts of Atia were washed away by the bitter sadness and anger at this place. "What are you saying?" Alex dreaded to ask, for he already knew the answer, but needed to hear it from Jared.

"Eric is no longer the head and last of his kin... it now appears he is the last of his kind altogether. My lad, when Eric goes to join your father... well, it appears that there shall be no more Cyclops left on this green world. But it's worse than even that, lad, for I do believe now that the so-called 'Wisdom's curse' has at last broken! And that bodes ill for all us folk, for our shield against mankind is broken with it!"

Jared cried and tears watered the ground before them for a long time, for he knew that he could never tell Eric the truth, for it will end him completely. So, he would mourn for him, and the passing of all these other good men and women and even children who had been so brutally massacred here. Finally, he cleared his eyes and spoke once more, though his voice was weak, shallow and nothing but a whisper. "O, my boy, what monsters could have done such a thing, what evil hate, drives them to complete such atrocities."

"I don't know," said Alex. He was sad, though had not been sad enough to shed a tear, for, while death is heart-breaking, Alex knew from his time with the gods, that it is far from the end. "But whoever did it, they must have had some real fire power," he remarked, for from the ash he had unearthed an armour-piercing bullet.

Chapter XIX:
16 Months AP, Venice.

Not a lot happened for the rest of that day. Alex and Jared buried the bodies on top of the hill in shallow graves, for they had but stone, sticks and their hands to dig with. Then, they got out Jared's map and plotted a new route, for there were tracks heading south from the hill and neither Alex nor Jared wanted to risk running into whomever had done this. So, they decided to go east instead, crossing the alps and heading to Italy. They told Eric nothing of what they found, dodging his repeated questions on the subject, such as why they had changed route, and, why Alex had suddenly come back. Neither wanted to put Eric through that, not when he would never expect to see any of the other Cyclopes anyway.

So, on the trio went. After the hill, Alex had not the need nor desire to leave them again, and Eric seemed happy because of his presence, so thought there was little point in doing it anyway. So, they carried on, from the hill, they crossed the border into Switzerland, going around Lake Geneva, to Corbeyrier. From there, they followed an old railway track through the mountains until they reached Visp and then dropped south, crossing the border again and into north Italy. Avoiding Milan like a death trap, because it could well have been, the three, still accompanied by Eric's twenty-nine golden sheep, continued East through north Italy, to

Verbania. Barely stopping for rest, they walked each day from dawn to dusk, the three pushed on from fear of being caught by the same gang that massacred the Cyclops on the hill. They travelled from Verbania to Lecco and from there on to Venice, where Jared planned to 'commandeer' another boat to take them the rest of the way via the Adriatic Sea.

"Do you think it's safe?" asked Alex as the three approached the city from the North via the Dese River, looking from across the bank at the bright, blue sea and the City beyond. It was mid-morning when they arrived at the suburbs of the floating city and already the sun was beating down upon them and not one of them was dry of sweat.

"No human left! What not safe?" said Eric as they strolled through the small village of Praello on the banks of the Dease River. His remark made Alex and Jared exchange sad and worried glances. It had not been all that long since they had had to bury the dead Cyclops upon that hill, a place that bore fear and pain for them even now, and was marked in their minds forever.

"No!" said Jared, hobbling a long a bit faster.

"I'm sure you're right Eric! But one can never be too safe now, can we?" He stopped all of a sudden in the middle of the road, surrounded by golden-fleeced sheep. He shakily lit his pipe and took in deep breaths of smoke to keep his emotions in check. He coughed a little, and Alex saw from a bit back with Eric as he spluttered up blood, spitting it on the floor. Before he quickly recovered himself.

"Something wrong with Alex and Jared!" remarked Eric as he looked down at the boy. Alex could barely look back at the big soft brute, and his big, blue eye, filled with concern and worry over the two. "No lie, what up?"

Alex shook his head. How could he tell someone that he was the last of his kind? How could he tell a friend that his last days will be the last of his entire species? *The dodo, Thylacin, Steller's sea cow, Quagga, Atlas bear. The great auk, Caribbean monk seal, the laughing owl, Falkland Islands wolf, Grey's wallaby, Elephant Bird, Schomburgk's Deer, Barbary Lion, Syrian wild ass, Caspian Tiger, Baiji, Pinta Island Tortoise, and now the Cyclops. All animals driven to extinction by man. How does one tell a friend that he is soon to be added to this list? How do I tell someone that his kind is just one of many driven to death by man, like a faceless mass? That he will be nothing more than the Syrian wild ass. That man has yet to learn the most simple and obvious of lessons? What can be more heart-breaking? Dream-crushing? Life-destroying than to know your fate is sealed and that your name will be plastered on the walls of history as another victim of the serial killer of earth?*

"So, what up?" asked Eric, his face and eyes showing only selfless kindness.

Alex smiled, blinking away the sadness inside. *It's better he doesn't know,* he thought to himself. *At least that way he can make the last days of his kind happy, and not so grief stricken.*

"Nothing!" he replied with the most cheerful smile he could muster. "Nothing at all, just tired; all this traveling has taken it out of me." It was the best he could think of to cover up the truth – after all, it was not entirely untrue, they had crossed the alps, walking along a railroad track, across north Italy, walked the length of France and England. Though in truth, it was the length of time that he'd spent away from Atia that had really worn him thin.

"You think hard? I got pull this thing from York to Venice! That hard!" Eric exclaimed with a chuckle and a smile, making Alex laugh as well as he gestured to the cart-like thing strapped to his back. It turned out to be just the thing that Alex needed to cheer up a little, as they gained on Jared who was hobbling in front, smoking his pipe and coughing.

Quite unexpectedly, and without any warning whatsoever, Jared stopped, turned on his heels and took his pipe from his mouth, waving it about. "Right!" he said all of a sudden, having calmed himself and thought long enough in the peace of his own company to formulate somewhat of a plan. "Now! I have an idea."

"Go on?" prompted Alex, as Jared had stopped mid-sentence as they caught up and he began smoking his pipe once more.

After taking out his pipe, coughing a little, he began again, "I have an idea," he began, pushing through the sheep to get closer to the pair. "Venice is a big city, and we have to go through it to get a boat. Now, it is out of the question for us to go," he said, pointing his pipe first at himself then Eric, who countered something under his breath in complaint as he had been quite looking forward to seeing the city. "So, Alex will go into the city, commandeer us a boat with whatever supplies can be found, then we shall meet up down the coast at Briccola resort. That should be plenty quiet enough, don't you think?" he said, now pointing his Pipe at Alex. "You remember what I did at Dover?"

To which Alex nodded his head as if to say *sort of.*

"Good," continued Jared, now getting rather excited that

his plan was coming together nicely. "We will meet you tomorrow morning, that should give you plenty of time to get a good boat and us to get to the rendezvous!" he said. "Where are we to meet?" he asked Alex again, just to make sure he got it.

"Briccola resort." he said with a sigh; he felt a bit foolish, in complete honesty, having to repeat Jared's words, not that he seemed to notice.

"Good! Right! okay, off you go, then, make sure it's a good boat and be there at dawn, sharp tomorrow morning, good luck, now go!" Jared said, turning Alex in the direction of Venice and pushing him away with a smile and a wave.

Alex walked alone, the heat of the sun now beating down upon him more intensely than ever, like a child playing with a magnifying glass. To make matters worse, he had no hat, dressed all in black and was walking on tarmac. There was no wind and no escape, the sea was like a mirage before him as he approached, heading towards the floating city and a chance to cool off in some form of water, he hoped.

Stripped down to his skin, with his father's trench coat tucked under his arm and completely out of water, he saw neither man nor beast on his march up to Venice, walking along the A57 till he reached the sea. The heat was made worse by the fact his journey was taking place on a dual carriageway. *So much tarmac!* he complained to himself as he walked round a rather large roundabout and onto the SS14, yet another dual carriageway, running along the sea towards Venice.

Walking for several miles, Alex couldn't be sure precisely how many, and, stopping for several breaks out of the sun, he passed a place called Tessera. From here, the dual carriageway turned into a smaller road. He rested a while amongst the abandon cars in a car park as he came into the village, under a tree by the road. But he didn't stop long. He needed to get to Venice as quick as he could, and wished to waste no time in doing it. The village, from what he saw, was a small place, with nice, whitewashed homes lining narrow streets. A place that he rather liked, but, to the contrary of Jared's fears, there was no sign that anyone has been there for a long time, apart from the occasional dead body that had been left on the roadside to rot.

So, Alex carried on out of Tessera and continued towards Venice. He continued through a place called Campalto, then through Bagaron, places of high-rise flats and boarded up hotels and villas, long since used. It was a place nowhere near as nice as Tessera, and Alex did not think to stay long in this place, though, here, neither did he find any men. As the heat turned ever and ever more intense, and as the day approached its hottest, Alex was forced to stop and raid a local shop for something to drink, though quickly thought better of it when he saw, and smelled, a rotten plague-ridden body lying on the floor. "Not much in it anyway!" he said as he looked at the mostly bare and lifeless shelves.

Still, he was parched and needed to find something to drink soon. It was not long from there until he walked into the more built-up area of Triestina and the road once again got bigger and hotter. As he approached a rather large roundabout and looked at the rusty signs (with paint that had begun to wear thin) for the right road to take, it may as well have been the Sahara Desert in his mouth.

"There'll be something to drink soon," he told himself.

"Just keep pushing on." So, after determining that it was the fourth exit to the right that he needed, still following the SS14, he pushed on harder than ever, and, in no time at all, reached a bend in a river like complex that, not that Alex knew this, was called the *Baia del forte*, a spider's web of rivers and waters that lay just beyond the road. It was so hot that Alex cared not for the depth of the water, nor what could possibly be lurking within, ready to try and take a bite out of him. He was simply too hot to care, and jumped in for a swim. "After all," he said to himself as he climbed out after being completely refreshed and cooled, "who's going to see me, everyone around is dead!"

Indeed, Alex hadn't seen any one so far. The water was cooling, though even Alex dared not drink it. "I'll have to find something else!" he said to himself as he contemplated taking some. "It looks a bit mucky to me." The sun dried him in a surprisingly quick time and, before long he was back on the road walking from Baia del forte to the SR11. The complex piece of road between the two rather messed with Alex's head, and it took him several attempts to get on the right road.

From there, he continued across the great bridge; the Ponte Della Libertá that linked the mainland to the floating city. It was a long stretch, and it took Alex a surprisingly long time to get across, but when he finally reached the city, his breath was truly taken away by the city before him, but he didn't stay long.

Where the bridge met the city, there was a small, triangular lagoon filled with vaporetto boats. Alex's first idea was, in the words of Jared, to 'commandeer one.' As Alex looked out across the city, he believed that Jared's worries were wrong, but, though the little boat would do them no good on the open sea, it would make getting around the city a little easier. So, Alex quickly climbed aboard an abandoned Vaporetto and set off.

After commandeering the boat, Alex set sail cautiously through the city via the Canal Grande. He presumed that any kind of boat fit for their needs would be near the open sea on the other side of the city, and the canal, being the biggest, seemed the simplest way to get there. It had well-passed the hottest part of the day now, and, to Alex's relief, the heat had begun to wane a little. "Wouldn't want to be doing this in the full heat!" he exclaimed to himself.

As he rowed on down the canal, something strange began to hit his eye. At first, he didn't think anything of it, though as he rowed through the silent and still city, a worry began to creep over him. Something that sent shivers down his spine and set him on edge.

Not just one, but all of them! "What happened here?" he asked himself as his eyes darted nervously about, for all the bridges along the Canal Grande seemed to have collapsed, or had been collapsed. The Ponte Degli Scalzi, the Ponte Della Costituziond, the Ponte dell'Accedemia and even the Rialto; bridges that had stood for hundreds of years, gone, only their stumps on the northern side remaining and the rubble in the water showing that they ever stood there at all. Sad as Alex was to see such history gone, his mind at the moment was completely preoccupied and filled with fear, and, from this fear, he found himself, completely unintendedly, starting to whistle. It started quietly at first, but before long it echoed into a great noise that filled the silent city with sound. Indeed, Alex found that he had never been so scared in his life, not even on his first day of school, or that time he faced up to that bully, or when his father died and the plague started, nor when his mother and sister died and he was forced to fend for himself, or when he had to leave his home or met Atia. Out of everything, this had to be the scariest moment of his life.

Turns out Jared's fears were right after all! Alex thought to himself as he kept on rowing, and, from his right, faces started to appear from the windows of the homes. Plagued faces, marked with boils and death. The sight gave Alex shivers, as the sight brought back memories from long ago at Sherwood where he met Atia, something that felt quite a lifetime ago now. But the dying was not the only thing that his whistling attracted, for, from up the river in front, came another boat like his, with three men on board, all draped and hooded in black cloth. Their faces where covered by masks from fear of breathing in anything that they shouldn't. There was one rower and two men with weapons, or rather, a stick and a bit of iron rod that they could use as weapons if the need arose.

Alex's heart was in his throat as he approached, the sight reminding him of paintings of Charon on the river sticks, and equally, if he didn't know better, he would be ready to believe that was where he was. The man at the front, not saying a word, held out his hand in a gesture to stop. Alex did as he was commanded, and stopped whistling, too frightened to do anything else.

The other boat now stopped, the two bumping next to one another slightly. The man at the front shuffled a little, giving away that he too was scared, as he said rather quickly in his most menacing voice, "Qual è il vostro business sentire e da dove vieni?"

Alex was nervous and hoped beyond hope that one of them spoke English, as he said as slowly and clearly as possible, so as not to anger or give the wrong impression, "Sorry... but I, err... don't speak... Italian!"

The first hooded man turned to the second, fear in his voice when he hissed "Americano!"

The second hissed back "Americano!" As did the rower; "Americano!"

Alex could tell from their voices that these were no friends of America. He never stopped to ask why; he was too scared that they would kill him out of anger and fright before he had the chance to tell them that he was as much an American as they were. Scared, he began to creep back on his boat, trying to get as far from them as he could. They seemed to take this badly, as the first one shouted at him, "Stare ancora, Americano!"

Alex froze in fright, gathering from the way the man was pointing his iron rod at him what he meant. The first man then turned back to his comrades, keeping his rod pointed at Alex, both seeming equally scared of one another, like a man and a tiger that have crossed paths.

"Non parlo inglese!" he said to his companions.

The second man nodded his head and repeated, "Non parlo inglese!"

Their attentions then turned to the rower at the back, who gave a sigh and gestured for one of the others to come and take the ore.

"Muoviti! Posso parlare inglese!" he said as he took the club from the second man, and pushed his way past the first, holding it out before Alex in a malicious way. He pulled down his hood to show his masked face. Immediately, Alex was surprised to see how old the man was. He was too old to have worked for many years, and the strain of holding the club and rowing the boat seemed to have taken the strength from him, as he was breathing heavy through his mask. "They want know your business. American!" he said, spitting in the water as he said the last word.

They seemed to hate the Americans more than anyone had hated anyone before, and that made Alex nervous for *what the hell could have made them like that?* He couldn't help but ask himself. "Not American!" he was quick to say, not wishing to stress them out. Not that they seemed to believe him. "I'm English! Not American, from Yorkshire," he begged, for the fear and hate in their eyes was enough to make an atheist run and pray.

"New York?" asked the man now at the ore of the boat. "Americano!" he cried, pointing his finger at Alex and setting his other companion off, who started trying to beat at Alex with his iron rod.

Indeed, it was only the old chap that could speak English that got the difference, and put out his hand to stop his companion, almost pushing him into the canal at the same time. "Non-Americano," he said, "Inglese! Britannico! Yorkshire!" Finally, the others seemed to understand, who settled back a bit and, to Alex's utter surprise, seemed to become quite friendly. Putting down their weapons, they pulled Alex aboard. The first man quickly inspected him to make sure he was healthy before putting a friendly arm around him and gesturing for the old chap to take them away.

"We are friends of English," said the old chap while he huffed, puffed and started to row them down the great canal. "Americans we no like! You welcome here in Venice. Home to all healthy. Last Italian community," he said with a great beaming smile as if he'd known Alex his whole life but not seen him for a decade, as did the others, making him feel as welcome as they could on their little boat. "You can stay as long as you wish my friend, all healthy are welcome. All but the Americans," he said as they turned into a smaller side channel at the northern side of the Canal Grande. Alex was amazed at what he saw.

Never before had he seen so many humans in one place, not since the plague started anyway. Every home was lived-in and cared for; there were sheets and washing draped from the windows and all people of this place seemed to be going about business as usual.

The old chap Alex now knew was called Renzo. The other two were known as Jeno and Kosmo, and both were older than even Renzo, neither under seventy and both with long, untidy, grey hair, olive skin and plump bellies. Renzo seemed to be a bit of an 'odd one out' for he still had some black in his hair and was as thin as a twig. "I have worked Venice all life," he told Alex, "taking tourists along canal, Jeno was a farmer before, grow oranges and wine. Kosmo was soldier, fought in army. Discharged and retire here, to Venice."

Kosmo turned to Alex and asked, while drinking from a bottle of Jeno's old wine that was stashed aboard, "Per quanto rimani?" he asked Alex, who in turn turned to Renzo for a translation.

"We want to know how long you stay," Renzo repeated.

"Just passing through, really. I'm looking for a boat that can take me out to sea." Renzo repeated his words in Italian, and all three men looked at each other, rather concerned, setting Alex's nerves off again. Indeed, he was just about to ask what was so worrying when the boat came to a stop outside none other than Saint Mark's Square, and Jeno and Kosmo helped Alex climb off the boat. Jeno disappeared into the square.

The square was larger and more beautiful than Alex could have ever imagined, with the large white pillars and arches decorating the sides, and the great tower rising up to look out across the city, with the sun hanging low in the sky and painting it even more red than it was before. It was truly inspiring. The whole place made one humble, and reminded Alex of the feeling he had when he first stepped through the portal and into the temple of healing. He looked this way and that, bathing in its magnificence and the warm light of the evening sun, and people were gathering in the open square, where tables had been laid out.

People were beginning to find their seats to have their evening meal all together. *A glimmer of a better world*, Alex couldn't help but think, *with food and drink free and plentiful, and everyone coming together as a community, helping each other! This is what humans are capable of when they're not trying to kill everything. This is surely the best this race has to offer.* Alex let out a smile, but sadness over, Eric still lingered within his mind. As more people took their seats, talking, laughing and drinking all together under the red sky and the wakening stars and moon. Here, there was no hate, no wrath, no anger, no malice nor murder. Here, humans had been given a chance to start afresh and make good the sins of old.

Chapter XX:
16 Months AP, Venice

As Alex marvelled at the wonderful setup of long tables, draped in white cloth and with cutlery laid out neatly in the middle of the square and all the people of Venice coming together to eat as one big family, he failed to notice a man walking towards him. An old man in his mid-sixties, short and olive skinned, no taller than Jared. His short hair was white with flecks of black mixed in, and his goatee was no different. He had hairy little ears and an air of authority surrounding him. Dressed in green shorts, sandals, and a buttoned-up red checked top like that a grandad would wear.

He had dark, brown eyes like bottomless pits, and a large grin on his face that never left, no matter the circumstances. "Hello, stranger." He spoke in the most fluent and superb English, as he held out his hand and embraced Alex, who had been caught quite unaware and didn't quite know how to take the situation. "You like our little setup?"

"Yes," replied Alex. The little man was too friendly to make him feel uncomfortable and offset, so much so that, though Alex had just met him, he felt he'd known him his whole life and could trust him with his deepest secrets. "It's quite amazing."

"My name is Nickolas Miliato. But please, call me Nico," he said, putting his arm round Alex's back. "Come," he chuckled, extending his hand and showing him the way to the tables. "Sit and eat with me, friend, and let us get to know each other a little better." Alex followed the little friendly man without complaint. He followed him through the crowd, though it took a long while for Nico greeted everyone with a smile and referred to them by name, shook their hands, shared a joke, and made them feel important and precious. Finally, they made it to the head table in the square, to which all others ran at a right angle to, and he sat Alex down next to him at its centre, as an honoured guest, while the other members of their community slowly moved to their seats.

As soon as Alex has sat down, there was a glass of wine before him. He's never tasted wine before, nor any Alcohol for that matter. It's good, very good and the glass is emptied rather quickly, and immediately refilled. "Alex Smith." Alex introduced himself to Nico, "and can I just say, I'm amazed at your English."

Nico laughed and smiled, as he does always, never does his mood seem to dampen, "I lived in England for many years, when I was young. Before I came back to Venice, when I married."

"Are you their leader?" Alex asked, though he has already guessed the answer to his question by the way the little man mannered himself.

"Yes," he nodded, "I guess you could say that I prefer to be called the head of the family. That's what we are here, just one big family."

"I like that," said Alex, with a smile. He liked the idea of that, a city that's one big family, everyone looking out for everyone else. *This place is truly heaven!* He thought to himself.

"Before I retired," continues Nico, "I was in charge of the police in Venice. I knew most people here, that's why they looked to me to take control. Now though, I'm just Nico. I look after them and keep them safe, no matter myself, but I am nothing more than plain old Nico."

"Well, you've done a good job," said Alex with a smile, looking out to all the happy and laughing faces as they sat at the long tables, "there doesn't seem to be a gloomy face amongst them. Though, if you don't mind me asking, what about the sick?"

Nico's smile wavered just slightly, but did not fall, though Alex can see the guilt that weighed him down in his eyes. "It has not always been easy. we had to knock down the bridges and we put the sick on the other side of the canal... we didn't want to but..."

"The plague is the plague." Finished Alex.

Nico nodded, "we gave them the best we can," he said, perking up a bit, "they have all the food and comfort they can have, to make sure their last days are good..." Nico choked on his words a little. "I've put many a friend and family member over there, everyone is heart breaking, but there is no more plague in this side of the canal at least. Aha!" he cried, far more cheerfully now, "here comes dinner!" and as he spoke, from the basilica behind them, comes old women carrying plate after plate of lasagne. Alex was the first to get his food, as their guest, and Nico was the last. When all the plates were served and all have sat down to seat he stood and said grace, as well as introduced Alex, not that Alex could understand any of it as it is all in Italian.

As he spoke though, Alex noticed something that has slipped his attention before. There were three long tables in the square, as well as the one he and Nico sat at, and he was the only person in the whole square that was under Sixty or not disabled of some description, by far, he's the youngest among them by at least ten years, and even then, the others were disabled in some way.

"Where are all the young?" asked Alex when Nico had concluded and sat back down, "I don't see any one under sixty."

Nico smiled, though, it hid the gloom and guilt in his eyes. "Tell me Alex," he said, changing very quickly the line of conversation and dodging Alex's question, "what do you think of a proper Italian Lasagne?"

Alex took a mouthful. It's good, very good. Though the texture of the meat seemed rather strange. "It's really good, but that meat, I can't say I've ever had anything like it before."

Nico's large smile bursted into a great laugh as he leaned over to Alex and said, "pigeon. Not the best meat but it's what we've got!"

The night drew on and on, though it can never be described as boring. There was a lot of talking and eating and drinking at first, then this broke into dancing and Nico called on his musicians. Traditional dancing, down near the canal. There was storytelling, lot more drinking, singing, and more drinking followed by a bit more eating. Nico introduced everyone to Alex and Alex to everyone, individually. Most couldn't speak English, but all were friendly, and those who could, would joke, jest and marvel at Alex's story of traveling from York to Venice, though, he failed to mention the nature of his comrades. Then there was more eating, bit more drinking, dancing and more singing. Nico attended to some matters of his little state and Alex found himself sat with Renzo, drinking.

Renzo had a stash of figs; they were all gone rather quickly. Renzo told Alex all of his life. They must have drunk three or four bottles of wine between them before Nico came over with a bunch of grapes each, and shared a fifth with them.

All in all, it was a very jolly night and there was not one man nor woman even close to being sober by the time people began to disperse. From what Alex could tell they must have been at it for close to six or seven hours. Though all the while, Alex couldn't escape the feeling that there was a shadow looming over them, something dampening the mood, something that no one was telling him. "Come, my friend," said Nico, half-drunk bottle of wine now in his hand, putting his arm round Alex, who had never been drunk before. "You can stay in the basilica with me tonight," he said, leading him inside.

"Wow!" gasped Alex as he walked inside. The great main chamber stretched up before him, all the chairs still sat out. Everything was preserved and kept immaculate, and you would be wasting your time if you went looking for a speck of dust.

Nico led him from the main chamber and into a smaller side room that had turned into his office. There was a bed made up inside.

"Will this do you, Alex?" he asked as he showed him in, and, taking out a bottle of Veneziano, a traditional Venetian drink, poured them two glasses of the red-orange liquid, as if Alex hadn't had enough to drink already. Alex sat, or rather slumped, down into an old woven chair in the corner, taking the Veneziano from Nico.

"Thank you, my friend," he said, taking the drink and trying to sound as sober as Nico seemed.

"Tell me, Alex," he said as he sat down at his desk, acting surprisingly sober considering the amount of drink he'd supped that evening. "What is your plan? I presume Venice isn't your final destination?"

Alex shook his head; he was too drunk to lie and make things sound sane. "I came to get a boat to take me to Greece."

"Really," exclaimed Nico, suddenly sounding very uneasy. "My grandfather was from Greece. Pylos to be precise."

"That's where I'm off," slurred Alex, "well, Sparta to be exact."

Suddenly, Nico went pale as a ghost, and Alex, even in his drunk state, could see the fear in his eyes. For the first time since they met, the smile left Nico's face. "And what madness would send you there?" he said, very angrily.

"What aren't you telling me Nico?" Alex asked in return, sitting up in his chair, feeling suddenly very sober and concerned, his nerves starting to creep back in.

Nico looked at the boy and calmed himself, sitting back with a sigh and smiled a sad smile, remembering that Alex is no harm. "Not six weeks ago, a party of Americans came through. Horrible, horrible people, their leader's name was, err… Howard! Yes, that was it, General Howard. He stayed several days, drank our wine and ate our food and took our hospitality. But they were off to Sparta. Before they left, though…" Nico began to choke on his words a little as his eyes swelled a little with tears. "Before they left, they told us

275

they wanted you! Our children! Anyone strong enough to do whatever they wanted. He told me to hand them over or he'll blow Venice from the water. Heavily armed, they are, tanks and jets and helicopters! I had... I had... I had no choice, Alex, I had to let them go."

Alex nodded and looks at the floor. Suddenly everything clicked in place. "I understand," he said, his voice the voice of hope for Nico. "I think they've taken someone dear to me too. A girl, a divine girl."

"Red hair?" asked Nico.

"You know her?" Alex asked, perking up, "You saw her? Is she ok? Have they..."

"She was fine when I saw her," said Nico, "they had her tied and blindfolded in the back of a lorry. I only saw a glimpse, but the image stuck in my mind."

"Well, I plan to set her free! That's why I need a boat." Nico looked up in hope. "If I help you Alex, will you free my children? Will you make sure that they come back to us? Will you?"

Alex nodded, it may just have been the drink talking, but he couldn't have the thought of such good people suffering such a horrid fate. "I'll do my best," he said. "I'll do my best to set them free!"

Nico began to cry, though not from sadness, but joy, joy and hope. He cried and celebrated and was fuelled by the joy of hope. "Then you shall have all you need, Alex." He was too desperate to think that Alex might fail or be overwhelmed, for how can one man face an army, but that did not cross Nico's mind. "We are too old to come with you, but you shall have plenty of food and wine and a boat, the best boat we have!" Tears streamed down his little, old cheeks. "God bless you, my friend, god bless you!"

Chapter XXI:
The Next Morning

Alex woke well after dawn had broken over the city. His head was spinning to the extent that at one point he felt as if he had been hung upside down. It took all his strength to stop himself throwing up. His first hangover was one of wine, made worse by his feeling of urgency due to the fact that he was running late. He got up and out of bed as quickly as his spinning, aching, head and his churning stomach could allow and left Nico's office. He was met, quite unexpectedly, by Renzo, who bid him to follow him out into the Square. The sun was high, and the citizens of Venice were all up and about at their business, with the square being cleaned and prepared for yet another night of celebration this evening, like every evening, apart from Sunday as he was told by Renzo. By the canal, he found Nico sat eating a breakfast of fruit and watching his people paddle up and down the canal, making all manner of preparations for Alex. "Come, my friends," he bid them, gesturing to vacant seats. "Share breakfast with me.

"Thank you," mumbled Alex the best he could, and he nursed his head before the completely unaffected Nico and Renzo, who found it amusing that the lad had a hangover at all. Alex tried to force himself to eat some of the fruit, but barely managed half an orange.

"You are to leave as soon as all is ready?" asked Nico, who, despite being excited at the prospect of his people being returned, quite liked the lad, and would have much preferred him to stay another day or two, for he knew in his heart, even if Alex succeeded, he would unlikely see him again.

Despite this, Alex remained strong. "No, I will go straight away, thank you!" he said with a pleasant smile.

Nico and Renzo finished the fruit between them and before long, all was ready for Alex to depart. Before the sun was at the climax of the day, its heat already becoming rather stifling, all the people of Venice gathered in the Square once more to bid farewell to Alex. In a small community such as this, news travelled faster than a wildfire in a land that has not seen rain for a year, and, before Alex had even awoken this morning, all knew of his heroic offer. Nico accompanied him as Renzo rowed him out to where his ship had been moored; the best ship they had, something they thought might just do to get out of reach of the Americans and, the only ship they had capable of standing up in a fight if it came to one. Laden heavy with food and wine, plenty for a return journey for a large number, the ship was not the most modern in the world, but its suited Alex just fine, and before he knew it, he was sailing off alone, leaving the floating city far behind as he made for the meeting point with Jared and Eric.

"Where the hell is, he?" asked Jared who was impatiently stood on the beach where they had agreed to rendezvous. "I said dawn! Did I not say dawn to him? It's almost mid-day! Where the hell is, he?"

Eric simply gave a shrug of his big shoulders as he sat on

the warm sand, his favourite ewe, Eve, was sat on his lap, bleating happily as he groomed her thick, golden fleece. "No know."

"Well, he should be here! His father was never this rude! Where the hell is, he?" Jared asked again, his nerves starting to get the better of him and doubt beginning to sneak into his mind as he began to fear the worst. Shakily, he lit his pipe and hobbled about a bit, filling his head with smoke to calm himself. But it was not to be, for Eric put an end to all chances of Jared calming down.

"Maybe dead."

"What?" exclaimed the old satyr. He hobbled over to Eric all worried and flustered, though he made sure that the cyclops did not pick it up, puffing on his pipe heavily as he left goat tracks in the sand.

"Maybe he dead!" Eric remarked again, scarily unemotional as he never even took his eyes off his favourite sheep in his arms and barely noticed Jared's presence at all. "He may be dead!" Eric repeated himself again, as if Jared was too stupid or young to understand what the three words meant, and required extra explanation as to what Eric was saying. Not that he ever gave it; Eric never repeated himself, it made him mad and he was not hiding the irritation in his tone at having to do it this time. *Twice bad, three repeats ridiculous!* he grumbled in his head, but, by far, Jared was the angrier of the two.

"The lad's bloody stronger than you think!" Jared said in anger, overwhelmed with a feeling of fatherly love for the boy. Perhaps it was due to his close friendship with Fred, or a feeling that it was his job to look after the boy, or just an uncharacteristic feeling of caring for anyone other than himself and Daisy. No one could have said, but nevertheless, Jared suddenly became very defensive. "He survived the initial wave, six months on his own in a dead land! He lived with the gods for Christ's sake! Not to mention everything he's done for us! How could you say something like that?"

"Could be right!" Eric grumbled. In truth, he too was worried for Alex. He had been a breath of fresh air in his cave, and he made much better company than that of Jared, but, in classic Eric style, he showed as little emotion as possible, and the more emotional he got, the colder in hatred he appeared from the outside.

Of course, Jared had absolutely no clue of this, despite living with him since they were children, such was his god-complex, which was unfair to say, since most gods were not as self-centred as himself. They were much too wise and old for that.

Jared, in his anger, stormed off, smoking his pipe, grumbling and muttering to himself as he went, back down to the sea to look out across the endless blue once more, that stretched out to the horizon and to the place where the sky and the sea met and merged together. He stood, smoking his pipe until his rage began to subside, listening to the gentle, timely lapping of the waves on the shore. A seagull caught his eye as it flew from some hidden nest and out to sea to search for food for its demanding chick. It flew out to the blue, the hot sun hitting and warming Jared's face as he followed it on its journey, the smell of sea air filling his smoky lungs.

As he followed the mighty seagull in its great task, full of fortitude and determination as it flew on, a small wisp of cloud blanketed the sun and cast a shadow over Jared and the sea, and here, like a speck of sand on distant tides, he spied what he hoped to be a...

"Ship!" he gasped, and coughed and spluttered and blood-stained the sand. Jared recovered himself and sped off as fast as his lame right leg would carry him, crying at the top of his black lungs, "ERIC! ERIC! A SHIP! COME LOOK!"

Eric climbed to his feet, his favourite sheep was taken with shock and ran and bleated back to the others, grazing on a grassy sand bank not far away. Using his great cyclops eye, Eric peered out to sea. He covered his eye with his hand, for by now the wisp of cloud had passed from over the sun. His eye saw clear and far, and could easily pick out the boat on the horizon. A bored grin formed on his face as he began to chuckle to himself in deep bouts.

"What is it?" Jared puffed, as he struggled to catch his breath as he came hobbling up to the cyclops. "Is... its Alex?"

Eric simply kept chuckling. "You gonna like this," he laughed, his eye not leaving the boat on the horizon.

"Is it a yacht? A really expensive yacht?"

Jared was deeply hoping for a yacht, something that was comfortable and luxurious, high-speed and reliable. Jared loved yachts, he could never have even dreamed of affording one before the plague, but now he could have anyone he liked, he really wanted a yacht.

Alex hadn't gotten a yacht. Long and slender, cutting through the water like a great snake, two great masts raised from the deck, where giant sails caught the favoured southerly wind blowing from the Alps in the north. The red and gold flag of Venice flapped atop the main mast. Along the hull were many empty gun ports for cannons. This was not a yacht, and Alex stood on the beak at the front of the ship as he approached. Spying the great Cyclops on the shore, he let out a cheer and a wave, which Eric replied to.

Nico indeed had given Alex a war ship, the best warship that he had. A full-scale recreated sixteenth century Venetian galleon. His sales catching the wind, it cut through the water as sleek as a blade. For the history-loving Alex, this was better than a yacht, or any other boat that Nico could have gifted him. The opinion was not shared by Jared, as he dropped anchor not far from shore and rowed over in a little boat.

"Was there nothing a bit... nicer, lad?" he grumbled as he looked on in dismay at the great galleon that bobbed in the waves before him. "No yacht?"

"What's the matter, it's great!" replied Alex, rather happy with himself.

"It's a miracle you even sailed it alone this far! How is a cripple and a Cyclops supposed to sail this all the way down the bloody Adriatic lad?" he said grumpily, but was quickly out-voted.

Eric, with joyous bounds and laughter, and a sheep tucked under each arm, cried, "This great! Well done!" Without even stopping, he waded out into the sea, heading for the ship, for he was far too big to fit in the little boat that Alex had rowed to shore. The other twenty-seven sheep quickly found their way on his boat and bleated impatiently, wishing to follow their master.

"Look, it's well built and well supplied! Eric is as strong as ten men and the sails are big. We can do this. Now get aboard or get left behind!" Alex said, rather putting Jared on the back foot with his strength of will.

"You're dull in the head, lad!" he grumbled as he climbed on board Alex's little boat, giving him a light slap round the head to show his unhappiness, and Alex set out back to the galleon. "Really?" he said as they set off. "Was there nothing else? Not even a fishing boat?"

Sparta

Atia sat miserably in her little cage in the ruined city. *I'm Divine,* she thought to herself over and over and over again until her head ached with the effort. *How can these mortal chains hold me?* But, try as she might, no reasonable explanation came to mind. However, that was not the worst bit. She was underfed and tormented, shot at as a joke by the men, who called her 'little birdy' and given nothing to keep her warm from the damp and elements but a sack cloth blanket. Truly, she longed for the sight of Alex. Every time she heard someone approach, she hoped beyond hope that it was him, but it was never him. She was about ready to break, but she kept thinking to herself, *He's coming! Death won't let me down! He wouldn't abandon me! Alex is coming!* And that kept her strong, but she didn't have much hope. By far, the worst of it was the Scotsman, Dr Bryon Mcherring. Since the death of the solider, General Howard had commanded Mcherring to torment her and torture her. He never asked any questions. It was more of her punishment than anything else.

The little, round-headed, bold, fifty-year-old Scotsman, with a drinking problem and a kilt that hid about as much as a tea towel, was standing over Atia with a cruel smile on his face. He'd been at it since mid-morning; now it was mid-day. Atia could hold back her tears no longer. To get a single tear from her was hard enough, but Mcherring had managed to get bucket loads of them. He knew how to extract pain, indeed, it was the only reason he'd been left alive and kept by the General at all.

"Please," croaked Atia, a rough metal collar rubbing her neck sore as she was pinned to the wall, cuts and bruises all over her body. "Stop," she mumbled.

"What was that, lassie?" said the cruel doctor, bending down to listen closer.

"Please, stop!"

Mcherring gave a horrid smile and a crackly, high-pitched laugh. "Stop?" he chuckled, smiling at Lieutenant Gabbles behind him. The American had no love for Atia, but he was not as heartless as he may have seemed, and felt, quite rightly, that this had gone too far.

"Now why would I do that? I'm just getting started!" And with that, Mcherring turned and grabbed off Lieutenant Gabbles a bottle of whisky, who resisted a little but soon gave in. He wanted to punish Atia for being who she was and for what she did to his friend, but in his heart, he knew that Mcherring was going too far, and his desire to hit the cocky Scott was getting overwhelming.

Mcherring took the whisky and poured it over Atia. The alcohol stung her cuts and scrapes and her screams of pain echoed out across the whole of Sparta. Mcherring emptied the contents of the bottle, then looked at it as if surprised that it was empty at all. "What ya gone and wasted that for!" he said, raising the bottle high above his head. "Wasting my whisky! You bitch!" He brings the bottle down on her head and smashed it. The glass cut into her crown and she fell to the floor, dizzy and sick. She coughed up silver blood all over the floor, but she was far stronger than a glass bottle, and no real damage had been done. Still, it hurt like hell. But Dr Mcherring was not done yet. He put his booted foot under her and kicked into her belly, sending her back against the wall. Atia coughed up half her last meal onto the floor. "You can fall down when I tell ya!" hissed Mcherring as, from the floor, he picked up the broken neck of the whisky bottle.

Gabbles was at bursting point. To see even an enemy being treated in such a cruel way; it was not human, and not even a monster deserved such a thing. Part of himself held back out of anger and hatred of Atia, but that wasn't the part that won out. His father was a priest, taken by the plague with his mother. *To stand and do nothing in the face of sin is to commit the sin yourself!* he thought to himself. They were his father's words, not his, but he lived his life by them. *A rat still has a life to live, as does a fly or a worm; who are you to judge if they should be punished?* His father had often told him. Watching the torture brought back all his father's words, and suddenly that part of him, binding himself back and stopping him moving, was gone, and he broke free.

Just as Mcherring brought the broken bottle neck down on Atia, there was a sharp pull at his arm as Lieutenant Gabbles pulled him off, twisting his arm until he let go of the broken glass, and shoved him back towards the cage door, stepping in between Mcherring and Atia.

"What is the meaning if this?" he hissed.

"That will do today, doctor! The general told you not to kill her, under any circumstance!"

Mcherring hissed again as he began to try to get past Gabbles by pushing him out the way, but as he approached, Gabbles drew his side arm and pointed it at the scot. "Go! Or

I'll shoot you dead! Do not think the General gives a dam about you! GO!"

With that, Mcherring, who was a coward at the best of times, turned and ran from the cage, disappearing into the ruins beyond.

Atia was too drowsy and in pain to really know what was going on. She heard the cage door close and open again a few moments later, or minutes, or hours, for she could not tell in her numb state. She flinched in fear and opened her mouth to scream as she felt cold water on her skin, but, to her surprise, was shushed gently by the Lieutenant.

Gabbles gently lifted her head and moved her bloody hair from her face, filling her weak eyes with light. "Shush," he said again as he began to pick bits of glass from her hair and wiped and washed her cuts and bruises, that quickly healed, with a damp cloth. "You'll get me shot! I'm trying to help you," he said gently.

Atia only managed to mumble one word in her state; "Why?"

Gabbles gave a sigh as he continued his work, checking over his shoulders in case he was spotted and dubbed a traitor. "Because I'm not as evil as the rest of them!" he whispered.

Atia didn't really listen, she was to numb with pain, so numb that she didn't even realise that, as Gabbles clean her, she called out aloud to Alex.

Chapter XXII

Lieutenant Gabbles stood at attention in his general's tent. The large canvas of fabric had, much like Atia's cage, been pulled over the pieces of broken wall, forming three sides of the tent and down to the dry, dusty, floor, though it was much bigger and cleaner than Atia's cage. Standing atop the mound in the old acropolis and overlooking the camp, its position made the general like the kings and priests of old. The air in the tent was cool and much more protected from the heat of the sun, sheltered from wind by the higher wall to the west and to the east. Outside the flaps to his tent lay a great pine tree, though a little to its left, under which General Howard had placed a chair from which he could look out across his camp and to the mountains, rising like a great wall of stone, beyond, and keep an eye on the comings and goings down below. Nothing missed his attention, not even Gabbles cleaning Atia, which was why he was here in the first place.

The General was sat in silence at his desk, an old wooden thing laden with not a lot of anything useful, but enough useless pieces of paper and battle plans to make it look like he was rather busy. But the thing that caught Gabbles' eye, as it did all who entered his tent, was the human skull at the end of his desk, looking out through empty eye sockets at all who entered, like a guardian of the pointless paper. Nevertheless, it sent an icy shiver down

Gabbles' spine.

Finally, General Howard looked up from his desk and straight at Gabbles with a stare that cut deeper than any knife, and suddenly Gabbles wished he was anywhere else but here.

"Soldier!" he said, standing up from his desk, his voice far more gruff and horrid than usual, beer in hand. "You better start fucking explaining yourself before I have you shot as a traitor! I gave Mcherring an order to torture the monstrous bitch! Do you respect my orders son?"

"Yes, sir!"

"Then why in the name of god did you go against them, err?" snarled the General, making his way round the desk and towards Gabbles, the reek of beer filling the Lieutenant making him want to gag.

"You said keep her alive, sir!"

"Fucking bullets don't stop the lass! You think little Mcherring can do a better job than an M4, soldier!?"

"No sir!"

"Then you did disobey my orders, impede on Dr Mcherring's duty?"

Gabbles didn't answer straight away, which was always a quick way to annoy General Howard.

"What do you say, soldier!?"

"No one is immune to everything, sir!"

"So what? A monster that can stop bullets but not bloody glass!?"

"I simply think he took it too far, sir! She seemed close to death to me, sir!"

General Howard gave a sigh and a huff and went back to sitting in his chair behind his desk. "Well, soldier, did she say anything useful to you at least?"

Gabbles stood, not answering for a moment. She had muttered something to him as he cleaned her up. He knew that he shouldn't say it or bring the wrath of his prisoner. *But what can she do?* he thought to himself in the split second of debate before his answer. *It's not like she's a god!*

"Sir!" the soldier's loyalty to humanity said, finally winning out. "She did mumble something, sir!"

"Well," pushed General Howard, suddenly leaning forward in his chair out of a sudden spike of his cold, hard curiosity. "What did the bitch say?"

"She said something about a boy, Alex, she said he was coming to rescue her, sir!" immediately after Gabbles' words had left his mouth, he was regretting them, but it was too late now. A sinister smile had formed across General Howard's face as he saw a gleaming opportunity falling into his lap.

"Well then," he said, murderous intent in his eyes. "Let's see if this Alex is what his made out to be." He chuckled to himself as he spoke, and swigged his beer. "Dismissed, soldier!"

Gabbles waited no longer than needed and quickly turned and marched from the tent, past the large pine tree and back towards his station, mumbling to himself, "you bloody idiot," all the way. He had served under Howard for many years, and though the general has always been this way, something seemed to have changed in him, since Atia had arrived, at least that's what Gabbles believed anyway.

Inside the tent, Howard was still smiling maliciously to himself, as he plucked from his desk the skull that rested nearby, and, whispered to it as if the old owner could still hear him from beyond the grave. "So, Alex comes to Sparta! I'll give him a Spartan welcome!"

It was dusk, and the sun cast long shadows across the ruins and the camp. The temperature was still high, in the mid-twenties at least, and the air was still windless, the sound of cicadas singing into the night was all about. The smell of dinner from the long mess tents drifted through the camp like a ghostly fog, silently calling the men to supper. Atia, from her cage, could taste the burgers in the air as the smell drifted from the tent on the hilled acropolis above her. She was starving, and her stomach complained like an earthquake.

Though starvation would not take her life, she needed food to keep up her strength. She longed for more than stale bread and dirty water, but she doubted she'd get anything else. Suddenly, she was distracted by the sound of footsteps coming in from beyond. Instinctively, she curled up in a ball in the far corner, terrified of being tormented, shot at, or having muck thrown at her, or tortured or stared at like some kind of eagle in the local zoo. But none of those things happened. It was her captor, Lieutenant Gabbles, who turned into the little ruined building and up to her cage, bearing gifts in his arms and a smile on his face. Atia, of course, didn't trust this act of kindness, nor the act that he committed before. After all, *What cause can he have for helping me?* she thought to herself.

"It's ok," said the Lieutenant as he entered her little cage. "I'm not here to hurt you. In fact, I shouldn't think that Dr Mcherring will hurt you again either.

Atia perked up a little at the good news but knew all too well that such mercy always came with a price. "You told them, didn't you? You told them about Alex!" she hissed from the end of her chain like an angry lioness, making even Gabbles back off a little.

"No!" he replied quickly, not wishing to anger Atia, and so denying his entire conversation with General Howard.

"No! Of course not."

"Then how?"

"I can be rather persuasive you know," said the Lieutenant with a smile after cutting Atia off mid-question. "Now calm down, I've got some gifts from the men... or rather, I nicked them from the men."

Atia smiled in amusement at this, and slowly came closer to Gabbles, as far as the chain around her neck would allow. Closing the door securely behind him, Gabbles approached Atia, putting his gifts down by the bars, he came and knelt down with her. "Now, promise me, you're not going to do anything stupid."

Atia simply nodded her head, not entirely sure at this point what was going on at all. To say she was surprised would be a bit of an understatement, though she was becoming ever more trusting and grateful at any rate.

"Okay, then," Gabbles said as he reached round her neck and unfastened the necklace of metal that shackled her, and removed it slowly and gently with a loving touch.

As soon as the metal collar had left her neck, Atia gasped in the cool air of freedom. Her throat had been rubbed red-raw and was scraped and bruised by the rough metal that had been tight around it. Atia reached up with unsteady hands to feel and massage her painful neck.

"Thank you." She croaked in her shallow voice, as, for the first time since the Lieutenant put the collar on outside the hotel in France, she had been able to breathe freely.

"I have something else," said Gabbles with a smile.

Turning to the gifts, he pulled out a hamburger stolen from the mess tent. "Here, have some proper food."

Atia smiled more sweetly than she had done in an age. She was more grateful to the Lieutenant than she had been to anyone before. But the hamburger wasn't all that Gabbles has brought her. As she ate, or rather gobbled, the food down in a couple of huge bites, Gabbles presented her with a blanket, much larger and softer than the sack cloth that she had been given, and covered her shoulders with it before taking out some linen to bandage up her wounds, though he had little idea how to do it or apply the cream he had stolen. Atia, of course, helped with that, instructing the Lieutenant on all things medical.

"You know a lot about medicine," he remarked once all her cuts and wounds had been tended to.

"I should do," said the extremely grateful Atia as the pair sat down together in the almost pitch black of the night, seeing only by the moonlight that penetrated through the holes in the sheeting that made the roof of her cage. "My mother is Health."

"Your mother's Health?" replied Lieutenant Gabbles, rather confused.

Atia smiled. "I forgot; you earthlings don't understand the gods."

"Gods?" Gabbles suddenly became cold with fear as his spine froze, the only thought in his mind was, *What if she finds out I dropped this Alex in it?* "You mean…"

Atia nodded. She found it amusing how ignorant humans from earth could be; such is the curse Wisdom put over them. "Yes, I am a goddess' daughter."

Gabbles nodded slightly; he, after all, was a devout Christian. His father was a priest, and he couldn't be sure if

Atia was simply having him on as a joke or something. "Right, well that explains a few things." Gabbles shivered. The sun had long gone now and the temperature had fallen rather a lot since. The lieutenant leaned a little closer to Atia, trying to share in the small amount of warmth created by the blanket he had given her.

Atia shuffled a little, a bit uncomfortable and suddenly worried he had a more lustful motive behind his kindness. She looked at him suspiciously. "Now, now Gabbles, don't get excited," she said, sounding a lot less grateful than before.

Gabbles looked at her and smiled. "Don't worry," he said, "you're not my type!"

The pair sat and talked long into the night and all the way to the break of the next day. Rising above the mountains to the east and casting long shadows over the camp as the air heats up once again as the sun returns. The pair had talked of all manner of things; Atia had told Gabbles of the truth about the Gods and of her time with Alex, which she looked back on now very fondly, and Gabbles told her all about his life, his father, his many tours of duty and his time since the Great Plague began. At dawn, he had left her to go about his duties, thinking it not good to raise attention to their new friendship, and so leaving Atia alone to her thoughts.

"Where the hell are you, Alex?" she asked herself. She was ever grateful to Gabbles for his kindness, but when it came to trust, she had very little. "What makes one change so much over night, I don't know, but it can't be good!" she whispered to herself, suspicion filling her mind. "At least Alex is trustworthy, and least I can count on him! Right?"

Chapter XXIII:
16 Months, 3 Weeks AP, Agios

From Venice, Alex, Jared and Eric sailed south through the Adriatic Sea. Eric did most of the rowing of the great galleon, where Alex looked after the sails, steered and navigated the ship. Jared, sulking mostly because it was not a yacht, sat at the stern and fished, with a makeshift rod and lore, dragging it in the wake of the vessel, and, perhaps unsurprisingly, he caught as many fish as if he had been fishing in the Sahara Desert in mid-summer. Before long, however, the trio found that they had to make landfall, mostly because all that Nico had seen fit to give Alex to drink was wine, and Eric supped his fair share and before long was rather drunk and quite unable to row. The Galleon made landfall twice before they arrived at their final destination. Once on the coast of Italy in a small port that Alex never found out the name of, and the second after they crossed from south Italy into the Aegean and towards their long-awaited destination of Greece.

Passing down the east coast of the island of Cephalonia and port of Sami, the galleon was refuelled with water for the last time before making its last leg. Alex, because Jared had refused to help in the slightest, changed their port destination from Plylos, which would require a long, cross-land, march to Sparta, to the small port of Agios Nikolaos. This was where, at the end of the third week of the sixteenth month of the Plague, the Venation Galleon arrived in the small port,

294

and its passengers, the cyclops, the man, the Satyr and the twenty-nine golden sheep disembarked and prepared for the final leg of their long journey from Yorkshire to Sparta. The only thing standing in their way was several miles of olive groves, and a great mountain, on the other side of which, to the east, was the ancient city and their destination.

It was dusk when the three made landfall and Alex suggested spending the night on the galleon before moving out. Jared's response to this was, "I will not spend one moment longer than necessary on that uncomfortable pile of driftwood." Though, not long after they had gotten off the ship and Jared had some time with his pipe, he appeared to settle down and come out of his unbearable sulk.

The three made haste through town as always on this journey; they had tried to avoid towns as best as possible, only passing by from a distance in order to get their bearings from time to time, and the last settlement they passed was no different. Alex's first impression of Greece was a good one; clear waters, warm air, olive groves all about and the sound of cicadas, like a great chorus, at first deafening, though before long becoming a beautiful sound all about him. The smell of olives was in the air, and he could almost taste the thousands of years of history all around.

"Did you know," Alex remarked as the three, and twenty-nine golden sheep, passed through the olive groves and away from Agios in search for a suitable place to make camp. "The Spartans worshipped the Goddess of Love, Aphrodite, not just as a goddess of love, but also of war. And indeed, it is Aphrodite, according to the Greeks, that started the great Trojan War by offering Paris the hand of Helen of

Sparta."

"Fascinating," replied Jared, truly not that impressed, unlike Eric.

"Wow, that amazing!" Eric Blue-Eye replied, who quite marvelled at Alex's knowledge of history.

"And also, Spartan women had more rights than women in any other place in Greece, more so than Athens, even, and that women were able to own and inherit their own land, which was something quite..."

"Shush!" cried Jared all of a sudden, bringing the party to a halt and cutting Alex off mid-sentence just before a clearing in some trees, where, the Golden sheep stood huddled all together in a flock, staring at something out of sight beyond.

The events that unfolded next happened in a blink of an eye for Alex, his heart leapt into his mouth and adrenaline filled him like rocket fuel. This was Howard's Spartan welcome.

"Something isn't right," exclaimed Jared.

Eric whistled and called his sheep, who began to run from the clearing.

There was a loud crack in the dusky light. A deafening bang consumed the chorus of the cicadas, fire burnt and spread and where there were once twenty-nine golden-fleeced sheep, now there were but four.

Alex stood there speechless, looking at the devastation of the rocket launcher on Eric's flock. Among the four remaining was Eric's favourite ewe Eve, bleating and running, begging her master for help and protection. But Alex, Eric and Jared were rooted to the spot out of shock and fear, like the ancient olive trees about them, and no help could be given to the loyal sheep until it was all too late.

The final surviving ram, Boris, with great, golden horns, turned to make a final stand, to try and protect his girls from the fate of their sisters. He charged, alone, head down at the Americans beyond. Running across the clearing fearlessly towards the trees. All time seemed to stop in that moment. The last charge of the golden ram, bravely giving his life for theirs, but none survived what came next. Boris, Eve, Shirley and May, one by one, were all cut down by the volley of bullets that came from the clearing. Boris, in his bravery, fell first, a bullet splitting his head in two. Then May fell, and Shirley after that, the bullets shredding them to pieces. An anti-aircraft gun was over the top, mowing them down and leaving nothing but tufts of golden wool blowing in the wind. Even Eve was helpless and died, her cries of pain and disappointment at her master echoed into the night, and would haunt the three for the rest of their lives.

"Go!" Eric cried breaking through his fear, the sight of his dead flock igniting the unquenchable fire of fury in his eye. "I hold them off!" And with that, Eric was off towards the clearing, armed with nothing but a great branch he had torn from an old tree, but this olive branch did not mean peace.

"Come on!" yelled Alex, the ringing of the rocket still in their ears as he yanked Jared to the side, and they began to flee the best they could with Jared's lame leg.

Behind them, through the ringing in their ears, they thought they heard cries of help, then gunshots. Then everything went quiet. The two struggled and limped on into the olive grove, further and further away from Eric.

The shadows were becoming long in the olive grove.

The sounds of men were hot on their tails when suddenly Jared came to a halt.

"What are you doing?" screamed Alex. Jared looked all about him; he could hear the men closing in in the darkness.

"I'll never outrun 'em, lad!" he cried, slight tears in his eyes. "Not with my leg! I'll hold 'em off, I'll use the last of my Kamari to help you escape!" Alex shook his head, but didn't disagree. There was no time to. He turned to run.

"Wait!" Alex turned back to the old satyr who was lighting his pipe for the last time. "Take this!" He took out a leather-bound book and passed it to Alex. "You wish to know about your father, lad, read this! You're not the first to make a journal of his life. NOW GO!"

But Alex suddenly found himself having second thoughts of leaving the Satyr and hesitated. "No, I can't leave you." Jared sighed, putting his hand up onto Alex's shoulder.

"My lad, save yourself," he said grimly, and hurriedly, for now, the sounds of men were dreadfully close to them. "I've cancer lad, found out just before the Plague, and said it would kill me. This journey was always going to be my last. Now, I didn't get to sail a yacht round Italy like I wished, but at least this thing in me won't be my end. Now GO!" he said and pushed Alex away. Alex, with tearful eyes could not argue and so quickly ran off, vanishing into the long shadows and not a moment too soon.

As soon as he'd vanished, the men were all about Jared, their guns armed and ready. Jared looked about them, took off his top hat and placed it on the floor, showing all his horned head. The men prepared to fire. Jared took one last puff of smoke from his clay pipe before dropping that too to the ground. "Aye, lads," he said with a smile, "this is a good way to die."

The men shot.

The bullets did their work.

But so, did Jared, and he went up with a tremendous bang as he released the last of his Kamari like a belt of grenades had been strapped about his waist.

Alex found himself running through the seemingly endless olive grove all alone. There was a great commotion behind him, and then, like before, all fell silent. Fear took him and filled him with dread. The adrenaline forced him to run on, through the gnarly, old olive trees. He could hear men from all directions closing in on him. He ran faster, but in the dark gloom he could hardly see where it was, he was going. He was lost, surrounded, afraid and all alone with no sign of help arriving. Suddenly, he was very aware that he might soon be dead, with no real knowledge of what would happen to him on the other side, or Atia if he failed to help her. *Why was I so obsessed with my father!* he couldn't help but think to himself, possibly his last thoughts being of how he should have done so much differently. *I wish I could do it again! I'd listen to Destiny like I should have. How things could have been different if I had. Perhaps Daisy may never have been able to force me back here in the first place! At least there'd be some fond memory of Atia in my mind!*

Suddenly, with the sound of soldiers on his heels, Alex emerged back out into the clearing where the sheep had died. It was deserted, save from the bodies of Eric's flock.

Alex gasped. There, across the clearing, leaning up against an old tree with Eve's limp body, sleeping soundly at last, lay Eric, coughing up his last.

Alex rushed across the burnt and steaming ground to where Eric was laying. There was blood pumping like a fountain from his belly. "Alex!" wheezed Eric Blue-Eye as Alex tried desperately to stop the bleeding, but there was little hope. "I glad, you here when I die!"

"Don't worry, big feller, you aren't dying yet!" Alex said, fighting back the tears in his eyes. *I can't lose you!* he screamed to himself. *Think Alex! What would Atia do?*

Eric took Alex's hand in his and looked down at him with his great, big, blue eye, understanding that there was little that Alex could do. He smiled a thin and wispy smile, and his eye seemed to fade. Blood spluttered out his mouth and he wheezed his last. "Alex... I okay... let me die... I... not sad... being last... of my kind," he said through his dying pains. Alex could hold back the tears no longer, but looked bravely up into Eric's now-fading blue eye as Death got ready to take his soul. With his last mortal words, Eric whispered to Alex something that would change the course of history.

"Don't..." he moaned with pain as the life drained from him and watered the old olive trees about them. "Trust... Daisy!" Eric's great blue eye closed, and his body went limp and cold.

Suddenly, everything turned black.

To be continued...